Henry Spicer

Acted dramas

Henry Spicer

Acted dramas

ISBN/EAN: 9783337304577

Printed in Europe, USA, Canada, Australia, Japan

Cover: Foto ©Andreas Hilbeck / pixelio.de

More available books at **www.hansebooks.com**

By HENRY SPICER

LONDON
CHAPMAN AND HALL, 193, PICCADILLY
1875

PRINTED BY TAYLOR AND CO.
LITTLE QUEEN STREET, LINCOLN'S INN FIELDS

TO

𝕵. 𝕱.

IN MEMORY OF AN OLD FRIENDSHIP

WITH WHICH THE WRITER'S EARLIEST INTEREST IN THE

POETIC DRAMA

WAS GRATEFULLY AND PLEASANTLY ASSOCIATED,

THESE PLAYS ARE DEDICATED BY

H. S.

PREFACE.

Tʜᴇ publication of any work claiming affinity with the poetic drama is—even without a view to profit—in these days so manifest an anachronism as to demand actual apology.

Mine must be found in the kindly remark of the critic of the 'Times,' who, in reviewing, not very long since, the drama of a far more distinguished author, took occasion to observe that *my* pieces deserved to be better remembered, and thus inspired me with the idea that those friends, still living, whose interest in their production afforded me such sincere gratification, might be not unwilling to possess them in a collected form.

H. S.

HONESTY.

𝕬 Drama,

IN FIVE ACTS.

DRAMATIS PERSONÆ.

	Covent Garden, 1845.	Olympic, 1848.
SIR PHILIP LANCASTER.	Mr. Archer.	Mr. Archer.
DOUGLAS TRAFFORD (*Cousin of Julia*).	Mr. Vandenhoff.	Mr. Stuart.
PEMBROKE.	Mr. Rae.	Mr. Lee.
LORD SEYLE.	Mr. Butler.	Mr. Fitzgerald.
MORDAUNT. (*Suitors to Julia.*)	Mr. Richardson.	Mr. Mazzoni.
GOSSELIN.	Mr. Stott.	Mr. Farrer.
SANDELL.	Mr. Martin.	Mr. Jones.
GRAEME.	Mr. Young.	Mr. Harcourt.
FRANCIS GAGE (*an Advocate*).	Mr. J. Vining.	Mr. H. Holl.
CYRIL (*his Brother*).	Miss Fitzjames.	Miss S. Kenneth.
DEVERELL (*a knavish Usurer*).	Mr. Rogers.	Mr. C. Perkins.
FAIRFAX (*Steward to* TRAFFORD).	Mr. Bass.	Mr. W. Davidge.
STEPHEN.	Mr. Biddle.	Mr. Buxton.
GILBERT. (*Servants.*)	Mr. Henry.	Mr. Pidgeon.
ROGER.	Mr. Thomas.	Mr. Jennings.
JUDGE.	Mr. Braid.	Mr. G. Almer.
CONFESSOR.	Mr. Hollingsworth.	Mr. Lawrence.
JULIA (*only Child of* SIR PHILIP).	Miss Vandenhoff.	Miss M. Duret.
INFELICE (*an Italian, betrayed by* TRAFFORD).	Mrs. Brougham.	Miss May.

CREDITORS, SUITORS, *etc. etc.*

ACT I.

SCENE I.—*A saloon in* TRAFFORD'S *house. It appears in great confusion as from an overnight feast. Chairs displaced, cups strewn about, with cards, dice, etc.*

GILBERT, STEPHEN, ROGER discovered.

GILBERT (*yawning*).
Faith! a wild revel. Be there many such?

STEPHEN.
Seven in the week, sir,—seven.

GILBERT.
     The Sabbath—

STEPHEN.
           Kept.
Dice are forbid; 'tis true the wine cask bleeds.
No songs, but then the jest and roaring tale
Fill up till midnight—*Monday*.

GILBERT.
       Well, 'tis said
That where the master's thriftless the man thrives.

STEPHEN.
Well said, but something tardily. My friend,
This is a world of change, a slippery world;
Laggards and slumberers, while 'tis whizzing round,
Oft wake to find its prizes filched away

B 2

By hands more wakeful.   Mark this cup now ;
                         (*takes a chalice*) gold,—
Chaste, sir, and precious.   See it ?

GILBERT.
                         Plainly.

STEPHEN.
                                   Good.
I put it in my pocket (*conceals it*).

GILBERT.
                         Well ?

STEPHEN.
                         That's all,
Pure gold is marketable.

GILBERT.
                         Well, but—

STEPHEN.
                                   Pardon,
There stands a pepper-caster, massive gold,
Worthy the chalice.   Who shall separate
These plighted lovers ?   No, be wedded here,—
My pouch your altar (*puts it up*).

GILBERT.
                         But is it honest ?

STEPHEN.
                                   Is it
Dishonest to take wage ?

GILBERT.
                         Why, no.

STEPHEN.
                         Then take it ;

You'll get it no way else.   Must I explain ?
The master's finished.

ROGER.
Eh ?

STEPHEN.
Concluded, sir,—
Thrown his last cast, disbursed his final crown,
And some few more.

GILBERT.
Nay, then to business.   These (*secreting plate, etc.*)
For wage this year, and next.   This to requite
My loss of service.   This but poorly pays
My wounded expectations.   This—

STEPHEN.
Away.
(*As they retire,* TRAFFORD *enters,* FAIRFAX *following with papers, etc.* TRAFFORD *paces the
room in agitation.*)

TRAFFORD.
Plate, jewels ?

FAIRFAX.
Gone.

TRAFFORD.
My armoury ?

FAIRFAX.
Gone too.
Lord Seyle bought that—

TRAFFORD.
The miser !   Wherefore ?

FAIRFAX.
Sir,

For hatred, as I think, or, as he called it,
Charity. Heaven pardon him, his eye
Flickered with malice as he mumbled that
The rats, which did infest his household might
Henceforth have lodgings cheap. 'Twas slight avail,
For fifty parched and droughty mouths did catch
The golden drops,—aye, almost ere they fell.

TRAFFORD.
Go, sell my horses.

FAIRFAX.
Pardon, sir, that's done.
There's not a hair, black, sorrel, brown, or bay,
Housed in your stalls, but what might truly call
Another man its owner.

TRAFFORD.
Am I mad,
Or do you mock me, sir? What's left?

FAIRFAX (*counting on his fingers*).
Your rings,
Your garments, your—

TRAFFORD (*furiously*).
Fellow, you've robbed me.

FAIRFAX.
Yes,
Even as for thirty years I robbed your father,
Hoarding the wealth you've squandered.

TRAFFORD.
Sell my jewels?
Who gave you licence? Horses too? Come, come,
You have used too much freedom.

FAIRFAX.
'Tis most true,

A freedom worse than bondage ?   Would you *hear ?*
I told you we were beggars.   Your reply
Was a new revel.   If I showed two files,—
On this a thousand bills unpaid, on that
One poor receipt, you laughed.   If, in despair
I dashed my empty coffer on the floor,
So to compel your notice, " Out ! " you cried,
" No temper, or no business."   Oh ! good sir,
How can you marvel, since I failed to rouse
Manhood or masterhood in you, I should thus
O'erstep my natural duty ?

TRAFFORD.

                Faith ! you have me.
Forgive me, good old man.   And now to work
At last in earnest.   If the need be pressing,
Pinch me once more our golden sponge ; I mean,
Seek Deverell out, the crafty usurer,
And bid him—

FAIRFAX.

        Sir, he'll lend no more.   Nay, worse,
He has been so loud for present satisfaction
Of moneys long fall'n due, that more I dread
His sudden quiet.   He's a beast that loves
An ambush to his soul.

TRAFFORD (*agitated*).

                To be struck down
Within a leap of safety !   These three months,
Used with the foresight of a boy, had won me
The richest dower in England.   Oh ! sweet cousin,
Ev'n now so fair, what art could paint thee, coming
With rescue in thy hand ?   What noise is that ?

FAIRFAX.

The proof and witness of my story, sir,
Who will not be denied.
            (*Opens a door at the back, through which enter a
                number of persons of mean appearance, creditors
                of* TRAFFORD.   *He then retires.*)

TRAFFORD (*starting back*).
How's this?   Beset
With thieves?   My steward, sirs—

FIRST CREDITOR (*Scrivener*).
He bade us hither,
Saying that when you saw our wasted mien
And ragged robes, you could not choose but hear
And give us moneys,—he himself had none.

TRAFFORD (*after a pause addressing one*).
Your claim?

SCRIVENER.
'Tis quickly said.   You owe me, sir,
A poor five hundred crowns.   That's to your worship
A supper missed—to me, existence.   Sir,
Fever attacked my house ; no leech was there
To stop the plague, no nurse to soothe, no priest
To whisper comfort.   My young son was seized,
And ta'en to sea.   I could not buy him off.
These woes broke down my father's heart.   Last night
The old man died.

TRAFFORD.
A sad tale, briefly told.
Well, sir, your claim?

SECOND CREDITOR (*An old man*).
Your steward came to me
Weeping, and cursing the hard fate that made him
Slave to a thriftless lord.   He knew my soul
Did teem with gracious feelings, as my purse
With cash ; and still his cry was gold—gold—gold—
Give him but gold, and—so Heaven prosper him—
It should be paid, yea, trebly.   By my heart,
I could not see the old man weep, and tear
Locks white as these.   I pledged my house, my land,
And, for return, am beggared.   For the debt,
I will forgive it, noble sir, I will—

Being no usurer—give but *half*, mark that,
But half mine own.

TRAFFORD.
Enough.　Stand back, old friend;
We'll speak again.　And *thou?*

THIRD CREDITOR (*Jeweller*).
I dealt in gems.
The Lady ——

TRAFFORD (*hastily*).
So—the pearls!

JEWELLER (*sullenly*).
My credit's gone
From too much faith in your nobility;
And I, once rich in good report, am called
Rogue, cheat, and thief!　Yes, you may pay the debt,
But you have crushed a fairer pearl than all—
Mine honourable name.

TRAFFORD (*apart*).
This work is mine.
I—*I* have made these poor homes desolate;
From infant mouths kept back the wholesome food;
Struck from the old man's hand the crutch and stay,
And left him prostrate!　I—O!　God, their tales
Cry to me with a truthful, hungry woe,
That sounds in spite of all.　Ho! there, within.
Fairfax.

(*Enter* DEVERELL *with Officers.*)

OFFICER (*to* DEVERELL).
Our man, sir?

DEVERELL.
In the gold brocade.

TRAFFORD.

How now, thou cozening slave !   Dost thou lift up
Thy heel against me?

DEVERELL.

Come, sir, better shape
Your language to your state.   Why do you pause ?
Arrest this man.   His three chief debts are mine.
To jail !

(Enter Servant with a letter.)

SERVANT.

Sir, from Sir Philip Lancaster.

(Exit Servant.)

TRAFFORD *(reads eagerly)*.

Lancaster to the rescue !   Glorious missive !
What a fair hand the old man writes !   All's saved !
All's well !   *(Reads again.)*

OFFICER *(aside to* DEVERELL*)*.

Shall we proceed, sir ?

DEVERELL.

       Fool ! keep quiet.
Would you hoist canvas ere you know the wind ?
Nearer the door.   Don't press the gentleman.
'Tis something from his honourable friend
That——

TRAFFORD.

Welcome, and well timed !   Still lingering, fellow ?
Read, then——

DEVERELL.

Good sir, your lowliest creature.   (*To
Officers.*)   Go !
Curse ye, be off !

TRAFFORD.

Lend me your purse.   Now, skip.

'Twould pose the devil which side of thy double face
Shows uglier, slave or bully !
            (*Exeunt* Deverell *and Officers.*)
           Leave me now,
My friends, and mark, to-morrow each man's claim
Shall meet due justice.   Stay, there's gold for those
Whose wants are loudest tongued.   At noon, I tell you,
And fail me not.   *To-morrow !*
        (*Exeunt Creditors.   Re-enter* Fairfax.)
          Now, good Fairfax,
Is not this well?   Sir Philip writes me here,
That conscious of my suit, so fondly urged
(He's pleased to say so) to his beautiful child
(Why doesn't he add, and heiress), and, good man !
Feeling that wealth so vast as must endow
That tender spirit, asks some hand to share
Its kindred duties, bids me put at once
My hope to issue.   If I win (*reading*)—I win
Her heart, then "Take her," it concludes, aye, "take her,
Good Master Trafford, *she is thine !*"   O ! joy.
O ! heaven !

FAIRFAX.

You love her, then, sir ?

TRAFFORD.

            Love !   I worship
Her and her wealth, alike.   And now to work,
Indeed !   To stop yon howling throats; to sweep
Out of my fortune's droughty channel, with
This rich and bounteous stream, yon carrion flies
That 'gin to settle there, and then—why, then
If there be surplusage——

FAIRFAX.

What then ?

TRAFFORD.

            To build
An altar, Fortune, to thy goddess-ship—

For ever when my need has blamed thee most,
Thou cam'st most bounteously!

FAIRFAX (anxiously).

You are sure—

TRAFFORD.

Of her?

Will the sun rise to-morrow?
(Exeunt.)

SCENE II.—*A magnificent apartment in the house of* SIR
PHILIP LANCASTER.

(Enter SIR PHILIP and JULIA.)

JULIA.

How! leave you, sir?   Is your poor nurse become
So rude and careless in her ministry,
So drowsy in her vigil——

SIR PHILIP (fretfully).

No, girl, no.

I said not that.   Why do you ever thus
Strive to pervert my meaning?   You believe me,
Aye, by your winks, side-looks, and sneers, you think me
A weak old man, a pettish, weak old man!
One to be dawdled, humoured, trifled with ;
Told fondling lies—

JULIA.

Nay, nay, dear sir.

SIR PHILIP.

A child

That must be put, with soothing, sugared words,
From dangerous asking.   Why, what's seen in me

To argue dotage?   When do I sit at gaze,
Gibbering and making mouths at vacancy?
Call the stars comfits; think this chair my steed;
Wash hands i' the moonlight?   Julia, Julia, child,
'Tis hard that thou shouldst mock me!

JULIA.
                              If one thought,
Untempered with its most fit attributes—
Dear love and deepest reverence—ever stirred
Within my breast, or quickened on my lip
In words, may the great Ear of heaven be sealed
For ever 'gainst my prayer, and mostly *then*
When my poor soul hath need.

SIR PHILIP (*in a low, fond tone*).
                              Let her speak on!
Still pausing, still, whene'er my soul grows warm,
And steals into the music.   O! my bird.
My melodist! whose song so gently chides
My erring fancies home—when thou art caged,
Must thou, as all thy prisoned woodmates do,
Give up thy wilding sweetness?   I'll not think
Of that.   Alas, me! warble as thou wilt,
I shall not hear thee.   (*Weeps.*)

JULIA (*apart*).
                  There's some painful thought,
Or half-born purpose, struggling in his brain,
That must be helped to live.   Father, dear father,
Why then fling forth your happy bird to find
Some rough, exacting master, who will change
The songs you love to weeping?   Is't to mend
Her fortunes?   They are whole.   Win pleasures?   Why,
I would not give, no, not for twenty thrones,
This low stool at your feet.

SIR PHILIP (*quickly*).
                  Nay, but you must,
And shall!   I'll have no glittering, foppish fools,

Pert, feathered popinjays, come swaggering here,
Peeping and pointing at a fond, fair girl,
Who, to their envy and her own lost pain,
Wastes the bright sunshine of her happiest years
Upon an old, gnarled tree. Owls as they are,
There's truth in their dull croakings.

JULIA.

        Aye, enough
To give the lie to their wisdom. Dearest father,
Let me be still your—

SIR PHILIP.

        Child, I need thee not—
Love thee, how dearly; but I need thee not.
Yes, *thou*, my music, light, and strength, and eye;
The one green leaf crowning my wint'ry age;
My comfortable book, wherein I read
Sweet tales of heaven! thou must be gone, and gild
One of that covetous myriad. To that end,
I have bid them hither.

JULIA (*faintly*).
Whom, my father?

SIR PHILIP.

         Whom!
Your suitors, child. All that desire to win
Your love or gold. Proud Pembroke, Douglas Trafford,
Mordaunt, the soldier; Scyle, the miser; Graeme,
And flocks of meaner note, all craving. I
Proclaimed an open field, and there shall be,
I trow, no lack of champions.

JULIA (*starting up*).

        How, sir! make
A market of your child?

SIR PHILIP (*seizing her hand.*)
Aye, girl, a mart,

Where thou alone shalt purchase.   Dare but cross
My will in this, and—darling as thou art,
The knot that ties together my old life—
I'll sever thee !   Say, 'tis my will herein
To prove thy wit and judgment.   Choose, thou shalt ;
Not as I point, no, no, take or reject ;
Break hearts or heal ; patch fortunes ; frown or smile ;
None shall say nay.   I would not seek to bind
Thy judgment to an old warped will.   Within :
(Enter Servants.)
My daughter needs her tirewoman.   The guests
Arrive.

SERVANT.
The hall is thronged, sir.

SIR PHILIP (signs to Attendants).
Here, I come.
(Exeunt.)

END OF ACT I.

ACT II.

SCENE I.—*The street exterior of* SIR PHILIP'S *mansion.
Guests arriving from time to time.*

(*Enter* F. GAGE, *a Pauper following.*)

GAGE.

Nay, spare thy thanks, man.   I rejoice with thee.
Not I, but truth, put forth thy stifled wrongs;
Not I, but justice, gave them victory:
Come, come, no more.   Go, and make glad thy home,
And husband thy new gain.

PAUPER.

But, sir, dear sir,
Touching the wage wherewith I said (I don't
Mean to deny it) I would pay your toil,
Should it avail aught—

GAGE (*aside, observing Guests*).
Still they come.   Still more.
A churlish revel.   No fair woman's face
In all their gilded rout.

PAUPER.
Sir, as I said—
True, I am rich; but wealth, so hardly won,
Should be spent sparingly.   If these ten crowns—

GAGE (*aside eagerly*).
The strangest concourse!   Mordaunt, too, and Graeme,
Lord Seyle.   Here will be jarring interests,
Or rumour lies.   Who next?

PAUPER (*aside*).
　　　　　　Nay, if he cares
No more for't, these five crowns, or three, or none—
Sir, hem ! Good morning.

GAGE (*starting*).
　　　　　　Stay, I had forgotten.
Pray you, return. Listen, your suit is won.
You are rich, have plenty ; I have no wealth, nor friend,
Save a poor brother, hunger-sick at home !　(*Aside.*)
Still they throng in. Hark, man, I am distressed,
Give me, or lend.

PAUPER (*aside*).
　　　　　　So poor ! A trifle, then,
Will answer all. My good friend, if this crown
May help thee, take it. Justice won my cause,
Not thou.　　　　　　　　　　　　(*Exit.*)

GAGE.
Alack, poor honesty ! What, Trafford !
　　　　(*Enter* TRAFFORD *and* PEMBROKE.)
How the knave porter cringes, as to one
May be his lord. They pause.　　(*Retires up.*)

PEMBROKE.
　　　　　　You've caught the mien,
And speak the language glibly ; yet, I think,
You never loved.

TRAFFORD.
I've watched the sufferers, sir,
From the disorder. When the wretch sits thus,
With knitted brow, thinking he thinks, speaks short,
Refuses wine, looks sheepish, cares not much
(Bad symptom that) for play, he's sickening. When
This calm is streaked with passion, the locked lips
Open and curl with sneers, that man's deceived,
And convalescent. But if three long months
Pass o'er him and no change, the pulse still high,

Sleep troubled, mind abstract, and language wild,
He's dead and gone in love ; he's fit for nought
But to be scarecrow to the rest.   No, no !
I'll be no lazar in love's hospital.   (*They pass in.*)

GAGE (*advancing*).
I can endure no more.   To question now
Yon lackered menial.   Stoop, good pride.
         So, friend,
  (*Approaches a Servant at the door.*)
Sir Philip feasts to-day ?

SERVANT.
   If that your worship
Except not to his purpose.

GAGE.
   Courteous sir,
One other question.   What event imports
This throng of manly feasters ?

SERVANT.
    Sir, my master
Holds, as it were. a tournament ; the course
Being love, arms, purses,—sword and lance, sweet words—
The prize, my Lady Julia ; free to all
Of worth and breeding.

GAGE (*eagerly*).
   Say'st thou ?   Stand aside.
Let me go in.

SERVANT.
 O ! yes, a likely tale.
Yonder's the tavern, sir.

GAGE (*seizing him*).
   Fool ! knave and fool !
Did you not tell me— Back, or—

SERVANT (*calls loudly*).
                              Ho! within.
                                        (*Enter Steward.*)
Well, sir.   What now, sir?   Is your humour tamed?
Shall we—

STEWARD (*to Servant*).
              Peace, fool.   Get to thy work within.
We know this gentleman,   (*Exit Servant.*)
                              And honour him,
Good Master Gage.   Yes, but for your bold hand,
That stayed her maddened palfrey ere he reached
The turn where death stood waiting both, good lack,
We had been mistressless!   *We*, sir, remember.
Do you think *she* has forgotten?   No, sir, no—
As you shall find, belike.   Will you go in?
Here lies the guest-room.   Ah! sir, that you might—
Ah! that you might—   (*Exeunt speaking.*)

SCENE II.—*Saloon in* SIR PHILIP'S *mansion.*

(SIR PHILIP *seated.* JULIA *beside him.* TRAFFORD
    stands near her. PEMBROKE, LORD SEYLE,
    SANDELL, GOSSELIN, MORDAUNT, *and others,
    suitors.*)

GOSSELIN.
Psha! sorry jesting, was't not?

PEMBROKE.
                              'Tis so old.
A loser's fashion to abuse the game,
I hold my tongue; but I had no chance—none—
Nor hope to win.
                                        C 2

SANDELL.
Nor I.

MORDAUNT.
I simply came
To laugh at your long faces!

LORD SEYLE.
I at *yours*—
The longest. (*Aside*). Cost a hat, though!

SIR PHILIP.
How, my friends!
Silenced so soon? Your merits and your claims,
So deftly weighed and rated? When I wooed,
I would have ta'en my sword-knot for a rope,
And hanged myself i'the gate, ere I'd have been
So quickly answered. One would think this wench
Had better patience—less desire to quit
Her old, weak, whimsical, tyrannical sire,
Than hath been boldly spoken; and must this—
This beauty own no lord; this wondrous wealth
(For, let me warn you, 'tis a duchess' dower)
No master? Fie! What's to be done in this
Sad strait? You, master Trafford, you alone
Have not, of all the goodly company,
Essayed that open palm. Find the right spell;
'Tis a woman's, it will close.

TRAFFORD.
O, sir, I wait
My turn. What champion next?
(*Enter a Servant.*)

SERVANT.
A gentleman
Claims audience, sir, and—

SIR PHILIP.
Bid him come.

TRAFFORD (*aside*).
Another !
Good. *Then* I'll end the show. Some city fop.
(*Enter* F. GAGE).
No, as I live, the cunning man of law
That pleaded 'gainst me when yon beggar won
Redress—'twas called so—for the means wherewith
I wrested from him what I thought my own.

SIR PHILIP.
Your name is—

TRAFFORD (*insolently*).
Francis Gage, sir, elsewise styled
" The beggars' advocate."

GAGE.
I thank you, sir.
I could not ask a better groom of the chambers ;
A humble name, but spotless.

SIR PHILIP.
Master Gage,
Know yourself welcome. Outward fashion, sir,
Plain though it be, endangers no man's fortune,
So there be that within may challenge claim
To my child's love.

TRAFFORD.
Sir, he has none.

GAGE.
No claim !
Aye, great and manifold, yet shadows all
If cast to your arbitrement. I love
This lady, deem that love so hopeless, yet
So true, doth draw into itself some part
Of the perfection of the thing beloved,—
Breathing an essence, a sweet, natural life,
In what might else seem worthless. I am here,

Compelled to speech, for who, at call so open,
Stands mute, denies his faith.   When *you* profess,
Could *I* be silent ?   'Twas a moment's duty ;
I have done it, and farewell.

SIR PHILIP.
                              Well said ; but wait
Your answer.   Speak, child.

JULIA (*in a low voice*).
                              Sir, I can but say
What, to no stranger—like this gentleman—
Can sound ungracious : Thanks.

GAGE.
                              When we give alms—
Nay, when withhold them—charity will deign
One look.
                  (JULIA *looks at him, then averts her face*).

TRAFFORD.
          What's this ?   By heaven, her brow is flame !
And 'tis not anger, nor amazement, nor
Confusion.   Cousin, know you him ? or by
What right he stands among us ?

JULIA.
                              Tell me, first,
What's yours, to challenge it.

GAGE (*aside*).
                              Pity and pride
At strife.   Will she deny me ?   Be it so.
I will forestal the falsehood, sweet, and spare
Thy wavering heart a treason.

TRAFFORD.
                              Sir, you see
Your part in the pageant's done.

GAGE.

                              You, sir, take care
Yours shall not pass unheeded.

                              Pardon, madam;
We that do fill the social deeps, and prop
The rude side of that bright and polished floor
Whereon our betters walk, hear from above
Sometimes sweet echoes.   It is said, your voice,
Out of its strangely soothing melody,
Can make the hearers weep.   O, speak to me !
One word in pity—one—pronounce me beggar,
Base, peasant, menial, slave ; thy worst shall lift
A million worlds above *their* ribaldry
This soul that worships thee—

TRAFFORD (*fiercely*).
                              Withdraw, I say.
(GAGE *remains unmoved, standing with folded
arms before her.   She does not notice him*).

TRAFFORD (*enraged*).
Will you not hear me, fellow ?   Feel, then !
(*Strikes him with his riding-rod.*   GAGE *seizes
him, and wrests it from his hand.*   TRAFFORD
draws.*)

SIR PHILIP (*starting up*).
Desist, young sir !   Cease, Douglas Trafford, sheathe
That coward sword.   O, cousin ! does the word
Offend you?   Draw upon a man unarmed,
Who but repels unmannered passion, shown
Before this girl, my child ?   Good sirs, I thank you.
The fault of this alarm is partly mine.
You have indulged an old man's whim.   Let that
Blunt the slight sting.   As yet, my child is left me ;
But there's one still to—well—Heaven's will be done.
Come to the board. You, sir, be welcome, too.
No?   As you will then.   No constraint.   Farewell.
                              (*Exit* GAGE.)

Come, cousin Trafford, know thy fate, but keep not
The arbiter long in council.   'Till she comes
I fast.   (*Exeunt all but* TRAFFORD *and* JULIA.)

TRAFFORD.
So, madam, this performance done,
And one sole puppet left upon the board,
Will't please you touch the wire?

JULIA.
It needs not.   Go.

TRAFFORD (*impatiently*).
Julia, no more delay.   In candour, cousin,
I do believe my happy fortune gives me
That precious heart of thine, with all its gifts,
Too numerous now to reckon, and outward charms,
I should but wrong i'the painting.   Speak, beseech you,
And with one gracious word, heal every insult
Borne for thy sake.

JULIA.
Provoked.   Ill borne.   No matter—
I loved you, cousin—once.

TRAFFORD.
I hoped so.   Well?

JULIA.
Well! Is that lover-like?   Well, as you say,
Ev'n so it is—*was*,—for 'tis grown a legend—
One of those greybeard venerable tales,
At which we first thrill with delicious awe;
Then ponder, pause, smile; lastly, melt in wonder
We ever gave it credence.

TRAFFORD.
How?

JULIA.
In short,

We've snuffed the candles, sir, put out the ghost,
And clipped the fairy's wings.   I love no more.
You are my cousin ; at that pleasant distance
I like you well, no nearer.

TRAFFORD.
Julia, Julia,
Beware of jesting with—

JULIA.
With what ?   With whom ?
What do I wound worth pity when I spurn
Thee and thy passion hence?   Restrain your rage.
I will not be commanded.   I am proud,
And, as the proud do, hate my haughty peers
More than the humble that offend me not.
Am *I* a bird, at the first careless whistle
To perch upon your shoulder?   To your revels,
Your wine, your dicing ; but, for *love*, ah ! cousin,
Erase that misread monosyllable
Out of your memory's book, till your heart own
Its sad significance.   Storm if you will,
I heed it not, but, if you *can*, lament ;
There's grace in that, it were retributive,
And I might bear you company, for both
Have from a nobler heart than either owns
Drawn anguish worse than tears.   Cousin, farewell.
(*Exit* JULIA.)

SCENE III.—*The hall of* TRAFFORD'S *house.*

(*A crowd of persons.* FAIRFAX *at a table with
money, etc.*)

FAIRFAX (*paying several*).
There, there, and there.   Still crowding !   I have but

Two hands, and that's a couple more than men
Like using for this sport. There, sir ; take back
Thy burly form—give room. This is a court
Where justice' scales weigh truly. Hold, man, so—

A MAN.
Good sir, you've paid me double.

FAIRFAX.
       Heaven and earth !
Have we an artist here ? Take this man's face,
Get it thrice copied. Hang up one i'the market,
One in the palace, (hold, sir, take thy gold,)
One in my lady's bower. 'Tis honesty
Disguised as man. (*Looks round.*) Content ?

MANY VOICES.
      All, all !
(TRAFFORD *enters cloaked, and pauses unobserved.*)

FAIRFAX.
       Off then,
Ye cormorants. Think better of the world,
I do already. One man claims no more
'Than his fair due. Another, that's my lord,
Strips his own shoulders, sells his horses, rings,
Begs, borrows ; yea, he pilfers (since 'tis theft
Fondly to trust the future), and all this
To see your claims amended.
    (*Exeunt creditors.* TRAFFORD *advances.*)

TRAFFORD.
    Fairfax.

FAIRFAX (*starting*).
      Ha !

TRAFFORD.
This is the truth ?

FAIRFAX.
Ay, sir, what matter now?

TRAFFORD.
Man, I have played ; I have trifled with the game
And lost it.   Do you hear?   Have we no rope
Save that?   'Tis shipwreck, and all's done.   E'en now
We drift upon the rocks—lost, shattered, sunk,
Beyond a hope or succour.

FAIRFAX (*aghast*).
   And—and—*Deverell !*

TRAFFORD (*gazing round*).
Death to the hound !   Smells he the blood already?
What's to be done?   Go howl to Lancaster
For his proud child!   No, dotard as he is,
He will not cross her.   Might he die this night,
Much would be mine.   And, Julia, but to bend
Thy haughty neck!

FAIRFAX (*aside*).
  How pale he looks !   Dear sir—

TRAFFORD.
Give me my cloak.   I'll taste the air.   I want
My sword, too.   Never look so frightened, man ;
I know what fancy moves thee.   Were it so,
Wherefore should I go forth?   If I sought death,
My soul would pierce these roofs as easily
As 'twould the yielding and invisible air
Before my footstep.   Follow *not*, I say.
       (*He goes out.*)

END OF ACT II.

ACT III.

SCENE I.—*A meanly furnished chamber.*

(F. GAGE *writing by a feeble lamp.* CYRIL *lies
stretched upon a rude mattress on the floor.*)

GAGE (*after looking up impatiently*).
No rest! No peace! Boy—Cyril; boy, I say!
Now you feign sleep. Come, come—your lips but now
Shaped out articulate words. Could you be still;
Vexing yourself, you torture me, and turn
The idle loathing of a petted child
'Gainst slumber's medicine. Why so restless, boy?

CYRIL.

I cannot sleep.

GAGE.
You sigh, too. Why is that?

CYRIL.

For idleness.

GAGE.
Tut—tut!

CYRIL.
For pastime, then.

GAGE (*aside*).
He will not say for hunger.

CYRIL (*starting up*).
Stay. I'll work.

I've strength enough, and courage enough, to share
This labour with you.   See, a page half filled ;
While yours is scarce begun.

GAGE (*snatching* CYRIL'S *pen*).
                    Do you forget
I am your elder, sir?   What folly's this?
You shall do no work, I say.

CYRIL (*faintly*).
                    Yes, by your leave.
Must you, though elder, slave for both?

GAGE (*falling on his shoulder*).
                    My Cyril,
Not in reproach I spoke ; but boasting, rather,
The right of elder birth to bear the load
That fortune lays upon us.   Patience, patience.
Seed-time is weary, but the harvest comes.

CYRIL.
There is more blessing in your love, dear brother,
Than fear in that word, death.   I do not wish
To live.   Do you?

GAGE.
                    Do I ?   What! Cyril, fold
Our idle arms and sink, because the land
Is hard to reach !   Come, 'tis a coward creed.
Why those, my boy, whom giddy Fortune showers
Her costliest favours on, who glitter by
Wrapt in her flimsy shows, drunk with her smile,
Are Heaven's least favoured children.   Come, to rest.
So there, to rest.   (CYRIL *lies down and sleeps*.)
                    At last.   Thanks, kindly sleep.
Unfee'd physician, work thy cure.   For me,
I can nor rest nor labour.
                    (*He moves restlessly about, pauses*.)
                    Morn already !
Another night has crept into the void

And silent space of that eternity
That went before the world.   If I have scorned,
O restful night, thy brief and priced hours,
I have robbed them of their sterner portion too,
Dark dream and bitter fancy.
                              (*A knock, he does not heed it.*)
                              Julia, Julia !
              (*Knocking repeated.   Enter* DEVERELL, *bursting
              in the door.*)

DEVERELL.
You keep me knocking at your beggarly hutch
As though I were your servant, fellow, not
You *mine.*

GAGE.
      You have supplied the reason.   'Tis
A beggarly hutch, and not a palace.

DEVERELL.
                              What ?

GAGE.
I say 'tis not a palace.

DEVERELL.
      Well ?

GAGE.
                              No need
To thunder at a poor man's door.   'Tis free
To all, as 'tis to death.   (*Turns away.*)   I am a fool
To rail.

DEVERELL.
      Proceed, sir.   Where didst learn this fine
Philosophy ?

GAGE.
In sorrow's school.

DEVERELL.
                    I thought so!
There's not a student, under his wise rule,
But he's a paragon of virtue.   Come,
My papers; are they finished?

GAGE.
                No.

DEVERELL.
                        No!   Not—
Not finished?   And you dare sit idling here.
Why, sirrah, 'tis a loss of fifty pounds,
If 'tis a penny.

GAGE.
                And to me a loss
Of, let me see, five groats.   Is't not enough
To starve?

DEVERELL.
            Hark, sirrah!   I have known you long,
And learned your fashions.   In the eyes of men
You do affect a breathless industry—
A very lust of labour; a fine love
Of honesty, which, much exalting thee,
Of all men else makes thieves; yet here you sit
In sullen laziness, that hardly deigns
Move hand to lip, charged with the unearned food
That better men provide thee.   As for *him*,
The indolent whelp, I'll quickly—   (*Approaches* CYRIL.)

GAGE (*starting up*).
                No.   Stand back!
He is too ill to labour.   You may read
So much in that white cheek.   Stand back, sir, or—
(*Aside*).   But patience first.   Good master Deverell,
Touch not my gentle brother.

DEVERELL.
                'Sdeath! I will.

Get up, sir.   (*Shakes him.*)   Work !   My papers ?   Up !
    No drones
Hive here.   (*Seizes him roughly.*)

                    GAGE (*rushing on him*).
            Thou thing of self—unmannered brute,
Aping man's presence.
                    (*Hurls him to the other end of the room.*)
                            Cheerly, Cyril.   Nay,
Lie down again.   Be tranquil.   *I* am here.

            DEVERELL (*who has risen slowly*).
Who houses serpents must beware their sting.
It is a perilous mercy.   I'll be quit on't.
Boys, we will speak again.   (*Exit DEVERELL.*)

                        CYRIL.
                    What !—is he gone?
What said he, brother ?

                        GAGE.
                    Nay, I care not.   Yet,
The red, malignant flicker his dull eye
Sent back to us, spoke mischief.   Had you but
The needful strength, we might go forth and seek
A better, friendlier shelter.   Back already !
                            (*Re-enter DEVERELL.*)

                    DEVERELL.
Now, gentle master Francis, aye, and you,
My pretty Cyril, though I'd willingly
Bear with some loss, I cannot entertain
Guests of such hot design.   If I mistake not,
There stands a brief account between us here
For food, for coin advanced, for lodging.   Now,
Pay me, or tramp.

                        CYRIL.
            Alas ! goodmaster.

GAGE (*pointing to* CYRIL).
Look.
He's ill.

DEVERELL.
The almshouse, or the hospital.
Come, sir. I wait, sir. What! no money? None?
Shall I be swindled thus; and when I come
Softly to seek mine own, be bowled aside
Like a king ninepin?

GAGE.
Fellow, give us peace
Till evening, I will then account to thee
For more than is thy due.

DEVERELL.
Do you forget
The blow? *I* do not. Were yon livid wretch
At his last gasp, he should not spend it here.
You know the law, sir. Out he goes! Away!

GAGE.
I *know* the law. He shall not.

DEVERELL.
Good. I'll help
You forth. (*Stamps, Bailiff and Assistants enter.*)
Now, Master Grasp, come in, and rid
This dove's nest of some cuckoos.
(CYRIL *leans faintly on* F. GAGE.

GAGE.
Force alone
Shall move us. Don't essay it. (*Enter* PEMBROKE.)

PEMBROKE.
Is— How now?
A brawl?

DEVERELL.
Another creditor !

PEMBROKE.
                    I come
To Master Gage.   Is this his chamber, sir

DEVERELL.
No, sir, 'tis mine ; though, 'faith, this advocate,
This man of law, disputes it with me.   What's
Your pleasure with him ?

PEMBROKE.
                    You're his clerk then?

DEVERELL.
                                        I !

PEMBROKE.
Who bade you ask my pleasure, then ?

DEVERELL.
                            His *clerk !*
This fellow's— 'Sdeath !   Sir, you shall presently see
Who's clerk, who master.   Troop, sirs.

PEMBROKE (*interposing*).
                            Patience, fellow.
Must we hear nothing but your brawling tongue?
I come to Master Gage, the advocate.
If I mistake not, *this* is he—and, sir,
I would entreat ten words.

DEVERELL.
                    Then take the street
For council-chamber.   This fine lawyer, sir,
Hath not a closet save what sparrows, daws,
Kites, and such vermin, share with him.   Come on.
My money, sir ; ten crowns.

PEMBROKE.
        Ten crowns ! There's twenty,
              (*Throws a purse.*)
Only to stop thy mouth. And now, begone.
A life's at stake, sir. Leave us.
      (DEVERELL *gazes a moment in surprise, then goes
      out with Attendants, etc.*)
              I am here
In anxious suit, seek honest aid, and take,
You see, the nearest way.

GAGE.
        A friendly face
Needs no apologist. Nay, I hold some clue,
For you have called me honest, and may know
It is my popular nickname, sir. Are *you* so?
Do you come fairly from the world to court
A man that's out of fashion ?

PEMBROKE.
        Fairly, sir.
Waste no suspicion on me. I am sent
By one in peril, whom *you* can aid—none better ;
Indeed none else.

GAGE.
      Not *you*, sir, but your gold
Roused my distrust. My clients wear no purses ;
They are poor common knaves, downtrodden mostly,
Under some golden wrong. We starve together.
Truth is a hungry calling. To the point !
Those twenty crowns—

PEMBROKE (*hesitating*).
      I fear that I—

GAGE.
          Say on.
You have a suit that must be pressed, and I,

You know, lack labour.   I'll not slumber on't,
Be sure.   And, for the cause, 'tis based, I know,
On right and honesty, else wherefore here?

PEMBROKE.
'Faith, sir, you bid me speak, and yet your words
 Crush mine i'the forming.   I'd invoke your aid,
To soften guilt scarce questioned.   'Tis indeed,
A monarch fault, a crime whose giant shape
Unfolds so redly on the eyes of men,—
Displays such foul and hideous leprosy,
It might almost be stamped a fellow-sin
To speak on such a side, or interpose
One breath, when justice, armed and terrible,
Awakes to strike it down.

GAGE.
'Tis.

PEMBROKE.
                    Murder?!

GAGE (*after a pause*).
                                        Well!
That's called so, which sometimes is none.   The fruit
Of madness, misadventure.

PEMBROKE.
                    Here 'tis linked
With a most foul accomplice—one that oft,
Working less bloodily, hath murdered too—
Filthy ingratitude.   Serene old age—
But I waste time.   Sir Philip Lancaster
Is dead—by poison.

GAGE.
                    Dead !   Then parricide
Is rife among us.

PEMBROKE.
Strange !

GAGE.
What's strange, sir?

PEMBROKE.

That
You touch the point so boldly.   Did you say—
Parricide ?

GAGE.
Aye, sir, not a wretch but found
A father in him !   You would have me plead
For his assassin !   *Me!*   I would not deem
That you intend an insult.   Pardon me,   (*Rises.*)
Time wears.

PEMBROKE (*going*).
Sir, God be with you.   As regards
Those coins, I—

GAGE (*starting*).
I had forgotten.   Take
Your offered— T'tis too late.   Sir, do not bind
My gratitude in such foul, loathsome chains !
Nay then, some cause, some colourable end,
Why this fair life was ta'en.   Not ev'n the savage
Will slay for slaying's sake.   What cause, sir?   Madness?
Nor wrong? nor insult ? nor revenge?

PEMBROKE.
There's none.
(*As* GAGE *stands irresolute,* CYRIL *leans upon
him.*)

GAGE.
'Tis a bargain.   Now, sir, to your tale ;
Out with it, quick.   Show me the ditch, the pool,
Where I must plunge these honest hands and wring

The filthy dregs. I am guilt's sworn brother. Come,
Show't me, I say!

PEMBROKE.
That's reasonable, now.
Listen. An hour past sunrise, you shall hear
Two blows on yonder panel. When you'd see
The murderer—

GAGE.
How, at large?

PEMBROKE.
But trebly girt,
With eyes that would outstare the basilisk.
Stay—you may need more gold. Here, here, and here.
Mark me; an hour past sunrise. (*Exit* PEMBROKE.)

GAGE (*after a pause*).
Cyril, Cyril,
Is—is he gone?

CYRIL.
Our *friend*, dear brother! look,
The gold.

GAGE.
Sweet Cyril, 'tis the wage of hell!
And I and honesty henceforth are foes.
   (*Falls on* CYRIL'S *neck.*)

———

SCENE II.—*A saloon in* TRAFFORD'S *house.*

(*Music heard within. Guests enter in departure.*
MORDAUNT, GOSSELIN, SANDELL, *and others.*
TRAFFORD *follows eagerly.*)

TRAFFORD.
Nay, come ; another round.

GOSSELIN.
Enough, already ;
Day blushes for us.   Look !

TRAFFORD.
Yet one more chorus,
Then part.   Fill up the goblets,—gentlemen.
A health (*guests going*).   Indeed !   Well if it must be so,
My good friends all, farewell.   (*Exeunt Guests.*)
Fairfax !   (*Enter Steward*).   The hour?

FAIRFAX.
Night should be past, sir, yet it is not day.
The lids of morning droop.   The sun was never
So loath to shine !

TRAFFORD.
So shamed, sir ; that were truer ;
O that, for one day, man might sleep supine,
And the surprised sun sink, as he arose,
The witness of no sorrow !   Hist !

FAIRFAX.
I heard
No noise, sir.

TRAFFORD.
Man, nor I, 'twas fancy raised
Those shouts and cries of— (*a roll of thunder*).   Hark !

FAIRFAX.
'Tis thunder.

TRAFFORD.
Groans
Wrung from the over-burdened element.
Not, as some say, the voice—   (*Enter a Servant.*)

SERVANT.

A woman, sir,
Craved shelter from the storm, who, having heard
Your name, fell swooning, and hath since besought
A moment's speech with you.

TRAFFORD.

Admit her.   Leave me.
(Exeunt Servants.   Enter INFELICE.*)*
Spirit of unrest!
Always prophetic of mischance and ill;
Pale star that sittest in my house of life,
To thwart my fairest auguries! alas—
Why dost thou ever haunt me?

INFELICE.

For revenge,
Or justice.

TRAFFORD.

Will you threaten?   Learn the truth.
The spring-day of my passion hath gone by.
The ghost of a dead love is loathlier far
Than was its being beauteous.   Do you doubt?
Look on my cheek, 'tis white; the eye-lid dry;
There, take my hand, 'tis cold.   You cannot trace
Love's fever in't.   The pulse, 'tis slow and dull,
Passion's quick foot skips like a bacchanal!
Farewell, and peace be with thee!

INFELICE.

Alas! alas!
For the dear quiet meadows where we passed
That first unconscious time?   Why did you teach
The wrong you will not mend?   Why roughly wake
This restless, inward monitor; then leave me
To bear the scourge alone?   Why say that we
Should, in like peace, with hands thus fondly twined,
And hearts thus bound, pass on from youth to age,

And I, *thy wife?*   Alas! I knew not then
What worth was in that word.   Both blest, and I
So rich in love, I would have given it for
A kiss, a smile, a word,—a very *word*
Had you so wooed me.

TRAFFORD.
Why this change?

INFELICE (*concealing her face*).
Because
It lacked the mirror of the world's hard eye
To teach my heart its nakedness.

TRAFFORD.
Enough—
My girl.   You speak in vain.   Between our souls
Is hung a veil through whose funereal gauze
Thy form, once fair, grows hideous.   You know not
What toils environ me—what frowning fears
Make death seem beautiful.

INFELICE (*eagerly*).
Dash them aside,
And live!   A gentle voice to our lost home
Recalls us.   Come away; quit these dark scenes,
And seek once more the valley where we strayed
From morn, not blither than our own glad souls,
Till languid eve, when to our lattice-pane
The prating night breeze stole with kiss and hymn
To chide our tireless talk.   Cheerly, sweet life,
Come; we have both been wanderers.   I, the first,
Have seen the peril of the way; and now—
By honour's path, to truth, to peace, to love,
To calm in this poor world, and bliss beyond—
I woo thee back.
     (TRAFFORD *turns, deeply moved, and holds her by*
       both arms apart.)

TRAFFORD.
My love! my own!

INFELICE.
Ah, Heaven !
He loves me yet ! *Thine own !* Oh ! let me die
Thus on thy breast, my weary sad heart's home.
Thou wilt not force thy worn and shattered bark
To warring seas again.   (*Enter a Servant. running.*)

SERVANT.
Sir, sir, alas !
Oh ! good Sir Philip—

TRAFFORD (*seizing him*).
Fellow, when—where—how ?
Who did the deed ?

SERVANT.
The murder, sir !

TRAFFORD (*eagerly*).
Away !
Call up thy fellows, arm them—

SERVANT.
Sir, 'tis vain,
The wretch was taken.

TRAFFORD.
Ah !
(*Servant approaching him, whispers. He drops
his sword.*)
Dog ! this is false.
Some palsied beldame duped thee with this tale,
Wrought out of drunken sleep. (*Servant whispers again.*)

INFELICE.
Alas ! alas !
What dreadful thing has chanced ?   Speak, dearest,
speak,
Let me partake thy sorrow.

TRAFFORD (*trying to avoid her*).
Woman, go.
You madden me.   Is this a time— Begone !

INFELICE (*clinging to him*).
Not in thy sorrow, then.   I love thee.

TRAFFORD.
Hence !
(*Throws her off, and exit.*)

INFELICE.
Hear, earth, sole parent !   Ere this humbled knee
Lift from thy dusty bosom life's dull load,
From throne and empire do I here depose
My o'er-enduring love ; thought, word, or deed,
By love engendered, do confess a sin ;
And every gift of nature, reason, strength,
Wit, courage, craft, devote to furnish forth
A vengeance worthy of my wrongs—and *thee !*   (*Exit.*)

SCENE III.--*The apartment of* GAGE.

(GAGE *discovered reading.*)

GAGE.
" Wherefore, to let the guiltie 'scape the law,
Is soe much mercie as he findes who slippes
The hangman's gripe, and, leapynge, is empayled
Upon the speares below."*   'Tis quaintly summed,
But with such close and cogent reasoning,
Thou plead'st for patience and the sheathed sword,
'Tis won ; and herein will I marshal me

* The remark of an old writer.

Upon the piteous side.   (*Shuts the book.*)
                            A sound—a step!
The murderer comes.   Oh guilt! what deadly fear;
What sick, expectant tremor, conscience-born,
Is eloquent in every glance and breath,
Footfall and finger-touch!   (*A knock.*)   Thou knockest
    timidly
For one of heart so bold.   Approach.
                    (*Enter* JULIA LANCASTER.)
(*Without turning*)   Approach.
Why dost thou hesitate?   I sit not here
To judge thee, but defend.   What, robbed of speech?
(*Aside*)   Perchance he weeps; and if he weeps there's
    shame,
And shame is pitiful.   (*Looks round and starts up.*)
(*After a pause*)   'Tis life!   It breathes!
Oh! lady, why—   Your will, beseech you?   Pardon,
I did not dream of this.   'Twas Pembroke's tongue
Bade me expect—not *thee*—

JULIA.
               My messenger
Did his kind mission faithfully.   All, save he,
Fled from my side, scared by this cloud of blood,
And left me to the storm.

GAGE.
              Grief, gentle lady,
For this most sudden and most foul misdeed
Hath hurt your reason.

JULIA.
             Are my words so wild?
I did not know it.   Pardon; I'll be brief;
Indeed, 'tis needful, for without stand those
Will not be long controlled.   Misjudge me not,
That's necessary too.   Know therefore, sir,
I am by nature cold and passionless;
An unemotioned, tearless wretch,—not so
The safer—happier.   Such mental mould

Repels the pigmy darts that slay the weak ,
But when the arrow pierces, it remains
And rankles to the core.   Not joy, nor grief,
Nor any sharp soul-sickness ever dimmed
Mine eye, nor spurred these pulses.   Place a hand
Here, on my bosom ; there's the heart within,
Coldly and sternly pacing to and fro
His natural prison.   I would kneel and bless you
If you could make me weep.

GAGE.

Pray speak your will;
Why breathe I but to hear it?

JULIA.

Softly, sir ;
Here will be recantations.   To be plain,
I am called Sir Philip's murderer.

GAGE.

Thou ?   Oh, Heaven !
Who dares accuse thee?   Tell me, let me seek
In his black heart—

JULIA.

I seek an advocate,
A man of peace, crafty, and wise, and cool;
Quick to discern, and patient to enlarge
Such flaw as chance may offer in that net
Spread to enmesh the guilty—

GAGE.

Yes, the guilty—
Not *thee !*—not *thee !*

JULIA.

Have I denied the deed ?

GAGE.

Nay, do so ; I had forgotten.   How long bear you

My questioning gaze ?   Must I, to win denial,
Ev'n feign suspicion ?

JULIA.

> To the work in hand ;
For my unliveried pages will abide
No longer question.   Listen.   I was seized—
The fatal goblet in *this* hand ; and *this*,
Glued to the old man's white and wrinkled brow,
Searching 'midst its dead pulses to discern
If more were left to do.   Thus was I found,
I—*I*, his nurse—his leech—his cupbearer—
Almost his pillow, for no sleep so calm
As that which visited those grey old lids
At rest upon my bosom.

GAGE.

> Thanks, kind Heaven !
All's clear, all's safe !   You knew not—could not dream
That death was in the cup.

JULIA.

> So well I knew
That silent agent's skill and potency,
That when I saw the baleful glitter hang
Upon his lip, I knew me fatherless
Ere life had fluttered forth.   Have I not said
None but myself did cater to his meal ?
None but myself watched o'er his slumbering ?
Hath any seen me mourn him ?   If not guilt,
It is a task well worth your eloquence
To give't an honest mien.

GAGE.

> Eternal power !
Rend off the veil from this strange heart, and show
Its natural colour.

JULIA.

Will you answer me ?

I sent for other aid.   Alas ! none came.
You have infected men with hate of crime ;
And not for gold—ambition—pity—pride—
Will *one* hold counsel with me.   You have cut
My hope away.   Defend—or let me die.

GAGE.

I will defend you, but—Oh, woman ! woman !
If you have done this, you have slandered Heaven,—
Lied to the hand that framed and sent you forth
A bright ambassador to teach mankind
Truth's grace and loveliness !   Thus, double traitress
To nature and to God, how can you hope
Emancipation ?   Speak, in mercy, speak !
For oh ! 'tis easier than to think thee guilty,
To hold that mirror false in which we view
Men's crimes inlimned,—the scales iniquitous
In which we weigh them.   Guide us now, great Heaven,
That, for some wise inexplicable end,
Hast let the rebel angels loose among us,
But veiled their thunder-scars.   (*He turns away.*)

JULIA.
Well, your reply,

And quickly ?   I am called.

GAGE (*eagerly*).
I am resolved ;

Guilty or not, strange being, I am thine,
Heart, soul, and brain.   Oh ! yet be merciful.
Hear me, thou shalt—
(*Throws himself madly at her feet.*)
Look !   By this constant earth,

The air that robes it, and the heaven that guides—
By every passion sown in human hearts—
Mine own unheeded love, by these fond tears
That, bursting some sealed conduit, will have way,—
With glance or gesture, if not word, reply—
Are you not innocent ?   Lift from my soul

The burden of this doubt, and all that love,
Such as man never felt, can urge man to,—
Art, eloquence, and skill, and zeal, and passion,—
I'll do for thee, and, Heav'n permitting, *save* thee.
Art thou not innocent ?
                (JULIA *stamps slightly.   Several persons enter
                    and surround her.*)

                        JULIA.
                        You see.   And so,
Farewell.   For ever,— or but till the hour
Of trial ?   Speak.   I may expect you?

                    GAGE (*hides his face*).   .
                                            Aye.
            (*Exit* JULIA, *guarded.*   GAGE *sinks into his
                chair.*)

END OF ACT III.

ACT IV.

SCENE I.—*A room in* TRAFFORD'S *house.*

(Enter FAIRFAX, *with* INFELICE *disguised.)*

FAIRFAX.

Eat, drink, and sleep ; 'tis well, sir. What beside ?
Canst lie, too ?

INFELICE.
    No.

FAIRFAX.
Why, there, thou dost ! How old ?

INFELICE.

Eighteen, sir.

FAIRFAX.
    And no falsehood yet ? Tell truth,
For eighteen years ! A page, too ? 'Tis the first
Step of thy calling.

INFELICE.
    An it please you, sir,
Under tuition, I'll soon—

FAIRFAX (*pushes her away*).
    Out!

INFELICE.
           But I've
Some lighter arts, sir. I can sing a stave,
Dance, strike the cymbal—

FAIRFAX (*turning*).
                    Sing! boy.   Canst thou sing?
Then serve my master.   'Faith, one strain shall more
Bestead thee than a score of silken lies,
Spun from the devil's own loom.   My master's sick
For music.   If thy warbling can allay
His frenzied spirit, we are thy debtors all ;
For since his kinsman's murder, he doth fright
All duty from him.   Go, my boy, get food,
Dress, and come hither.
            (*Exit* INFELICE.   TRAFFORD *enters slowly and
                dejectedly, his dress neglected, etc.*)
                    Sir, I've chanced upon
A minstrel page.

TRAFFORD.
            I met him yonder ; 'tis
A fair, well-seeming boy.   There was a thought
Troubling my mind.   Ah! Fairfax, didst thou give
Those alms I spoke of?

FAIRFAX.
                    Aye, sir !   Gratefully,
The poor souls took them ; will repay, too, nobly
With poverty's sole coin—its tearful prayers.

TRAFFORD.
This wealth was lent, 'tis bought.   But *will* they do so ?
Will they remember, Fairfax?

FAIRFAX.
                    On my faith,
I think so.

TRAFFORD.
        Go !   (*Exit* FAIRFAX.)
            I am restless, sick, and sad,
Faint at the heart, and weary in the limb,
Could bluster with a sparrow, chide the wind
That, with the music of its westering moans,

Mocks my tumultuous—   (*Re-enter* FAIRFAX.)
                How, sir!   I have said
I'll speak with none.
                (*Enter* DEVERELL.   FAIRFAX *retires.*)

DEVERELL.
But *friends*.   (TRAFFORD *turns away.*)   Aye, friends,
    good sir,
If you'll hear all.   You owe me, as I think,
Some seven thousand—   (*Looks at tablets.*)

TRAFFORD (*impatiently*).
                Know at once, old man,
I cannot pay thee.

DEVERELL.
            Nay, most honoured sir,
Who talked of payment?   Thomas Deverell
Feels for his friends.   He's not a post, a stone,
And seeks no further than to 'scape the losses
Men daily thrust upon him.

TRAFFORD.
                Master Deverell,
Show me your drift.   You knew my hopes, and how
This most unhappy——

DEVERELL.
            Murder!   Aye, I know
What's said, and I suspect that—You look pale!

TRAFFORD.
Proceed, man.   Never heed my looks.   (*Sits down.*)

DEVERELL.
                    'Tis plain
She's guilty; and, as lucky fortune wills,
Old black-browed Gisborne sits in judgment,—he
Whose life his own child sought.   He'll not be found
Too hard of faith!   What slender proof soe'er,

He'll hang her for ensample.   But the law
Is complex and unsure, and those wise brains
Who lend, for wage, the talents Heaven assigned,
In aid of its worst foes, might haply light
Upon some nook of refuge.   Now, admire
My prudence, sir.   I have seen these gentlemen ;
Some I have bought, persuaded some, of some
Deep in my debt, made sure ; and so 'twill fall
That no lip opens on the accused side ;
No witness called to palliate, nor quaint rule
Be twisted to her safety.   What remains ?
The murderess once disposed, her forfeit wealth
Due to the crown, shall, on petition, fall
To you, her kinsman.   Is this—Ha ! how now !
Fall'n senseless !   Ho !

(Re-enter INFELICE and FAIRFAX.)

Look to your lord.   Poor fool ! (*aside ; exit*).

TRAFFORD (recovering).

Then he is gone ; nay, leave me ; all is well.
I will o'ercome this weakness.

FAIRFAX.

Sir, the Court

Send to require your presence.

TRAFFORD (to INFELICE).

Alan, haste

To master Pembroke.   Bid him follow me
To—to the court—of—ah ! he knows.   Away.

(Exeunt.)

SCENE II.—*The street.   Exterior of the Court Hall.*

*(Many persons assembled and passing to and fro.
Enter* PEMBROKE *and* INFELICE.*)*

PEMBROKE.

This note, boy, to your master.   As you pass,
Note well the prisoner—looks she red or pale—
Stands she—or sits—who's speaking ; if the judge,
The elder of them, he with sluggish brows,
Fingers his robe, *thus.*   Then to me again ;
Here will I stand beside this pillar.   Fly.

(*Exit* INFELICE.)

Myself I dare not trust.   Here's one comes forth—

(*Enter a clerk.*)

How goes the day, sir ?

CLERK (*with a conceited air*).
Very gloomily
For justice ; well for those, sir, who possess
Light consciences, and skill in drugs !   (*Exit.*)

PEMBROKE (*approaching nearer*).
All's still !
What beating hearts anticipate the birth
Of fate, that pregnant pause may furnish !   Ah !
(*A sudden and loud murmur heard within, then
enter two Advocates, eagerly conversing.*)

FIRST ADVOCATE.

Well spoke, I grant !   But 'tis a dangerous zeal
That o'ersteps nature.   Never was truth so mauled,
So daubed with fancies hypothetical,
Andthrust in reason's room !   (*Exeunt.*)

(*Enter another Advocate.*)

PEMBROKE (*meeting him*).
Whither so fast ?

THIRD ADVOCATE.
To burn my books, sir, sell my gown, and give
My tongue a lasting holiday.   No hope
For plain dull plodders more.   Gage is the man !
In the rich field of mortal eloquence
He hath not left a flower.   No sophistry
Forgotten, shift unventured.   Sir, he forced
Belief from weak hearts.   Where the strong refused,
He took his tribute out in womanish tears,
Dropt on the yellow scrolls his pained, pleased hearers
Sought to seem studying !   Hearts of adamant,
And nerves of steel ! else is yon fair wretch free,
Half England at her footstool.   Ha !
            (GAGE *staggers out.   They surround him.*)

OMNES.
            Huzza !

GAGE (*struggling through them.*)
Off   I breathe fire !

A CLERK (*follows him eagerly with scrolls*).
        An hundred crowns, sir, hold—
Plead but this cause to-morrow.   We have long
Beheld your rising.   No !   Then, fifty more,
A hundred more !   *Two* hundred, sir, for *this*—
And every future—

GAGE (*distractedly*).
      Lost ! lost ! lost !   (*Rushes out.*)

CLERK.
        O ! mad.
         (*Returns.*)

(PEMBROKE *to* INFELICE *who enters*).
Alas ! condemned.   Away !   Let's after him.
        (*Exeunt.   Crowd disperse.*)

SCENE III.—*The Court.*

(*Judges and officials seated. JULIA stands before them, guarded. TRAFFORD as accuser, with Advocates, etc. The court, crowded with persons of both sexes, is dimly lighted, and the whole wears a dismal aspect.*)

FIRST JUDGE.

Record the verdict.

CRIER OF THE COURT.
Julia Lancaster,
Duly convict of blood and parricide,
Hold up thy hand.   Keep silence.

SECOND JUDGE.
Stay a moment.
If, Julia Lancaster, thou hast ought to urge
In stay of lawful sentence, speak it now ;
Our duty bids us hear.

JULIA.
O, good my lords,
Abhor me not, that I have learned to rule
Those mental furies—passion, hate, and fear ;
To see nought strange in any giddy height
That guilt may reach at ; nothing beautiful
In innocence assumed, or worthy blame
In that too-eager justice which o'erleaps
The crouching guilt, and hunts the innocent
For that it seems to fly.   Great griefs are dumb ;
And, as the heart-wound leaves but little trace,
The bitterest tears fall inward.   Tell me what
Shall nature build on, if her holiest fields
Are mined with murder ? cultivate what flowers,
If opening buds burn up the parent tree
With poisonous distillation ?   How, sirs, give

Death with caresses?   Steal my father's life
Holding his white head to my breast?   For so
Ye found him.   Yes, thence had he gone, and left me
Richer by nothing of the gifts of life,
And poorer, by a parent.   But, for I know
An iron fate, stifling my better will,
Shall, for a season, keep this mystery sealed
Out of man's knowledge, and my life, meanwhile,
A loathsome and polluted thing—*content*,
I give it ye.   (*Turns.*)   But, by this hand I raise
Up toward the source of truth, I now adjure
The doer of this dark and monstrous deed,
Shortly to meet me, and to answer there
The stain of double murder.   I have done.

TRAFFORD (*rising eagerly*).
Sirs, I beseech you, spare her.   Let her live,
If there be doubt.   Nature herself declares
This crime too hideous, and man's elder law
Soiled not its mighty page with parricide's
Impossible name.   If mercy—

MANY VOICES (*murmuringly*).
Mercy!   Mercy!

A CLERK (*aside to Another*).
He hath but clenched it.   Ha! mark Gisborne *now*.

ANOTHER.
Aye, dumb and white with rage.   Thinking, poor devil,
Of his own assassin-daughter.

FIRST JUDGE (*rising*).
Master Trafford,
You do mistake your office, lending breath
To that besotted cry.   Above your head
The murdered victim shakes his grizzled hair,
Moaning for vengeance.   Shall our cups be baned?
Harm dogs unpolicied mercy.   Life for life!

The sword that glances from the well-condemned
Stabs twenty guiltless.   Woman, raise thy head.
Hark.   As those cressets flicker and grow wan,
So ebbs thy life.   And, look you, since 'tis meet
That, in the scraping this unnatural blot
From God's disfigured earth, there should be shown
Some due abhorrence, though the rope be shameful,
And the axe keen, we here pronounce on thee
The penalty of *fire.*

JULIA.
I am very young.
How long, my lords, may be accorded me
To urge life's feelings, memories, hopes, and fears,
To this untimely harvest—pluck their roots,
And cast them, in one fair and living heap,
Into my gaping grave ?   How long ?

SECOND JUDGE.
Three days,
Which, by petition on the accuser's part,
May somewhat be enlarged.

FIRST JUDGE.
Not at my will.
Three days, thou murderess ! Aye, thou witch, three days.
Therefore, prepare.

JULIA.
I will, my lord, and when
I shall recount my catalogue of sin,
Murder and witchcraft, as my chiefest crimes,
Shall first be thought of.
(*As the Judge rises,* GAGE *rushes in eagerly*

FIRST JUDGE (*turning from him*).
Drag her to the cell.
Proclaim the Court dissolved.

GAGE.
Not so, my lords.
I have that to urge—

FIRST JUDGE.
You are too tardy, sir.
Not even your fiery eloquence can stay
The course of justice longer.

GAGE.
Keep your scorn
Till you have heard.

FIRST JUDGE.
Sir, sir, I've heard enough.
The day's, I trust, not distant far when guilt
Shall fee no devil's advocate. What need
Hath innocence of a mentor? Have you witness?
If not, I hear not.

GAGE.
Witness I have none.
But in those ancient volumes, by whose rule
Our fathers meted justice, it is writ,
That if a prisoner, howsoe'er accused
(The act not seen), shall by a champion's sword
Engage, and, ere the first star shines, prevail,
He shall be free. No scroll less merciful
Repeals this plain enactment. On the part
Of Julia Lancaster, I here demand
The wage of battle.   (*Sensation; a pause.*)

FIRST JUDGE.
Rather would I blot
One twelvemonth from this waning calendar,
Than stretch a life so forfeit. But the law
Cannot be curbed, nor lightly bent aside,
Even to good ends. 'Tis granted. Master Trafford,
Throw down your gauntlet. Do you pause, sir? How!
You are the challenger.   (TRAFFORD *drops his glove.*)

> There lies his gage.
And with his body in a listed field,
Will he defend our sentence.

GAGE.
> It is well.

FIRST JUDGE.
Where is your champion, girl ?   'Tis a short step
From field to scaffold.

JULIA.
> Aye, if Heaven so wills.

FIRST JUDGE.
Peace, thou profane one !   Should the appellant yield,
He dies before thee.

GAGE.
Aye.

FIRST JUDGE (*to* JULIA).
> Can I not shake
Thy stubborn spirit ?   To the cell with her.
> (*Exeunt Judges and others.*)

END OF ACT IV.

ACT V.

SCENE I.—*A large gloomy apartment in the house of the* LANCASTERS. *Old pictures hang round.*

(TRAFFORD *discovered at a table writing*.)

TRAFFORD (*starting*).
Again, thou boding voice !   Will no thought drown,
No reason stifle thee ?   Have I not said
She shall not perish ?   Can the eyesight weep
Red, visible blood, that wheresoe'er I turn,
A drop lies weltering ?   Dim shapes flit by,
Old men, with halting gait and grizzled hair,
While from the walls an hundred grim old sires
Glare hate like mocking demons.   O ! my soul,
Fear'st thou to wear thy dearly purchased crown ?
Cup of my life, art thickening to the dregs,
And yet no sweetness ?   I—I cannot bear
This shrieking silence.   Alan, Alan !   Boy,
                              (*Enter* INFELICE.)
Come hither.   In this tedious march of life,
The few steps thou hast walked with me have wrought
A pathway through my heart.   I say, my boy,
I do believe none, none in all this world,
Saving thyself, doth love me.   'Tis most strange
How like thou art to—there—'tis gone again,
Form, air, and voice and feature.   Sure, if those
We love—   (INFELICE *laughs*.)
          Why smilest thou ?

INFELICE.
                    Pardon me.   To think
Of the fantastic forms love takes.

TRAFFORD (*thoughtfully*).
                    'Twas much
To say I loved her then. But there's a thing
That bears so much love's semblance, that 'tis hard
To name it lowlier. The difference is,
It lacks the undying soul. It is a fire
That may be quenched, re-kindled, drowned again,
Yet hold a glimmering vitality,
Obedient to the hour ; but love, that curse,
That serpent, fostered in man's heart to turn
Its little good to ill, can know no change,
No, not an hour's death.

INFELICE.
                Do you yet repent
Your rage with Infelice? Would you—

TRAFFORD.
                        Boy,
I never knew repentance.

INFELICE (*aside bitterly*).
                'Tis to learn.

TRAFFORD.
What say'st thou? Alan, I did bid thee once,
Or 'twas my purpose, question of her fate.
What didst thou hear?

INFELICE.
Sir, she is dead.

TRAFFORD.
                Dead !

INFELICE.
                      Aye.
She, that did so adore thee, lives no more.
Heart-dead, she wanders through a world that hath,
Like thee, no pity for the fool that gave

The bright pearl honour, for the ruby love,
And failed of both. Beware! For with such rule,
As night treads out the dead sun's track, doth hate
Spring from the sepulchre of love that's slain
By him that was its keeper.

TRAFFORD.
Be it so.
Here's scarce enough of peace for her revenge
To flesh its tooth upon. God rest her! *Dead!*
I trust she is. The stamp of horse! Look out!
Beneath the window. Fly! boy. Wilt thou let
Good news stand shivering at the door, and leave
Its welcome to cold lips of—   (*Exit* INFELICE.)
Now—Oh! *Now*—
Pardon—reprieve—or—God!   (*Sinks into his chair.*)
Come, Alan! What?
To hear a laugh, a happy cry, a leap,
A bounding step i'the stair. O! crawler. Gone
An hour!   (*Re-enter* INFELICE.)
Thou hast it on thy cheek. Shriek, owl!
Is—is it—

INFELICE.
Death.

TRAFFORD.
Why there's a black page turned.
Leave me—to bed! Sleep, if thou canst. No; stay
Without awhile. These news have troubled me,
Even past belief. My prayer refused, though backed
With untold wealth. Not gone?

INFELICE.
So please you, sir,
You have guests to supper, bade to celebrate
The pardon you—

TRAFFORD.
Why, let them come. But—stay.

The little flask thou know'st of, let it stand
Beside me at the board.   I warned thee once,
Did I not, Alan, what a dangerous gem
Gleams in that crystal casket?   'Faith, of late
It likes me to consort with things of death ;
I love to raise that flask before the sun,
And think that every crimson mote that skips
And glitters there, can drag down to the grave
A giant's life.   It is a dreary thought,
And should not be indulged.   Thou'lt do this?
                              (INFELICE *smiles.*)
How?   My mission pleases thee?

                    INFELICE.
                              It ever does,
To serve my gentle lord.   (*Exit* INFELICE).

                    TRAFFORD (*starting*).
                              Again—wild knell!
                                        (*Exit.*)

                SCENE II.—*A prison.*

(JULIA *lies asleep upon a rude couch.*   GAGE
   stands beside her, his arms folded.)

                    GAGE.
She stirs not,—hardly breathes.   If flattering tongues
Brought this brief rest, these latest friends have proved
Thy falsest.   But a moment, I am loth
To snatch away the robe of this sweet calm,
Since deep indeed must be the rest that next
Shall marry those dear lids.   If *guilt* be here,
Then conscience, sick of torture, drops the whip,
And dozes o'er the wheel.   If *innocence,*

Would thou wast dead before me !   (*Clock heard.*
                                        To my task.
Wake, madam.   (*Kneels and kisses her hand.*)

        JULIA (*awaking and starting up*).
                Is it time ?

                GAGE.
                        Dear lady, yes ;
For life's great end.   Prepare.

                JULIA.
                        Look up ; I fear not !
Men hold my cause dishonour.   I must die.

                GAGE.
'Tis even so.   Death robes himself in peace,
And lays his dart aside, and takes your hand
To lead you past all ill.   Your sleep was calm,
And I was anxious lest that busy life
Should, with delusive and impertinent dreams,
Dress it unfitly.   Time is jealous of thee,
And, miser-like, weighs every grain that quits
Its almost drained exchequer.

                JULIA.
                        Thoughtful,—kind.
How—how repay—

                GAGE.
                You cannot.   My reward
Is this,—to seek none.

                JULIA.
                        You are cold.   I trust
We are at peace ?

                GAGE (*agitated*).
                At peace !

JULIA.
              Yes, for the wrong
My haughty spirit—

GAGE.
              Mine was haughtier, lady.
To wrong and smile is easy; theirs' the triumph
Who bear it and still smile.   Oh ! pardon me.
What do I prate of ?   Your disdain was just.
The sole fault mine, and for the punishment
Enough.   'Twas borne.

JULIA.
              You had that stay so oft
Enjoined to me, your pupil.   You could *hope.*

GAGE.
I had no hope.   Perhaps that's false, for all
Is possible to faith, and love is faith,
The blindest of all bigots,—holding trusts,
Sweet, simple, hard to blame, among them *this*,
That its immaculate idol, owning not
The low constraints of pride, makes to herself
A better law, spurns reason, knows no fear,
But that of leaving one true worshipper
Unpitied, if unpaid.

JULIA.
              But *you*, so wise,
So schooled, so doubting all that cannot show
Reason's calm countersign ?

GAGE.
                   The common law,
Retributive.   We boast our strength—and fall.
Ah ! lady, such temptations fronting him,
Man needs a better Ægis than his reason.
Warning,—example fails.   One falls ; we blame
His fortune, not his creed.   While woman breathes,
There will be idols to engender faith,

And fools to yield it.   I am mad, I think,
To mock your ear with this poor prate.   Forgive me
This, my last fault.

JULIA.

Good friend, what other?

GAGE.

Truth.

Lady, I said I loved.   To that confession
I thought my duty prompted.   It was pride.
Cowards bewail their hurts,—the brave man turns
Apart to hide them.   Which did I ?

JULIA.

'Tis easy

To pardon trespasses our bosom yearns
To copy.   I am dying ; and I use
The licence of a tongue, henceforth to keep
Its secrets better.   To these pitiless walls,
To me, that never nursed my own heart's peace,
Peace willingly came.   I am as one who sinks
In wearied slumber on some arid plain,
But, waking, finds it Paradise,—bright fruit,
And blue lakes, forest-fringed ; and mottled glades,
And waving stems, and delicate sweet flowers,
And valleys green and golden.   So my heart
Unfolds an inner life,—delicious, glad,
Exulting ; every thought a music strain,
And every pulse a joy !   Hence, pride and fear,—
Hence, womanly reserve.   Protector—friend—
I love thee !

GAGE.

Do not mock me —

JULIA.

Be it so.

It best becomes thine honour to reject
The humbled heart that, sought in fortune's noon,

Was gracelessly withheld. Poor triumph, to call
Its last few pulses thine !

GAGE (*in uncontrolled emotion*).
Life of my life !
Guide of my footsteps ! Thou sweet only star
That my hope's heaven gave throne to ! dost thou stoop
Earthward at last ? Too late, too late !

JULIA.
Dear friend,—

GAGE.
Is this a living hand ? Ah ! Julia,—Julia,
Why yield it now ?

JULIA.
To be embalmed in tears ?

GAGE.
Forgive them ; they are happy—   (*Enter* CYRIL.)
Brother, brother !
She has confessed—   *(Shouts within.)*
What cry is that ? You're pale !
What is the matter ? Speak !

CYRIL.
A mighty crowd
Is closing round the prison,—one huge sea
Of tossing arms and furious faces.

GAGE (*exultingly*).
Life ! (*Runs to* JULIA.)
'Tis life ! The storm breaks.   (*Loud tumult.*)

GAOLER (*within*).
Double the guard there. Ho !
Discharge the culverin ; we shall need more aid.
(*Shot heard. Tumult increases. Gaoler and
Guard rush in.*)
Come,—to the western tower.

ANOTHER (*rushing in*).
No,—'tis assailed.
(*The gates are attacked.	Guard defend them.*)

GAOLER.
Up to the parapets.   Arrows, lead, and stones
Are there in plenty.   Comyn, Hugo, Gray,
Surround the prisoner.   Should your iron yield,
Ye have daggers.   Use them.
(*They rush out. Attack continues.	Shouts of
"Rescue."   The Guards stand bewildered.
Gate burst in, and Guards forced off.*)

GAGE.
See,—the gates give way !

FIRST MAN.
The litter, there.   Madam, we bring you life.

JULIA.
Life !   What is life ?   The privilege to wear
Humanity's frail garb ?   Friends, you misjudge
My purpose and my will.   I seek not life
Unsanctioned by the high and unbought grace
Of justice.   The proud gratulating joy,
And honest welcome of all good men's eyes.
Hence will I pass to death,—or with a name
Clear as the heart within,—a felon doomed—
Or else an honoured sister, 'scaped more fair
From slander's noxious handling.   Oh ! away
To aims more hopeful.   Seek the guilty, or—
If Heaven so will it—one devoted arm
To meet the accuser *there.*

FIRST MAN.
Who dare do that?
Beast !—liar as he is—a man must own
He's good at sword-craft.

JULIA.

Then to your homes.   Fall down,—
Plead for the soul whose earthly house must fall.
Die not to save the dying.   Hear my words,—
There is more pain in serpent-slander's tongue
Than any mortal death.   (*Takes* GAGE'S *hand.*)
Within this hand,
As in a sacred casket, have I lodged
That dear bequest, mine honour.   Heav'n shall aid
To whiten my stained name.   Blessing and health,—
I mean the heart's health, friends, wait on ye all,
Till next we greet each other.   (*Noise of arms heard.*)
The guard ! Oh, hence !
Call you this love,—to stain my parting soul
With true blood vainly poured?

GAGE.

Away,—away !
Seek out a champion.   Still there's hope.
(*They retire slowly and sullenly as the Gaoler
and Guard rush in.*)

GAOLER.

On ! Seize
The prisoner.   Charge.   Take her alive or dead.

JULIA (*walks towards him*).
Behold her.   Brothers, fare ye well !
(*They surround and lead her off.* GAGE *staggers
across and falls in* CYRIL'S *arms.   Exeunt.*)

———

SCENE THE LAST.—*Old Smithfield, showing the Old
Priory of St. Bartholomew, founded by Rahere; the
Convent of St. John, Old St. Paul's, etc. To the
rear, the place of execution, scaffold, pile, etc. Lists
prepared, Judges' chairs, etc.*

(PEMBROKE *enters slowly.*)

PEMBROKE.

'Tis as I feared.   The day is come, and Fame,
So loudly vaunting Trafford's skill in arms,
Hath done us mortal hurt.   O ! never debt
Did gall so bitterly an honest heart,
As mine to Douglas Trafford, which hath bound
My rapier here, when—

(*A Servant enters with missives.*)
What says Mordaunt ?   (*Reads*)   That
" His honour and his love hold strife."   Why then
We know who's conqueror.   What more ?   " That he's
His country's soldier."   Pah, the coxcomb !   " Owns
No foe save hers."   Hence with thy *love*, and teach
The zephyrs lightness.   Seyle, my generous Seyle !
Hath this harsh need stirred thy two drops of blood
Into a warlike tempest ?   (*Reads*)   Out, alas !
" He is too old, and were his years more few,
Lacks gold to furnish him.   His *heart*," ha ! ha !
" Is with the right."   Now, Sandell, Gosselin.

(*Reads, and dashes down the letters.*)
False-hearted cravens !   Julia, must *thou* die,
And such lives mock the world ?   (*Distant trumpets.*)
'Tis the first challenge !
Now, Trafford, if thy bosom closets aught
That fears the face of day, look to thyself.
Thy witness comes.   Heaven guard the innocent now !

(*Exit.   Crowds begin to press on.*)

A WOMAN.

A goodly day, my gossips.

ANOTHER.
Very fair.

From Brentford ?

FIRST WOMAN.
    Aye. My little Michael, here,
(Your cap, sir) begged so takingly to see
The pretty lady burned, that—boy, don't tease
That butterfly! Let go, sir. It hath bones
And sinews like our own. Wilt never learn
Humanity? And so, ma'am, 'twas agreed
To make a merry day on't. And we go
To supper in Eastcheap.   *(They pass on.)*

A FORESTER (*pointing off*).
          Is that the man?
Beshrew him for a coward! You ne'er see
A fellow of such frightened aspect, but
There's a black heart to match it.

      (Enter on one side TRAFFORD *armed, and* PEM-
      BROKE *on the other.* JULIA *in white, her
      feet bare. A Priest beside her. Guards,
      etc.)*

CONFESSOR (*speaking as they enter*).
This holy resignation. Truly, they
Who take their fortune frankly by the hand—
You heed me not, my daughter.

JULIA.
        Father, yes,
I did but—I—   *(Still gazing around.)*

CONFESSOR (*in a low voice*).
    Nay, but if any link
Dearer than other—

JULIA.
    Nothing, no, 'tis nothing.
Only I thought I had one friend. Look, father,
Stand you between my heart and that false world,
For we have nought in common now but form,
And promise of decay.   *(Procession resumed.)*

PEMBROKE (*to* TRAFFORD).
                What would you, man?
Why do you catch mine arm?

TRAFFORD (*hoarsely*).
                        The world goes on.
The sun above us, the green earth below,
The living, leaping waves, the multitude
Of human atoms, dancing up and down,
All keep their wonted office, and no howl,
Nor strange eclipse, nor earth-engendered flame,
Striking the vain, presumptuous souls of men,
Consorts with what we look on.

PEMBROKE.
                Guilt should die.

TRAFFORD.
It should so.   Aye, and blench, and quake ; not wear
This martyrish visage.   It should not outface
Even death.   She was my playmate.   Speak, is't done?

JULIA (*pauses suddenly*).
I have forgotten something.   Father, hold.
And you, gentle my executioners,
Temper your zeal with patience.   I must speak
One moment with my kinsman.

CONFESSOR (*interposing*).
                Dearest daughter—

JULIA.
Father, refuse me, and your holy work
May lack fruition.   Drag me not to death,
Which I oppose not, so my soul be freed
From earthly cumberings which afflict an dstay
Its passion.

TRAFFORD (*shrinking away as she advances*).
        Back, sirs.   I withdraw.

PEMBROKE.

You cannot.
What, are you mad?

TRAFFORD (*attempting to pass*).
The air—the throng—the weight
Of arms—

PEMBROKE (*detaining him*).
She comes, man!   See, she comes!

TRAFFORD (*madly*).

Stand off!
I am not bound to hear.

JULIA.
Aye, but alone.
(*Approaches nearer.*)
Douglas, a word can save me.

TRAFFORD (*trembling and pale*).
What—what word?

JULIA.
Your fancy never set these terrors forth,
Ne'er dreamed what shameful rings should girdle me,
What fiery tongues lap up my bounding blood,
And stamp upon my thrice-accursed name
The brand of such a deed!   O! thy revenge
Went not to this.   Have pity on my youth?
Strike off these horrid fetters, quench the flame,
Give back my life—mine honour.

TRAFFORD.
Die for thee!

JULIA.
For that step through the lattice.

TRAFFORD (*eagerly*).
Hist!

JULIA.

You see
I might say something, yet I will not.   Speak.
At least they'll yield thee a more merciful death,
And but one murder done.   Have mercy, cousin ?
Speak, Douglas !   Douglas Trafford, speak.

TRAFFORD (*stammeringly*).

To innocence
Death has no pang.

JULIA.
And to the guilty, life,
What joy?   Farewell !

TRAFFORD (*eagerly*).
O ! pardon.

JULIA.

Seek it *there*.
(*Turns away.*)
I stay the pageant.   On, sirs.   I have said.

(*As the crowd close round, a distant shout is
heard.*)

TRAFFORD (*grasping* PEMBROKE's *arm*).
Lo ! you.   A champion !   Hark ! that cry—

PEMBROKE.

The howl
Of wolves that sight their prey.   Hold !   Hark, *again !*
Can there be hope?   Stay, sir, there may be yet
Work for thy puissant arm.   How now ?   You shrink,
You tremble, man !   (*In a whisper*)   Dost fear?

TRAFFORD (*passing distractedly to and fro*).
She dies !   Away.
Men—fiends—beset me not.   (*Stops aghast.*)
Ah ! what art *thou ?*
Blood-seeking phantom !   What is done, is done.

I cannot save thee now, nor my lost soul,
From thy denouncement.   O! be merciful.
Gracious thou wert in life, and in thy truth,
Most womanly.   Thou shalt have honour.   Aye,
Glory shalt grow from thy sweet blood.   But *now*,
Avoid me.   Oh! avoid.   (*Cowering down.   Trumpet.*)

PEMBROKE (*touching him*).
Behold!

(*Crowd opens, discovering* GAGE *armed, and*
CYRIL.   *They advance.*)

GAGE (*gazing around*).
With whom
Come I to fight?   Where stands the enemy
Of truth and Heaven?   The bold-faced, living lie,
That slays the guiltless with the accursed stain
Of his own murderous fingers?

PEMBROKE (*eagerly*).
Here's your foe!
Now let the truth be manifest and plain.
Awake, man, wake.   Yield you, or fight.

TRAFFORD (*looking up*).
With him!
A bookish stripling, a—nay, gentlemen,
Set me a soldier here, at least, a foe
Worth my reputed sword.

GAGE.
Come, to thy guard.
And know, vain braggart, truth requires not hands
Tutored in strife, but oft, by humble ways,
By poor, unpractised instruments, works out
Its righteous purposes.   Defend thyself,
Thou coward slanderer.

TRAFFORD (*with sudden rage*).
Give me mine arms!

Villain (*striking* INFELICE), *mine arms!* Stay'st thou to
    hear thy lord
Baited by beggars, and— (*to* GAGE) Thy wretched life
Come not to mine account.
        (*Arms, etc., brought. He dashes the corslet from
        him.*)
                      Trouble me not
With toys. The very glitter of my steel
Must end this quarrel.

INFELICE.

        Wine, there, for my lord,
He thirsts. (*Wine brought.*) My failing heart, hast thou
    not looked
For such an hour? Give *me* the goblet. Hold !
Look to his belts. Shall I give up mine office
At such a time? (*Offers it.*) Drink, sir, and nerve your arm
To victory.

TRAFFORD.

        I need it not. O ! heaven,
My brain. Nay, if thou wilt.   (*Drinks deeply.*)
          'Tis cheering. How !
         (INFELICE *drops the goblet.*)
Art sick, boy?

INFELICE.

       With a sudden fancy, sir.   (*Stoops.*)
Your dagger hangs awry. 'Tis mended now.
       (*Marshal and Guards advance.*)

MARSHAL.

Let no man aid, by voice or sign, the cause
Of either combatant.   (*A pause.*)
       Take your places. On !
And God defend the right.   (*Trumpets. They engage.*)

PEMBROKE.

       His step is wild.

His blows drop feebly, yet he shows no hurt.
What ails your master, boy?

INFELICE.
                  Sir, there are harms
Not of the sword.   Some hearts, I think, are most
Assailable within; and we have seen
Unwholesome drinks may strike—

PEMBROKE.
                  What do you mean? (*Shouts.*)
Ha! look.   'Tis over.
          (TRAFFORD *throws up his arms and falls.*)

TRAFFORD.
                  I am slain, but not
By thee.   The poison.   Help! I die.

GAGE.
                                Confess.
Speak, thou unhappy—she is guiltless!   Aye.

TRAFFORD (*hoarsely*).
Lift up my head.   *I murdered Lancaster!*
                            (*Exit* PEMBROKE.)
And, with my steel glued to her snowy breast,
Prescribed the oath which, wretched fool, she kept
Ev'n to the grasp of death.   The page! the page!
'Tis he hath done this.   Seize him!   Bring him near.
O fellow, tell me, what did I to thee?
What wrong hadst *thou?*
          (*He raises himself with a sudden effort, gazes
            eagerly at her, and falls back dead.*)

INFELICE.
                  He knew me.   It is good.
Now lead me where you will.   (*She is led back.*)

GAGE (*sinks at* JULIA'S *feet*).
                  Spotless and saved!

That shout.   My fainting heart, one moment hold,
Then, if thou wilt, be nothing.

                (*Shouts within*, " Pardon !   Pardon !")

         PEMBROKE (*rushing in with a scroll*).
                   Pardoned !   Free !
Truth hath prevailed.

            GAGE (*leans forward.*)
             O ! happy—

           PEMBROKE.
                  All our hearts
Rejoice with thee, sweet lady.

              JULIA.
                Not with me
Alone, my friend.   With love, with HONESTY !
                (*Gives her hand to* GAGE.)

THE   END.

PREFACE.

THE groundwork of this dramatic tale is derived from the event known in history as "Raleigh's Conspiracy," —a plot having for its object the advancement to the throne of the Lady Arabella Stuart (cousin-german to James I.), but so slight in its construction, and hopeless in its prospects, that, but for the celebrated name involved in its complicity, it might not have attracted even that slight notice since accorded by historians. The name of Lawrency (or, more properly, La Renzy), is scarcely alluded to, excepting by Sanderson, by whom that person is stated to have betrayed the conspiracy.

The author is unwilling to forego the satisfaction of recording that this, his earliest attempt at dramatic composition, received, at its first publication, the valuable stamp of Mr. Macready's approbation, and was indeed accepted by that gentleman for performance,—an intention, however, which circumstances unconnected with the piece ultimately prevented. The writer's connection with the Olympic Theatre being a matter of sufficient notoriety to most persons interested in theatrical matters, it may be as well to mention that the piece, whatever its merits or future fortune, is no less the choice of the company than of the management,—Mr. Brooke having

from the first entered into it with a warmth and interest
which assisted to create in others a similar feeling ; and
Mrs. Mowatt having devoted to a somewhat thankless
character a careful and discriminating study, which, at
all events, cannot fail to have its fruits in future suc-
cesses. These, however, must be achieved in that more
congenial sphere, where all that is earnest and beautiful
in the dramatic art yet commands the triumph it de-
serves, and which this true interpreter of woman's nature
has quitted, leaving, for a time, a prosperous career, for
the purpose of adding to her dramatic wreath the somewhat shrivelled leaf of European fame.

DRAMATIS PERSONÆ.

Dudley Latymer . . .	Mr. Davenport.
Lawrency (*formerly betrothed to* Edith)	Mr. G. V. Brooke.
Walter Vivian (*his Friend*) . .	Mr. H. Holl.
Sir Griffin Markham, *Hampshire*	Mr. Kinloch.
Sir Edward Parham, *gentlemen*	Mr. H. Mellon.
Brooke, *engaged in*	Mr. Darcie.
Peyton, *the conspi-*	Mr. Butler.
Farninghame, *racy in fa-*	Mr. Morton.
Watson (*a Priest*) *vour of the*	Mr. C. Perkins.
Lady Arabella Stuart.	

Hugh Kensell (*Gaoler and Heads-man*)	Mr. E. Stirling.
Bagot (*a King's Officer*) . .	Mr. H. Lee.
Grossvelt, } *Servants to* Lawrency.	Mr. Fortescue.
Wilhelm,	Mr. Fitzgerald.
First Servant	Mr. Mazzoni.
Second ditto	Mr. Buxton.
Third ditto	Mr. Pigeon.
Townsman	Mr. Lawrence.
Giovanni (*a Boy—Page to* Edith)	Miss Mandlebert.

Edith (*Wife of* Latymer) . .	Mrs. Mowatt.
Ethelind (*her Attendant*) . .	Miss K. Howard.
Marion (*Daughter of* Kensell) .	Miss Marie Duret.

Scene—(*in Hampshire*). A.D. 1603.

ACT I.

SCENE I.—*A room in the manor-house.*   LATYMER,
  EDITH.

EDITH.

So you evade my questions.   So you'd trifle
With a capricious child.   (*Goes to him.*)
            Husband, I take
My ample portion in your happier thoughts,
Deny me not the bitter.   Well I know
What threatens us, and, woman as I am,
Such humble sense I have as teaches me
That plots like these, on such weak warrant based,
Run one set course,—dissension ; reach one end,—
Death !

LATYMER.

      Be it so, then.   One word binds me, sweet.
Men call it honour.

EDITH.

      Truth might call it—   (*Pauses.*)

LATYMER.

                              What ?

EDITH.

Treason, my Dudley.   Think of your dead father ;
Or if that loyal heart could—

LATYMER (*rising*).
                  Spare me, love.

                              G 2

This only can I promise ; three days hence,
A secret council of our band is held
In the oak chamber—
              (*A Servant enters and delivers a letter.* LATY-
          MER *opens it eagerly.*)

EDITH.
              What ill words have stol'n
Your colour thus ?   Speak, Dudley.

LATYMER.
                    Nothing, sweet.
That is—Ha, ha !   How strangely this strange world's
Affairs are jumbled !   Here is—(*Aside*) Cursed chance !
Why tends he hither now ?—(*Aloud*)   Here is a scroll
From our good friend—our playmate, Lawrency.

EDITH.
From Lawrency ?

LATYMER.
              Even so.   How now, my love ?
Who loses colour now ?   You cannot think—
Not fear that—

EDITH.
          Fear ! 'Tis true he knows not yet
Our happy fortune,—dreams not that this hand,
By his wild life—his long neglect,—redeemed
From a most hateful bond, hath claimed the right
To choose its master. *Fear !* I fear not.   He
Hath, doubtless, other aims,—fresh objects—ties—
Myself forgotten.

LATYMER (*who has been reading in an agitated manner*).
                    Why, the insolent scroll,
From end to end, is honied with thy name !
Nought else,—nought else.   " Come quickly,"—" gone
      too long—"
(Who told him *that ?*) " Star of his hope,"—" a heart

Unworthy, but still true."   Ha, Ha !   *Forgotten ?*
Lo! here again,—" His rose, his pretty Edith "—
" His playfellow "—" his—"

EDITH.
Ha!

LATYMER.
Look, what he writes.
" His promised, plighted *bride !* "   What! do I dream ?
Are you not mine ?

EDITH.
What power can sever us
Till death parts all ?   Had he ne'er left me thus,
For years unheeded, like a thing he held
Not worth the search ; or grasped at will, and used
To patch his tattered fortunes, I had still
Been thine.   Love knows no bond, no counsel, save
Its mighty impulse, to select its throne.
Mine did so.   It is *here !*   (*Embraces* LATYMER.)

LATYMER (*regaining his composure*).
Why, let him come.
We'll welcome, in all cheerful confidence,
This sudden visitant, who treads upon
The heels of his despatch.   Have courage, love ;
Albeit he is our kinsman, trusted with
Life secrets,—dearest counsels,—soon I hope
To need his aid no more.   My gentle one,
Be thou alone my counsellor, my guide,
My bosom's hope and home !   Oh ! let me learn
Some fairer language.   I must weary thee
With this old, passionate, never-varying tale,
I love thee, and *I love thee.*   (*Exeunt.*)

SCENE II.—*A part of the grounds.*

(*Enter* LAWRENCY *and* VIVIAN *as from a journey.*)

VIVIAN.
Yon gipsy seemed to know you.—" Hound of Cecil ! "

LAWRENCY (*smiling*).
Small skill in divination.   I am just now
Less hound than huntsman.

VIVIAN.
                    Could the hag have seen
The warrant in your bosom ?

LAWRENCY (*feels eagerly in his vest*).
                    How should—   Ha !
What, Grossvelt,—Wilhelm,—knaves ! (*Servants enter.*)
                    A paper lost—
A scroll—it is of import.   Back, and trace
The way we entered.   Fly !   (*Exeunt Servants.*)

VIVIAN.
                    What names are writ
In the scroll ?   This may breed mischief.

LAWRENCY.
                    Every one.
Latymer first, Markham, and Farninghame,
Bold Brooke, young Parham—   (*Re-enter Servants.*)
                    Speak.   'Tis found ?

WILHELM.
                    So please you,
We think you dropped it at the end of the wood,
Where the old gipsy fronted us.   Perchance—

LAWRENCY.
Away—and seek her out.   An hundred crowns
When my hands close on it !   (*Exeunt Servants.*)

Walter, thou know'st

I come no stranger hither.   The last lord
Of these domains was my youth's earliest friend ;
But cast me from his bosom in the hour
I most did need protection.

VIVIAN.

In revenge,

You doom his son to the headsman.

LAWRENCY.

In revenge,

I come to save his child.   Aye, rescue *thee*,
My little rosy playmate of the wood,
My love, my Edith !   Thou hast been with me
In many an hour of peril, cheering, watching ;
Thy soft voice drowned the battle, the wild storm
Shrieked by unheeded.   All my inner world
Was peace—and Edith.

VIVIAN.
You are moved.

LAWRENCY.

My friend,

This prize was mine.

VIVIAN.
Was ?

LAWRENCY.

Was !   Did I say so ?

Honour and hope rebuke me !   We were pledged ;
Her father willed it.   She was but a child,
Nor thought to cavil at the fatal bond
Her riper years refused.   She never loved me ;
And was too fresh and innocent of soul
To feed me with false hope.   Beneath that roof

Five years were wasted—years of doubt and fear—
That laughed and sorrowed like a various May.
Well, she grew colder, frowns more frequent, smiles
Most chill.   At last,—Vivian, my patience failed—
On the strong faith of her dead father's pledge
I built the temple of my hope—and fled
For present peace—to ——

VIVIAN (*smiling*).

> Marion Kensell!   Well,
You might have found worse comforters.

LAWRENCY.

> I had
A different meaning, sir,—but since you name
The flower, I own the balm it bore.   Poor child!—
Poor Marion!   gentle—trusting—of my grief
She knew not—questioned not.   With patient tears
She wrapped me in her soft, caressing arms,
As I had been a wayward, peevish babe,
Upon her breast, and soothed with happy songs
The fiend that vexed me thus.

VIVIAN.

> You did accept
The love you could not give her?

LAWRENCY.

> With each morn
I swore that ere yon glorious sun had done
His course, I'd tell her all—eve after eve,
Still left the word unspoken.   Oft I turned
With a bold, studied, villain look—the sound
Died on my severed lips.   How could I gaze
Into those mild—those trustful, piteous eyes—
And say "*I love thee not?*"—how rend apart
The veil that drooped above my struggling soul,
And show her—Edith?

VIVIAN.
Where dwells Marion now?

LAWRENCY.
With the old brute, her father, gaoler here,
In Winchester. Enough of this. I would
'Twere night—all well.

VIVIAN.
What fear you?

LAWRENCY.
Did I say
I feared? But to the purpose; see you yet
My purpose here? Wherefore I seemed to join
This idle plot? Why, when I found 'twas known,
I flew to Cecil, and, for what I told,
Obtained this honourable spyship? Look,
Why did I this? To warn them, man—mislead
The subtle hounds of justice; cast a shield
Around my Edith's head;—to save her—save
Dear Latymer, her playmate—give her peace
For anguish—safety, for her hatred—life—
Life for her frowns! You hear? Why do you stand
So coldly mute? Is't not a blest exchange,
A luscious vengeance?

VIVIAN.
Calm yourself, my friend,
It is a generous aim. See, who comes here.
Our host. in faith, and the fair dame; what, man!
You flush—and pale. I swear they shall not see
A soldier shaken thus!   (*Leads him aside.*)
        (*Enter* LATYMER *and* EDITH, *attended by*
        GIOVANNI.)

LATYMER (*to* GIOVANNI).
                Said he no more?
Yet Parham minces not his words. Once more,
The message.

GIOVANNI.
"Three days hence, in the oaken room,
I'll prove thy wren a vulture.   Let your lord,
Meanwhile beware his talons." (*Retires.*)·

EDITH.
  He would say
That Lawrency's a traitor!

LATYMER.
  No! some jest.
He false! Lawrency false!   Dismiss your fear.
The man is brave and constant.   In our scheme,
None plunged with readier zeal.   Who know him best
Most wholly trust him.   Let us in.   Come, come—
All's well, my love.

EDITH.
I *fear*. (*Re-enter* LAWRENCY.)·

LAWRENCY (*meeting them.*)
  My kindest cousin!
Dear Edith!

LATYMER.
  Welcome.   By this very oak,
We parted—how long since?   No matter, cousin.
Here stands he yet to greet you—worn in limb,
But heart-whole, like true friendship.

LAWRENCY.
  A good omen.
I pluck an indented leaf—his honest hand—
And wish all staunch as he.
  (*Aside*) Great heaven, how fair!
Dream, memory, fancy, what poor things are ye!
O artists! feeble and incapable,
How are ye beggared all!

LATYMER.
     Time, as you see,
Makes little change.

LAWRENCY.
     I know it. Had a tree
Sunk down with years, or but a single stone
Of the old mansion changed its wonted hue,
I would detect it, trust me.   (*Enter* VIVIAN.)
         Latymer,
Here is a comrade, Walter Vivian ; give him
Some welcome too ; he's worthy.
      (*Aside*) Most demure
And smiling priestess, sits thy worship there ?
Her breath waits on his words ; her eye claims his,
And will not be denied. My soul grows dark ;
I'll hence and walk. ''Twere better far to gaze
On souls that float in the red streams of hell
Than longer on this pair !   (*Exit.*)

LATYMER.
     Hath aught occurred
To vex our kinsman ?

VIVIAN.
     Sir, he ne'er seemed merrier ;
These lovely scenes called many a pleasant hour
Back to his mind. No warrior to the field,
Lover to bridal, schoolboy to his home,
Passed with more gamesome mood. His generous heart
Dwells on it strongly. (*Aside*) Heaven forgive me !
      (*Re-enter* LAWRENCY.)

LAWRENCY.
     Cousin,
You will forgive my lack of ceremony.
A foe, that I had hoped to leave behind
In the damp fields of Holland, haunts me still,—
A sudden faintness, which the calm fresh air
Doth quickly medicine. (*Aside*) I will try her now.

(*To* Edith)   Dear   cousin—Edith—*Lady* Edith—
 madam !
What, is the harp strung with such chilling wires ?
I have no heart to touch.   *(Turns away.)*

EDITH.
 You spoke, sir ?

LAWRENCY.
          Something
To my kind cousin Edith.   Lady, *you*
Have struck it from my mind.

LATYMER.
 (*Aside*) So grave, my Edith ?
A word, good Master Vivian.   (*They talk apart.*)

LAWRENCY.
       Edith,—still
I call you so,—am I forgotten, Edith ?
Is *all* forgotten ?   All the pleasant things
That we have loved ? the rose-walk and the bower,
The tale of witch and fairy, conned beside
The gossiping brook ?   Shall I go on ?   What need
To play the tutor to your memory,
Which doth put on this dull and careless garb
In very wilfulness ?

EDITH.
 What joys are these
To fill the heart with ?   Our maturer thought
Sweeps brightly o'er the mind's expanding scroll,
And reason on the ready surface writes
In characters more loved, and lasting too.

LAWRENCY.
Oh ! do not,—do not preach so harsh a faith !
Drag not the fabric down in whose kind shade
This outcast soul hath hidden from despair ;
Nor, with such cruel sorcery, transform'

Memory's bright gold to ashes.   Must the heart
Crowd its fair mansions with new tenants, stern
And world-polluted, yet refuse its first—
Its innocent guests, a home ?   Would I had died,
Ere wandered back to find such heart as thine
Turned from its woman's truth and tenderness !

EDITH.

I am not changed ; and, since you challenge truth,
Then blame me not for its unwelcome mien.
I loved the roses *then*,—I love them now,—
Armed as they stand, their tiny points show fair
And patent to the eye.   The fount, the bird,
Have the same melody so loved of old,
They cannot pander the sweet gift of song
To falsehood's purposes.   No changeling I,—
What I have loved, I love ; what hated, I
Past words abhor, and that is,—would you know
Its name ?

LAWRENCY.
Aye, Edith.

EDITH.
Treachery !
(*Crossing, gives her hand to* VIVIAN, *and exeunt.*)

LATYMER.
You are not well.   Smile as you will, that cheek—

LAWRENCY.
It lies, sir ; don't believe it.   Are they gone ?
Why do we stay, prating of nothing?   Come. (*Exeunt.*)

END OF ACT I.

ACT II.

SCENE I.—*A summer parlour.*

(EDITH *alone.*)

EDITH (*pushes her harp aside.*)
I cannot recollect it.   It is strange,
The melody so perfect in mine ear
Should 'scape my touch.   My heart is ill at ease.
Pass but this day in safety—   Who is there?
The page!   (*Enter* GIOVANNI.)
          What news, good boy?

GIOVANNI.
                    Madam, this day
Shall make all known and sure.   There has been talk
Of some strange proof—
                    (LAWRENCY *appears at the door.*)

LAWRENCY.
          A word, I pray you.

EDITH.
                              Sir,
You see me.

LAWRENCY.
          I must speak upon a theme
That brooks not listeners.

EDITH.
          Well, Giovanni, go ;
Presently I shall need you.

LAWRENCY.
                    I accept
The warning, and am brief.   Wherefore these cold
Averted looks ?   What fatal hand hath raised
This icy barrier, still more sundering hearts
Never too dearly tied ?   Oh, Edith ! now
That time and grief—rude-handed mediciners—
Have tamed this soul, and made it teachable,
Be my instructress.   Show me how to win,
If not thy love,—thy mercy.

EDITH.
                    Will you learn ?

LAWRENCY.
As though a world were guerdon.

EDITH.
                    Listen, then.
I am loth to seem inhospitable,—but
Your horse has rested ; put him to his purpose.
Be silent as to all you may have seen
And noted here.   So will I school my mind,—
Confess I have judged you hastily, take back
Suspicion, and give—

LAWRENCY.
        What,—what ?

EDITH (*turns away*).
                    Gratitude,
Thanks, welcome, and—surprise.

LAWRENCY.
                    A prudent pledge !
    must, I fear, ask more.   For your own sake,—
For life's sake,—honour's sake,—lastly, for mine,—
Say not " despair."   Oh ! put not to the test
The frailty of this heart, nor set at strife
Gratitude, mercy, and the love of thee,—

Lest that the last prevail.   See, Fate has laid
Her sharpest weapons ready to my hand,
And fair occasion courts me.   Nay, no more.
Throw this ill-fitting garb of anger by ;
Oppose no longer your dead father's will,
And, even at mine own peril, these thy friends,
Though far advanced in treason's dangerous march,
Shall be, by friendly hands, drawn back and saved !
Reject me, and they perish with the boy
Whose blood is worth them all.   Do not speak yet ;
Pause on the final doom !

EDITH.
           Pause ! That were treason.
The life you threaten is my husband's !

LAWRENCY.
                Thy—
Thy husband's ?   Ha ! betrothed you mean.
                (*Seizes her arm.*)
                What right—
You jest though.   No, you dare not.   And the blood
Mounts to your temples,—voluntary witness
Of this foul falsehood.   Dare you give it tongue ?

EDITH.
I am wife to Dudley Latymer.

LAWRENCY (*after a pause*).
              Look at me.
I challenge you, proud as you are, to do it !
See, after all, you are but woman, Edith—
Woman, whose soul's first element is love,—
Whose nature's essence, mercy.   Woman never
Turns back on the neglected,—tramples never
Upon the fall'n.   Honour's her earthly god,
And her high creed and code admit no faith,
No law that wrongs the innocent.   Edith, you
Were mine, by promise, in the face of Heaven !
When did I tear that bond ?

EDITH.
                    When, with no word
Of parting or of promise, you—

LAWRENCY.
                    Were thrust
Forth from this home, that might have been my Eden,
By the fierce angel of your cruelty.
Alas! I hoped my absence might bring forth
A better angel,—pity! Latymer!
Why, woman, to *my* passion, this boy's love
Was but an idiot's fancy! Edith, thou
Sat'st empress in mine honour's throne. Thy hand
Wielded the radiant sceptre nought could hide,
Nor question, nor withstand. Have mercy, Edith!

EDITH.
Have I not said I am a wife?

LAWRENCY.
                    Forsworn
Already,—false to *me!* Be falsely truer.
Come, I will pardon all,—love still—will save you
From ills you dare not dream of. Storms are near;
Turn then and fly. Oh, Edith! fly with me
Back to bright lands, aspiring hopes, high dreams
I left, to bid you share them.

EDITH.
                    Are you vile
Beneath all scorn, or do I wickedly
Pervert your meaning? Have I wronged you? Well,
I relegate my cause to the sole Judge
That cannot err. *There* plead with me. Begone!
And know that I disdain your menace, man,
Ev'n as I loathe your love. Go, serpent, that
Would sting my more than life!

LAWRENCY.
                    Oh! yet be warned.

Send me not from you with such poisonous thoughts
Warring upon my reason. Edith, speak !
Have you no pity—none ?

EDITH.
             Take all the truth,
And *then* repeat that question. Lawrency,
We know your errand. You are Cecil's spy,
Worse office than the headsman's. He but sheds
Forfeited life. You traffic in the guiltless.
Shall I stay longer ?   (*Exit.*)

LAWRENCY (*a pause, he looks up suddenly*).
            Who—who spoke to me ?
What shapes are these that float upon mine eyes,
Glide o'er the landscape, glitter from the tree,
Inviting as to some rich banquet, each
With aspect fairer than his fellow ? Ha !
With what fell craftiness ye choose your time !
Such should not tempt in vain ! I know you all,
Ye smiling fiends and ministers of hell !
Whence ye arise, and whither lead, I know,
And who your master. Still, with heart enslaved
By your surpassing mien, and promise kind,
I make ye mine, and follow. Come, Revenge !
Come, sweet Revenge ! swift Hope for once outrun—
From nought I'll shrink, so 't be but quickly done.
                      (*Rushes out.*)

SCENE II.—*A retired part of the Gardens.*

(WALTER VIVIAN *sauntering listlessly about.*)

VIVIAN.
This will not do. I must shake off this calm
That steals, like some deceitful foe, on one

Whose life is action. Yet 'tis sweet. I like
Those sleeping skies, and, to my ears, there's music
In that brook's murmur—nay, in the wordless hum
O' the summer insects. Would I were a fly!
A soft and gentlemanly life he leads,
Without on earth a duty or a care,
Making his love and music to the flowers,
With honey for his pains. With day he dies,
The wisest act, and last, of his little life,
Night being too chill for his luxurious ease,
Too coarse for his gentility. Heigho!
Who would not be a fly?
   (*Enter* LAWRENCY *in a disordered manner. He
   paces up and down, as not noticing* VIVIAN.)
     What, comrade!

     LAWRENCY.
          Ha!
You here? I sought you.

     VIVIAN.
     What has happened?

     LAWRENCY.
          Lost!
Lost! lost! You jested at our speed of travel.
Walter, the horses must be foaled o' the wind,
That shall outgallop human treachery!

     VIVIAN.
She has refused?

     LAWRENCY.
     Refused! A puling boy
Has snatched my prize, as you would thistle-down,
And whiffed it from me. It is well—quite well!
I woo another mistress, now—and you,
Dear Vivian, shall secure her. Take this scroll,
I would have written something, but can trace
No characters that man may read. Mine eyes

Dazzle and throb—beneath my writhing hand
The letters turn to blood!   Horse—and away
George Bagot lies at Mallwood with his troop,
Not ten miles hence—away!

VIVIAN.
My mission first
What must I do?

LAWRENCY.
Oh! pardon.   In this scroll—
It bears the seal of Cecil—thou wilt write
The names of Griffin Markham, Farninghame,
Brooke, Peyton, Parham, and—and—*Latymer!*
To-night the witch of Discontent doth hold
High council here; and hither come her sons,
In strange disguises.   Choicest plotters they!
Oh! I could laugh, but for a demon thought
That burns me; here— Let Bagot draw his men
About the door, and when my rapier falls,
Unleash thy bloodhounds, and secure them!

VIVIAN.
All

LAWRENCY.
All I have named.   Dost understand me?

VIVIAN.
Aye;
But I have ate and drank with Latymer,
Looked in his heart, and now, to hang him!   Think
Of the poor girl, too!   Nay, my conscience shuns
This act of—of—

LAWRENCY.
Stern justice, thou wouldst say:
I'll help thee to the word.   Tax as thou wilt
My friendship.   Try it utterly.   Come, come,
To work.   (*Exit* VIVIAN.)

With every pulse I feel
My nature change and darken.   Edith—Edith !
This is thy deed, not mine. No, no, not mine !   (*Exit.*)

SCENE III.—*The Oaken Chamber.*

(LATYMER, FARNINGHAME, PEYTON, BROOKE,
SIR GRIFFIN MARKHAM, *and others carelessly
disguised.   Sitting as in deliberation.*)

FARNINGHAME.
Well, as you please.   I care not.   I have said;
And let him hear that, spite his pleasant mien,
I hold the gentleman too crafty far
To trust our necks with.

PEYTON.
                    Judging by its chain,
You value yours but slightly.   At what tryst
Bought you the gew-gaw ?

FARNINGHAME.
                    Spanish boots, bright spurs,
And jewelled dagger, harmonise so sweetly
With a butcher's frock and beaver.

PEYTON.
                    Gentle shepherd,
Wilt try a fall with me ?

FARNINGHAME (*rises*).
                    Good sir o' the shambles,
Tempt not your bullock's fate.

MARKHAM (*interposing.*)
                    How now ? how now ?

Here is a coil betwixt two honest men,
The butcher and the boor!   Our friends have yet
To learn disguises.   We, who breathe in courts,
Are the sworn masquers.   The world finds us ever
What we would be, not what we *are*.

         BROOKE (*aside to* FARNINGHAME).
                         Lo! now
Sir Griffin Markham (fifteenth page of state,
Deputy-usher of the queen's back-stairs)
Mounts his court palfrey.   You shall hear anon
The very words the Lady Clarice Mayne
Whispered the duchess in the presence-chamber,
That made her stiff grace smile.   Would'st know how oft
The king caressed his poodle?   He will tell you
These news, and more ; and for all rumours—'Sooth,
Commend me to these know-alls, who know nothing ;
Who skim the airy froth of circumstance,
But leave the cream behind.

             FARNINGHAME.
                 Our scale is light—
Be thankful to the very butterfly
That perches on the beam.   (*Aloud*) But this is strange.
The trysting time is past ; yon empty seat
Doth augur badly for our brotherhood.
What, can the blossoms of our sprouting tree
Drop off so quickly?

             BROOKE.
                 'Twas my own remark,
And, Latymer, I tell thee to thy beard,
Thou nursest carelessly our infant cause.
I do mistrust this friend of D'Aremberg,
Whoe'er he be.

             LATYMER.
             Rest you contented, sir ;
If freely I confide to this man's hand

My life—as deeply gaged as any here—
Why, so may you.

(*Enter* LAWRENCY, *speaking 'to one without.*)

LAWRENCY.
I tell thee, sirrah, no ;
Hence !—*I* will do thy message.   Cousin Dudley,
Here was some man of thine before the door—
A most importunate knave—who would intrude
Upon these worthy gentlemen, to bring
A pressing embassy from thy fair *bride.*

LATYMER.
From Edith ?—ha !

LAWRENCY.
That thou must keep in mind
To ride with her to-morrow, else she would
Believe—something, I know not what—

PEYTON.
To business.
Now, may no half-heart friends delay our deeds,
Nor discord mar our councils.   Let us first
Consult our letters.   What says D'Aremberg ?

BROOKE.
Oh ! *he ?*   But little to the point.   He writes
As if the paper were red hot.   Wise hound !
He never cares to open till the game's
Afoot, but then, hark to him !

FARNINGHAME.
Gentlemen,
There is a little custom, a mere form,
That's true, but still a safe one.   Our new friend,
Good Master Lawrency, hath not yet taken
The oath that binds our brotherhood.

(*Enter* WATSON, *closely muffled.*)

LATYMER.
Watson! Then
There's danger.

WATSON.
Not a whit. I am here to quicken,
And not to quench your courage. Pray take seat,
While briefly I unfold a project framed
Last night, and needing but a few bold hands
To make it perfect. Ten days hence the king
Will hunt at Hanworth.

MARKHAM.
Sport to his grace!

WATSON.
Amen.
And, to save fruitless questing, while he hunts
The deer, we'll hunt the king! That hart once snared,
We make our own conditions,—lift our lady,—
Set free men's consciences, work full revenge
On Hume and Cecil. Well?   (*A silence.*)

MARKHAM.
'Tis well conceived.
How rides the king? Much following?

WATSON.
But his band
Of thirty yeomen-foresters, lightly armed
With hunting-spear and knife. Stay, hear this first.
Then answer.

BROOKE.
'Tis the—

WATSON.
Wait and hear. You'll find
That he who should be foremost in reward,
As he is ever first in danger, claims

Nothing but honour. To my own lot falls
A high distinction, England's Chancellor.
The noble Cobham's kinsman, Master Brooke,
Lord Treasurer. Next him, his mate in talent,
Sir Griffin Markham, versed in court intrigue—
Quick in resources—who so fit as he
For our State Secretary? Last, not least,
The good Lord Grey, our Master of the Horse,
England's Earl Marshal.

> (*During this speech* Sir Edward Parham
> *has entered and placed himself opposite to*
> Lawrency.)

PARHAM.
>   There's one other post—

WATSON.
What, sir, is that?

PARHAM.
>   The office, sir, of—hangman!
If I mistake not, we shall have quick need
Of such a functionary. I, too, beg
To read my schedule.
>   (*He produces a paper, which* Lawrency *snatches
>   and tears.*)
>   Matthew Lawrency,
Thou art a traitor and a villain! (*All rise in confusion.*)

MARKHAM.
>   Ha!—.
How well he played his part! and yet, methinks,
He hath not lived at Court.

PARHAM.
>   Now hear me, sirs;
While here you sit, dispensing place and pay,
Honours and titles, by this gentleman

Our lives are bought and sold.   Look here, sirs! here
                              (*Points to the writing.*)
From this torn witness we may gather still
What will convict a traitor.   Seize the spy!
Pluck down the base informer!   'Tis but choice—
Our lives or his.   (*They advance upon* LAWRENCY.)

LAWRENCY (*aside, irresolute*).
            They prick me to the verge.
A leap—and over!   Edith !—I must gulp
The hellish potion.   Back, sirs !—I can use
My sword, if needed.   (*They press him.*)
            Rash and headstrong fools!
Your blood upon your heads !

        (*Strikes down* PARHAM'S *rapier.   The door and
            windows are forced open, and* BAGOT *rushes
            in with soldiers.*)

BAGOT.
                    Swords, gentlemen !
Secure that window—let no bird escape—
A brimming trapful !

PEYTON (*to the guard*).
            Let me pass, good friends.
Alack ! I knew not what disloyal mouths
I came to measure for to-morrow's feast.

BAGOT.
Good master butcher, not so fast.   Ho ! sirs,
Let him not pass—him in the fisher's frock !
'Tis Griffin Markham.

MARKHAM.
            Ha ! you know mine air.
Your courtier can't be hidden.   (*Draws.*)

LATYMER.
            In the toils ?

Draw, friends, and try the temper of your steel.
Rapier to partisan !   (*All draw.*)

BAGOT.
Hold—hold ! hot boy.
Your sires were loyal gentlemen.   I'd not drench
Their ancient hall in blood.   Let fall your swords,
Trust your king's mercy.

PARHAM (*to the guards, who secure them.*)
                     You have forgotten *one* ;
The master-spirit of our enterprise ;
(*Aside*)   And, as I think, its traitor.

BAGOT.
                     Sir, the list
Of disaffected shows no other name
Than those I deal with now.   (*Enter* VIVIAN.)

VIVIAN (*aside to* LAWRENCY).
                     You were not prompt
In signal.

LAWRENCY.
           Prompt enough, I fear ; less close—
Quick eyes observe us.

BAGOT.
           Forward, gentlemen.
Such treatment as may make your prison-hours
Less galling, shall be yours.
           (*As they are led out,* LATYMER *pauses, and beckons*
           LAWRENCY.)

LATYMER.
                     Cousin, a word—
Closer—come closer ; fix thine eyes on mine.
A dark suspicion rests upon thee ; tongues
Have freely used thy name : but I am slow
To see the cloud I would not, and prefer,

By greater love, and fuller trust, to shame
A fleeting honour back.   Think what is *there!*
A thing how loved—how fair—how friendless—how
Unused to sorrow's sting.   I think thee honest
I know that thou'rt a man.   Thou'lt watch this treasure?
Thou'lt guard her with all truth and tenderness?
And soothe and strengthen when my danger comes?
For well I know there's danger.   In a word—
All vile suspicion spurned like hate aside—
I give her to thine arms, a gem to be
Returned me here, as pure ; or else, redeemed
With added grace, in heaven.

LAWRENCY.
                    Cousin, I take
The gracious pledge, and will defend it so
That when thou'rt free, thou shalt suspect no more,
But know me—as I am.   (*To* BAGOT.)   Sir, with your
        leave
I'll journey with you.   I'll to London too,
And there partake the fortune, good or ill,
Of my dear friend and cousin, Latymer.

BAGOT.
Your presence may be needed.   Much I hope
This boyish plot may finish, as it ought,
Rather in jest than blood.
                    (*Exeunt all but* LAWRENCY *and* VIVIAN.)

VIVIAN.
                    Was it well managed ?

LAWRENCY.
Excellent well, sir.   The most diligent fiend
In Satan's train could make no better speed,
Were a lost soul just turning back to heav'n
That had been deemed secure.   'Tis done—no more—
I bargained with thee, not for praise, but gold :
Thou shalt not lose thy hire.

VIVIAN.

How !—pitiful !
Wast thou not mocked—and—

LAWRENCY.

Give me thine hand, good friend ;
'Tis very true.   What strange forgetfulness !
Yes, I was mocked ; thank God that *I was* mocked,
Insulted, spurned !   I know thou dost not heed
My sometimes churlish speech ; no, no, thou dost not,—
Thou'rt my good friend : come on, we'll follow them.

(Exeunt.)

END OF ACT II.

ACT III.

SCENE I.—*A cell in the old gaol of Winchester.*

(LATYMER *conducted by* HUGH KENSELL *and others.*)

LATYMER.
More of thy lantern, friend.   Scant light is here,
To thread such mole-paths.

KENSELL (*sullenly*).
                    Men have preferred our darkness,
To the sunshine of the scaffold !   Randolph, make
Those rivets sure.

LATYMER.
How ! Chains ?

KENSELL.
                    Up with him straight.
Secure, but not too close ; just room to reach
The couch.   Aye, so.   Let no tight tether spoil
The gentleman's repose.
          (*As they secure him to the wall, enters* MARION.)

MARION (*passing near him*).
          Be patient.

KENSELL.
                    Good.
Now for the banquet !   How, girl, what hast here ?
Black bread and water, wench, are prisoners' fare.

MARION.

But, father, he is gently bred.

KENSELL.
The better.
Luxury must learn temperance.   Off with you,
And fetch his fitting meal.

MARION.
But, father —

KENSELL (*furiously*).
School me ?
Are you the mistress here ?   (*Seizes her brutally.*)

LATYMER.
Hands off, you savage !
Base fellow, will you kill the girl ?

KENSELL.
Why—no.
She's useful yet—though she's —, no matter.   Go !
Avoid the cell.   Begone !
        (*Pushes her violently from him.   LAWRENCY,
        who enters, catches her in his arms.*)

LAWRENCY.
How now, Black Hugh !
At the old sport ? Grim keeper of hell-gates,
I've warned you once.   Take care.   (*Pushes him aside.*)
Nay, my poor girl—
Be calm—be comforted.   (*Exit MARION.*)
Well, cousin — How !
What trinkets have we here ?
        (*Examining LATYMER's chains.*)
Unlock them straight !
        (*To KENSELL who releases him.*)
And now begone, old ban-dog !   For the time
I take thine office from thee.   (*Exit KENSELL.*)

LATYMER.
                    By what spell
Canst awe yon savage thus ?

LAWRENCY (*coolly*).
                    Murder, my cousin,
Done in these walls—not 'twixt the night and morn,
But, day by day, with slow and lingering pains—
And for a price a hungry beggar would
Have flung in the giver's face.   Enough ! your look
Questions of Edith.

LATYMER (*eagerly*).
                    Speak !   How did she bear
The shock that parted us ?

LAWRENCY.
                    When first aroused
From that most kind oblivion which affords
Hearts breathing-time, she gave herself to grief
That awed all comfort dumb.   At length, her mood
Changed, and the mourner thenceforth wore her grief
With proud, calm constancy—as if wound up
To some fixed aim.   Hark, Dudley ! she is here !—
In Winchester—at hand !

LATYMER (*impatiently*).
                    Say'st thou at hand !
And not upon my breast ?

LAWRENCY.
                    Ah ! better there—
Word, thought, and sense joy-steeped—forgetting old—
Not shaping forth fresh ill.

LATYMER.
                    How ?

LAWRENCY.
                                She hath planned
A forceful rescue.

LATYMER.
            Worse than vain.   Ah, heaven !
A fond, yet fatal rashness—while one hope
Of mercy's left us.   Look you, I'll not pause
To ask why you so oft have crossed my way
For good or evil, for I deem the last
But cloak to the better future.   Tell me, then,
My strange, mysterious kinsman, who, since youth,
Hast been a dreamer—

LAWRENCY (*gloomily*).
                ·True, I have dreamed.

LATYMER.
                                Awake
And give us counsel.   Edith—

LAWRENCY (*hastily*).
                        Hush ! no need
For more.   Write comfortably.   Bid her note
How things that do obeisance to the storm
Rise up in fresher state.   Say life is dear—
Love-gilded—and so bid her seek to save,
By swift compliance—patience—gentleness—
Rather than dangerous schemes.   I must begone—
Vivian, I think, is here.   Give whom you will
The letter.   'Twill pass free.   (*Going.*)

LATYMER.
                        Then farewell, cousin.
How cold your hand is !   How ! no friendly gripe ?

LAWRENCY (*grasps his hand*).
What call you this—and *this ?*   (*Exit.*)

SCENE II.—*A meanly furnished room in the Gaoler's
 house.*

         (MARION, *watching by her child.*)

      MARION.
More quiet now.   That restless wail no more,
Grates on my heart.   O kind physician, sleep—
What balm can equal thine ?
      (*Sings, in a low tone, a melancholy song.*)
        Out on my tongue !
Why should it choose this discontented strain,
When I'd for once be merry ?   There's a time
For grief—that's hourly ; joy—that's when kind looks
And loving words, like visitors who know
How welcome is their coming, boldly knock
At memory's mansion.   In, sweet guests—come in.
Here's room for all—and lo ! the master's step
Sounds on the threshold !   (*Enter* LAWRENCY.)

     LAWRENCY.
     Where's your father, child ?
Came he not hither

    MARION (*runs to him*).
     Hush, dear love, he sleeps !
The baby sleeps at last.   The fever fit
Hath worn him sadly.   Heaven be praised thou'rt come.
I've much to say to thee.

     LAWRENCY.
     Then quickly, girl ;
I must away again,—my horses wait.

     MARION.
First look upon the little slumberer ;
Soft—soft—I pray you ; if you knew the pains
To win him to this sleep.   O Lawrency,
Looks he not lovely ?

LAWRENCY (*in a low voice*).
                    Ah, what ill hast *thou*,
My little folded rosebud, at thy core,
That paints thy leaf so dimly ?   Fade, my flower ;
Best fruit of earth—better thou should'st be worn
On angel breasts than here.   (*Turns away.*)
                    I'll harm thee not
With prayer or blessing.

MARION (*to* LAWRENCY).
                    Come and rest awhile.
Look, I'll sit here—   (*Places herself at his feet*).
                    And lean this throbbing brow
Upon thy knee.   I would not see thine eyes,—
For if I looked and found rejection there,
Methinks 'twould kill me.   Take me from this place,
And keep the pledge you gave.

LAWRENCY.
                    Again, again,
The weary, sad old tale.

MARION.
                    With added sorrow.
My father hates me, Lawrency.   'Tis true—
That sense, which in the sternest parent's heart
Hath some dominion, hath been changed to gall,—
To scorn,—to loathing.   Foul, contemptuous words,
And blows, less hard to bear.   Worse still, O God :
My child,—he struck my child,—even as it stretched
Its little arms, and would have flown to him
Had he permitted.   Pity—I can bear
This weary hope no longer !

LAWRENCY.
                    It is well ;
Thou shalt not.   Know then, thou canst never be
My lady-wife.   But, for that silken snare
Which binds so many discontented hearts,

I'll give thee—nay,—whate'er thou wilt.   I'll——Well!
Why do you turn so pale and clutch mine arm?

MARION.
Forgive me; I am faint—I scarcely think
I understand you——

LAWRENCY.
                When, in former days,
I talked of *love*, thou wast not wont to be
So slow of comprehension.   Plainly, then,
Thou hast no longer hold upon my heart,—
But for thy patient, thy enduring faith,
I'd still reward thee.   I am not ungrateful—
I will protect thee, Marion—nay, I will ;
But in the narrow and blind path I climb,
Not both may stand—and if thou meet'st me there,
Who falls?   Be wise, then.   Dost thou heed my words?
If thou didst love me—Marion——

MARION.
                            If!—I love
Thee more, because grown out of love with sin.
Oh, therefore, hear me.   Armed with honesty,
We may defy the stings of outward ill,—
Yea, laugh to scorn the malice of the world,
And teach it envy.   Load the heart with guilt,
And the calm look of that unconscious babe
Can set the cheek on fire.

LAWRENCY.
                    Hold me not thus ;—
I like it not.   Marion, I bid you rise.
Fond girl, thou should'st have known my nature more
Than to believe my purpose might be swayed
By such a whining homily as this.

MARION (*springing up wildly*).
Another voice, another look than mine
Must force a passage to this stony heart

Yet newly-closed !   Come, little advocate,—
(*She takes the child.*)
Fail thou, we're lost indeed.   Hush, darling, hush !—
'Tis nothing.   Look upon this cherub face—
The blue eye glistening through the half-formed tear,
The tiny fingers in each other twined,
As some sweet angel prompted him to join
His wretched mother's prayer.   Canst thou refuse
So innocent a pleader ?   Take us hence ;
Leave us in scorn, disgrace, and poverty,—
But, oh, not *here !*

LAWRENCY (*his head averted, waves her from him*).
Away ! I cannot—Heav'n !
Must I bear this ?   Woman—have mercy—Hence !
Thou wilt not ?

MARION (*clasping him*).
Never ! never !

LAWRENCY (*forcing himself from her*).
Stubborn girl—
Selfish and wilful.   Since you will not take
The good I offer, bear thy slavish lot—
Thy felon-father's menial.   Let me go.   (*Exit.*)

MARION.
My child—is this the end ?   To rest again,
My bird !   O heart—unwilling heart,—confess
The source of this rejection.   He has looked
Upon a fairer face.   Shall I die *thus*—
No pity—and no vengeance?   Let me think—
Not feel—that's over.   Man, man,—you have roused
A demon in me, and the strength that should
Have met and conquered it, thy merciless hand
Itself has plucked away !   Rest, rest, my child—
We will be both avenged.

SCENE III.—*Corridor in the prison.*

(*Enter* LAWRENCY *and* KENSELL.)

LAWRENCY (*impatiently*).
He does, I tell you.   What a fool art thou,
To think, because a man can gulp down wrath,
He shows you all his soul !   A slow suspicion,
Once wakened, is the strongest.

KENSELL (*sullenly*).
'Twas your fault.
(*Takes an axe from the wall, and begins lazily
to sharpen it.*)
You handled me too roughly.   Who'd believe,
That I—with knife at hand—

LAWRENCY.
Thou obdurate ass !
Learn then to curb thine instincts.   Keep thy blows
For men.   I tell you what, my worthy friend—
You've not looked well of late.   I'm a physician—
A dose of hemp might——

KENSELL (*aside*).
Curse him !   I would give
One hand, to stab with the other !   What's to do ?
Speak, sir.   I've work here.

LAWRENCY (*leans familiarly on him*).
Did we talk of health ?
What of my cousin's ?   Did you note, sharp Hugh,
A dim look in his eye—upon his cheek,
A more than prison paleness ?   These young spirits,
Endued with eager life—can't brook the cage—
I think he'll die.

KENSELL.
Yes—give him time.

LAWRENCY.

        Well, time.
But time, good Hugo, like a blundering leech,
Can cure as well as slay. Say the law fail:
He will come forth—a bright bird, newly fledged,
And with, besides, that smell of virtue on him,
Which to *my* nostrils, as to thine, good Hugh,
Wafts no such grateful incense. Time!—pshaw—time!
All men are beaten in that race. Old gossip!
Are there no graves *within* ?

KENSELL (*grinning*).
        For living men?

LAWRENCY.
Happily phrased. With your accustomed wit,
Keen as an axe—you've hit it. There's enough.
I know you.

KENSELL.
      Why, not quite; best speak out plain :
You want me to do murder?   (*Swinging the axe.*)

LAWRENCY.
       Well, you fool!

KENSELL.
I'm sick of this commanding! Look you, master,
I am your instrument, and abhor mine office ;
Your slave—and curse you for it. I had once
A child with cherry lip and silken hair,
A blue-eyed baby-face! She was the chain,
That to sweet Nature linked this bruted soul,—
My *penitence*—sole sphere where guilty eyes
Meet Heav'n unchidden. You—oh, curse you for it!
Passing the opened-armed, the wooing sin,
Sought, found, and plucked my cherished, innocent
    flower,
And tossed her, withered, back to me. E'er since,

Her wan cheek is my torture—her sad glance,
Like red-hot wire, thrills through me, and incites
My savage soul to madness.　First I sought
With wealth—blood-gained, or how I cared not—to
Purchase your tardy justice ; but that failed.
You smile !

LAWRENCY.
Go on, sir—finish.

KENSELL.
　　　　　　　　　Look you now.
You've a rough job in hand—you want my aid,
To win it.　Wed my daughter.　I'll do that ;
Nay more—what work soe'er, albeit your lip
Falter in whispering to me.　Wed my child.

LAWRENCY.
Well—and what then ?

KENSELL.
　　　　　　Why, stab her, if you list ;
She'll die—a wife !

LAWRENCY.
　　　　　I'll think of it.　(*Aside*)　At least,
There's little risk in promising.　Well—well—
It is an honest claim.　Be true to me,
As I have ever found you.　Have your way.

KENSELL.
Your hand upon it.

LAWRENCY (*reluctantly*).
　　　　　There—enough.　Next time
The thumbscrew, rather.　I'll begone.　　　　　(*Exit.*)

KENSELL.
　　　　　　　　Huzza !

We'll have the jolliest bridal!   Bolts and shackles!
These walls shall echo till the deepest cells
Heave up a sullen rouse.   Ho, there—what, ho!
(*Runs to door, back.*)
Girl!   Wench!   My Marion!   (*Enter* MARION.)
Spindles to the devil!
Give me a kiss.   Don't look so pale.   Go to!
Come hither, little fool.

MARION (*timidly*).
Don't beat me.

KENSELL (*exultingly*).
Tush!
You'll be a wife, soon.   Let your lord do that.
'Tis a good English pastime.

MARION.
Wife, sir?

KENSELL.
Yes,
A kiss, I tell you.   Thank your good old father!
'Tis a great price he pays, to make his lost one
A brave and honest dame.

MARION.
What price?

KENSELL (*fiercely*).
Why—blood!
(*Aside*) Old blockhead!   Can't I hold my tongue?

MARION (*seizing his arm sinks kneeling*).
This way,
Father, look on me.   Can that devil-man
So damn all brother-souls?   Will he reject
This hand when graced with honour—virtue—God!
And grasp it, dowered with murder?

KENSELL.

Why—why—

MARION (*faintly, as she rises*).
Hold—
I thank you, father.   I am very grateful.
I cannot tell how grateful.   But you'll see.   (*Exeunt.*)

SCENE IV.—*In a house near Winchester.*

(EDITH, ETHELIND.)

ETHELIND.
Your journey, madam, squared not with the will
Of Master Lawrency?

EDITH.
The eager zeal
With which he did oppose it, gave more strength
To my resolve.   Clothed with some secret power,
He sways our destiny; and 'tis no shame
To say I fear him.   Yet I would not stay—
Ha! here at last?   Leave us, good Ethelind.
(*Enter* LAWRENCY *attended.   Exit* ETHELIND.)
What of my husband?   Speak,—hast seen him?   Hath
He sent for me?   How fares my lord?

LAWRENCY (*to attendant*).
Some wine (*drinks*).

EDITH.
I pray you—

LAWRENCY.
Stay, sir.   Let me ne'er bestride

Yon dapple more ; she flung at every bush,
As if a lion couched there.   I would know
When Master Vivian comes.   (*Exeunt attendants.*)

EDITH.
                         Oh ! wilt not answer ?

LAWRENCY.
Ha, lady ! what with me ?

EDITH.
                         With thee !   Alas !
Much,—very much.   I'd have thee render back
A perilled life ; I'd have thee wash away
From thy stained soul the wrong that thou hast done
In making merchandise of the dear blood
Of thy familiar friend !

LAWRENCY.
                         I marvel what
The suit may be to which these kindly taunts
Are but the prelude.

EDITH.
Give me back my husband.

LAWRENCY (*after a pause*).
How, lady, are these clasped and suppliant hands
The same that waved me from thy presence once
With such a royal scorn ?   Are these the eyes
That scathed me with their lightning ?   This the voice
That, when I murmured of my passionate love,
Willed me to take my palfrey and depart,
And I should have thy gratitude ?   Nay, come ;
I fear me 'tis but jest.

EDITH.
                         Is this an hour,—
A theme for jesting ?   Lawrency, thy heart

Was noble,—*is* so; pause then, listen to
Its language, and my prayer.

LAWRENCY.
I will.

EDITH (*joyfully*).
I wronged thee;
And you, disdaining vengeance, greatly choose
A gift no gold may purchase,—that sweet peace
That self-approval brings.

LAWRENCY.
Come, this is well.
No thanks; I do my portion, richly paid
By this most blissful moment. Thus we seal
Our mutual compact, Now thou'rt mine indeed.
(*Advancing as if to embrace her. She starts back.*)

EDITH.
It cannot be; thou dost not mean it. Say
Thou dost not mean it! Listen, Lawrency;
Thou stand'st this moment where the paths divide
To good and evil. Choose the right, nor make
The devils blush at thine excelling sin.
I tell thee, could I list such fearful terms,
The sacrifice were vain, for *he* would cast,
In hate and scorn, the worthless life away,
Bought at such a price.

LAWRENCY (*after a pause, gazing at her*).
'Twill be a sorry sight,
When some dark locks we wot of are beheld
Wreathing the hangman's fingers! When low hinds,
While homeward wending from their honest toil,
Gaze on the blackening features, and cry, "See
The bloody traitor's doom!" while mothers raise
Their whimpering brats to touch the scaffold's rim,
And bid them love their king.

EDITH.
                Oh, God ! no more.

LAWRENCY.
Alack ! a flimsy thing is woman's love.
Lo ! how the winter of self-sacrifice
Doth chill it to the core !

EDITH.
                My life for his.
If not, accuse me.   Let me die with him.

LAWRENCY.
Thee, my sweet friend ?   Our gallant king might well
Forgive so fair a foe.

EDITH.
                Hold, sir.   Here end
This devilish mockery !   Love, I cannot give ;
It dwells within a cold and dreary cell,
Bound to the fettered prisoner with a tie
Stronger than chains.   Hatred itself might blush
To plant a scorpion on his couch of stone,
Or quench the last lone spark that cheers the night
Of his soul's darkness !   Take my gold, I pray thee,—
My land—my jewels—I will be thy slave,—
Thy mistress, *never !*

LAWRENCY.
                See, I want thy love,—
Thy love,—and thee.   Look you, I jest no more.
Be mine thou shalt !   Ay, sweetheart, never dream
That thine accursed minion can escape
My vengeance.   Know that, though the headsman miss,
My hatred shall be fed.   If one hour hence
Thou dost relent—

EDITH.
                Away ! I heed thee not,—
I know not what thou speakest.   Go ! thy words

Make a strange senseless murmur in mine ear ;
My soul rejects their meaning.   Tempter, hence !
   (*Exit* LAWRENCY.   EDITH *remains motionless,*
    absorbed in grief, till VIVIAN *enters.*)

VIVIAN.

Madam, my master,—that is, I would say,
My *friend*,—desired me bring this loving scroll
To your fair hand.   'Tis from your lord—
     (EDITH *snatches it eagerly.*)
       And say
That—but you chid him hence—he would have told
Much that had giv'n you comfort,—what calm cheer
Marked the discourse—

EDITH.

    Not see me !   Do I read
The words aright ?   Bid me return, and leave
My husband fenced with foes ?   Have I not sworn
To cheer and tend him through all grief and pain,
Ev'n as we shared our love ?   Alas ! what hour
So much demands the duty he disdains ?
Speak, sir.   I cannot read this riddle.   Speak,—
Canst *thou ?*

VIVIAN.

    If my poor judgment may presume,
He knows his safety best.   Doth he not write
Of love, of pardon, duty, gentleness ?
Nay, says he not his life's salvation rests
On thy most prompt obedience ?

EDITH.

     Ay, 'tis so,
Ev'n so 'tis written.   Heaven, my footsteps guide !
As he can scarce test that obedience more.
I am ready at your pleasure.
     (*Exit.   Re-enter* LAWRENCY.)

LAWRENCY.

    Bravely done,

Shrewd second!   Let not this consenting mood
Change by delay.   To-morrow we'll set forth
For those broad lands, which, fairly confiscate,
Shall call me lord.   For our caged bird—

VIVIAN.

For him?

LAWRENCY.

Hugh Kensell is his keeper.   Would'st thou more?
(*Exeunt.*)

———

SCENE V.—*The Prison.*

LATYMER (*as if suddenly awaking*).
Let go my arms!   Why do ye mock me?   Ha!
False villain!   I can reach thee still.   'Tis nought;
Thank God! 'twas but a vision.   Strange,—I thought,
While sadly musing o'er my numbered hours,
A silent angel came and set me free,
And pointed to my home.   There Edith stood
To greet her lord; when one like Lawrency
Leaped from the earth beneath my very feet,
And bore her shrieking thence.   'Twas terrible!
Still I behold that look of malice mixed
With fiercer passion.   Hark! the bolt revolves.
(*Enter* MARION *stealthily.*)
My mute purveyor, I ne'er hailed thy step
As now I do.   Speak to me.

MARION.
I am changed
Since you beheld me.

LATYMER.

So thou art, indeed
Or else this dungeon-light gives ghastlier hue
Than captive cheeks are wont to wear.

MARION.

I mean
My heart is changed.

LATYMER.

Gentler it cannot be ;
And that thou art not grown less merciful,
This visit proves.

MARION.

I bring nor hope, nor aid.
Hope mocks me ever ; pity veils her brow ;
The flowers I plant bear thorns.   Why should I deal
In mercy's sweet and tender offices,
Yet ne'er partake of them ?

LATYMER.

Why, art thou not
A woman ?

MARION.

You love life ?

LATYMER.

I court not *death*,
And would not meet him on the scaffold.

MARION (*sternly*).

See ;
I come to traffic with thee for thy life.
My price—revenge !   Look on me.   I am wronged,
And need the service of a stalwart arm
Like thine.   Do but my bidding, and thou'rt free ;
Refuse, and here I leave thee to thy doom.

Come,—choose. But three days past, I would have
    spent
My heart's blood, drop by drop, to save from harm
One hair of that fair brow. I'll not look back ;
Love lies behind,—hate onward. Would'st thou live?—
But now my thought grows wild, my senses reel.
Blood !—I will have his blood !

LATYMER.
                Can passion work
A change so fearful ? Thou hast not yet named
Him who hath wronged thee.

MARION.
          Lawrency.

LATYMER.
                My friend ?
Leave thy revenge to God !

MARION.
          Back to your straw ;
That fearless look misled me,—I mistook
Your nature. Fare you well.   (*She retires.*)

LATYMER.
        Oh, Edith ! Edith !

MARION (*returns suddenly*).
Stay, I have news for thee. Thy Edith lies
Within a ruffian's snare,—ev'n as we speak,
'Tis closing round her.

LATYMER (*starting up*).
        Ha ! the dream !

MARION (*going*).
              Farewell !
LATYMER.
Hold—hold—in pity ! Is this dungeon hell,

And yon fair thing a demon sent to prove
My spirit's strength?   I—I will follow thee.
Girl, thou hast raised a fiend, with which to dwell
Alone exceeds my power.   What of my wife?
My Edith?   Has she—   Woman, thou didst speak
Of danger,—of a snare!   Fool,—fool! 'tis plain,
It is—it is my dream's reality.

MARION.
Wilt thou revenge me?   Swear!

LATYMER.
                    I swear!

MARION (*unlocks the chain*).
                        'Tis well;
                    (*Brings a disguise.*)
Throw these rude garments o'er you.   Quickly; now
Follow,—but not a word.   (*Exeunt.*)

SCENE VI.—*A Street near the Castle.*

(*Enter* LATYMER *and* MARION.)

MARION.
Now thou art free; away, and quickly make
Thy ransom good.   (*Stops as she retires.*)
                Hist you!   Avoid the Tower,
For man to-day makes holiday to see
His fellow butchered.   Fare you well!   (*Exit* MARION.)

LATYMER.
                        The Tower!
What secret impulse bids me seek the spot

From which she warns me ?   I will go.   Good rags,
Be my protection.
     (*As he is going, enter some Townspeople.*)
    Hold, I pray you, sir ;
What do they at the Tower ?

    Townsman.
      What do they at
The Tower?   Curtail man's fair proportions, sir.
Would'st see the subjects they do practise on,
Thither with me.   (*Dead march without.*)

    Another.
   Back, neighbours,—back, I say !
Room for this lady.   Come, sirs, let us on.
   (*Exeunt;* Latymer *follows, and enter at the
    other side* Hugh Kensell *and others, armed,
    with a Townsman.*)

    Townsman.
By yonder corner.   Ha ! mine eye just caught
The flutter of his ragged cloak.   He makes
Straight for the river.

    Kensell.
   Twenty crowns I give
The man who grasps him first.   Jerome and Cole,
Round to yon corner, and head back the game ;
We follow on his track.   Who's for the crowns ?

    Townsman.
Start fair, sirs.   One must win.   The prize is sure.
    (*Exeunt, running different ways.*)

    END OF ACT III.

ACT IV.

SCENE I.—*The Garden at Ellingham.*

(EDITH—ETHELIND.)

EDITH.

Look on the dial, Ethelind ; the day
Is surely waning.

ETHELIND.
'Tis just noon.

EDITH.
No more ?
I would that it were evening.   Sit by me.
Did I not talk of dreams ?   I'll tell thee what
Befell last night.

ETHELIND.
What was't, dear lady?

EDITH.
Hark !
Put close thine ear ; are we secure ?   Methinks
The air is listening, it has grown so still—
The flowers seem glancing hitherward.   Come on,
Into this nook ; their bright eyes pain me.   Hist !
'Twas thus :—There sat a weight upon my bosom,
A crouching phantom, whose white ghastly hand
Beckoned my sleep away.   There was a sound
Of fluttering wings, as if a prisoned bird
Had seen her love-mate in the skies at play,
And would be with him.   Then—
(*They walk aside conversing.*)

(*Enter* VIVIAN, *muttering angrily*.)
>'Tis ever thus—
I see—with pride. While plotting, it doth sit
With drooping brow, and lips demurely pursed,
A humble suitor—till its end be won,
And then it doth begin to flout and scold
And show its blacker nature. I know not
When I have been so stirred ! (*Exit.*)

(EDITH *and* ETHELIND *return.*)

ETHELIND.
>You wakened then ?
The blessed Virgin shield us from all ill :
Would we might never dream !

EDITH.
>So thou wouldst cast
A world away ! Sweet soother ! gentle sleep !—
Who paints forgotten pictures on our hearts,
So that we deem them real ; gives despair
Hope's healthful whisper ; brings the beggar wealth ;
Plucks down oppression ; bursts the prison-door ;
And justice gives, unbribed. Nay, let us dream ;
For only then, if we perforce must err,
'Tis done in innocence. Whose form is that
Amid the trees ? Methought that here mine eyes
Might shun the presence of false-scheming men ;
But there's no peace—no peace !

ETHELIND.
>I know his gait ;
'Tis Walter Vivian. Look, he turns—now stops—
Now turns again. He's angered.

EDITH.
>Come this way—
I hate his scrutiny—the wicked tool
Of a worse master !

ETHELIND.
To the bower, sweet madam ;
I have a charm to lure this dragon hence.
Trust him to me.   (*As they go out, re-enter* VIVIAN.)

VIVIAN.
He grows in malice, too,
E'en as in villany.   Blind and sottish fool !
To yoke my fortune to so wild a car,
Which bears me breathless over rugged ways,
And depths scarce fathomed, from whose fearful leap
My cooler thought recoils.   And for what end
Have I done this?   For none.   Offence nor feud
Had I with Latymer ; no revenge to wreak
In blood or ruin.   By heaven, I'll move no more
In aid of Lawrency !   As yet—   (*Enter* ETHELIND.)

ETHELIND.
How now ?
What sturdy vagrant's this that dare approach
So near my mistress' person ?   Out !—Alack !
'Tis Master Vivian !   Pardon, sir, I took you
For some poor vagabond—some petty thief—
Some gaol-bird newly freed.   Kind sir, I hope
You pardon me.   (*Curtseying ironically.*)

VIVIAN.
I understand you, child.
No music soothes me like a woman's tongue
Tuned for a scold.   I am in a bitter mood,
And would be cheered ; so here I'll rest me ; now
Go on : let's see thy spirit,—in good faith,
Thou hast one.   Come, child.

ETHELIND.
Would that men might say
The like of thee !   Thou wear'st a sword, indeed,—
(Is't of true metal or a peacock's plume?)
And hast a manly swagger—airs would fright

My very grandame ; still, I dare be sworn,
The worth o' the picture's chiefly in the frame.

VIVIAN.

Again well said.   I'll kiss you.

ETHELIND.

You had better !

May a poor damsel know what mighty cause
Hath moved this generous ire ?   At shovel-board
Did Master Holdfast beat thee ?   Does thy back
Ache from a recent cudgel ?   Art dismissed ?
Was the last flask of Malvoisie too sour
To please thy palate ?   Tell me.

VIVIAN.

Worse than that.

What think you ?   The new lord took strange offence
At some misdoing ; struck the steward twice,—
A grey old man that might have been his sire,—
And hath discharged the cellarer, a man
I held in high esteem.

ETHELIND.

I know you did.

A most discreet old man.

VIVIAN.

True, child—'tis base !

And, but my pouch is empty as a drum,
I'd serve his beck no longer.

ETHELIND.

Are you mad

To tell me so?   What, if yon bird reported
That to your master ?   You'd be packing soon.
Ay, sir, right quickly thou'dst be fain to take
Thine honoured spyship hence.

VIVIAN.

My master, truly !

Since when wore I his livery?   Hark you, girl!
Were it my will to—Humph! I'll talk no more.

ETHELIND.

'Tis best.   Thou'dst else betray some confidence
That none but knaves should hear; some valorous plot
Against a woman, when no manly foot
Is near to crush ye.   By these heavens that shine,
One stained with deeds like this had better dwell
On savage shores, with things untaught and wild,
Than strut the world, clad in such garb as thine,
And call himself a man!

VIVIAN.
It was not I.
No deed of mine—I thought—   (*Aside; turns away.*)
Am I a fool,
To blush and stammer like a chidden child
Before this wench's eye?   'Tis bitter truth
Gives her words venom; she but drives more deep,
A thorn was fixed before.   I am not yet
So much at odds with virtue as to make
All reconcilement vain.   I'll speak to her—
Tell her the tidings; ask her—Ethelind!
Hem! Ethelind!

ETHELIND.
Mocker!

VIVIAN.
I mock thee not.
Nay, Ethelind, believe me,—trust me, child.
Less hardened than I seem, I here reject
An office fits me not.   I honour thee,
And pity thy poor mistress.

ETHELIND.
'Tis too late.
Alas—alas! too late!

VIVIAN.
For once thou'rt wrong.
Canst keep a secret safely ?   Spare thy fib,—
I'll trust thee, woman as thou art.   Then know
That, by a hand unknown, some instruments,
Useful for man's enlargement, were conveyed
To an imprisoned knight, one Latymer ;
Who thereupon escaped.

ETHELIND.
Can this be true?

VIVIAN.
'Twas thought he sailed for Flanders ; but of this
I have no certain knowledge.   To thy mistress ;
And, with these news possessed, sing in her ear
A song of comfort.   Say, withal, that I—
I, Walter Vivian, kiss her hands, in shame
That I have stained my erewhile manhood, thus
Joining her crafty foe ; but from henceforth
Am vowed her champion.

ETHELIND.
Never would I seek
A blither errand.

VIVIAN.
To thy charge, my maid.
(Exeunt severally.)

———

SCENE II.—*A Part of the Grounds.*

(Enter MARION *as a page.)*

MARION.
Well, I have traced this dark, corroding ill
Through nerve and vein, and, as I deemed, the core

Is—Edith !   Mocking villain, thou shalt make
A dear account !   'Twas well I waited not
The cold and sluggish aid of Latymer.
My ready path lies open.   I will seem,
False wretch ! thy faithful and most loving slave—
The tool and pander of thy hate and crimes—
Until the ripe hour comes ; and then I'll doff
This servile badge, and shew thee Marion !
(*Horns without.*)
What—from the chase ?   Hunter, thyself art snared.
(*Exit.*)

(*Enter* LAWRENCY, *with hounds, huntsmen, etc.*)

LAWRENCY.
Hang me yon spotted brach without delay !
Beauty, ye call her !   Hang her !   'Tis the won't
Of beauties to mislead.   Dost hear me, sir ?
Now what dost gape at ?

HUNTSMAN.
Did your honour say
The spotted brach ?   The best—

LAWRENCY (*impatiently*).
She shall be hanged !
Away, and do it.

HUNTSMAN.
Sir, the hound is staunch !

LAWRENCY.
Dost parley with me, fellow ?   Here, give up
Thy belt and horn.   Seek out another lord.
Take thyself hence.
(*The huntsman throws down his belt, etc., and
exit.*)
Where's Julian ?   Where's the page ?
Go, seek him.
(*Enter* VIVIAN.)

Thou here! lazy fellow—hence!
Did I not give thee hasty missives?   Now
Beshrew thee!   What dost here?

VIVIAN.
A quiet stroll
Did better suit my fancy.   I'll not ride
Unless the humour serve.

LAWRENCY.
Why, what means this?
Away, sirs!   (*Attendants go out.*)
Now, thou most untoward knave,
Where are the papers my rash confidence
Gave to thy charge?

VIVIAN.
Safe, sir.   The scrolls are safe;
Heed not for that.   But I'll no longer be
An unrewarded drudge.   The game is played—
And, while thou'rt fattening on the treasure won,
In purse and prospect I am lean as ever.
Give me a thousand crowns!

LAWRENCY.
Get thee to bed
·And sleep thy senses sober!

VIVIAN.
If I drink,
'Tis but to drown the devil.   He is here
Again—or, is it thou?

LAWRENCY (*turning away*).
There, get thee gone!
I'll talk with thee to-morrow.

VIVIAN (*following.*)
No, to-day.

LAWRENCY.

Tempt not my patience further.   Look you, Vivian :
Let us not quarrel.   I am hot as thou,
And, being provoked, more dangerous.   I say,
Beware !

VIVIAN.
    Beware thyself.

LAWRENCY (*grasps his sword, but looses it again*).
                    Go—go, thou'rt drunk.
This time I pardon thee.

VIVIAN.
                    Yon helpless girl
Is not thy victim.   *I* protect her, *I !*
Storm as thou wilt, and vapour with thy sword,
That bird hath 'scaped the snare.

LAWRENCY (*draws and advances on him*).
                    Stand from thy path,
Fool ! wilt thou tempt thy fate ?

VIVIAN.
                    I fear thee not,—
Come on.   (*They fight, and* VIVIAN *falls.*)
    The curse of English hearts upon
Thy French-taught tricks of fence,—thou hadst me there;
Thy bodkin's point has pricked me from the world
Ere I could make my peace with honesty.
This is Heaven's justice.   On this very spot
I sold myself to thee.   As thou'rt a man,
Undo thy guilt.   O me ! I faint—this blood—
                    (*He dies.*)

LAWRENCY.

Beshrew thee for a quarrel-seeking knave ;
Thou forcedst this on me.   When the whelp we rear
Grows to a lion with his teeth undrawn,
No marvel if those dangerous fangs be turned

Upon their feeder.   Vivian, this was ill—
The morning of our friendship promised not
To couch in bloody clouds.   Ah ! destiny.   (*Exit.*)

(*Enter* Edith *cloaked.*)

EDITH.

Alas ! my shadow warns me that the day
Is older than I thought.   My champion, ho !—
Soft—here he lies !   Great Heaven—to slumber thus
At such a moment.   Hist !   Good friend, awake !
'Twas not my will to keep thee.   Sentinel,
Is this thy watchful faith ?   Up—up, for pity !
Alas ! what stain is on my robe ?   'Tis red—
'Tis blood—the sleeper's blood—and he will wake
No more till angels summon.   Now, indeed,
Am I deserted.   Ah !
          (*Re-enter,* LAWRENCY, *attended by* GROSSVELT
              and WILHELM.)

LAWRENCY (*approaching her*).
My truant bird !

Would'st slip thy jesses ?   Grows thy perch so dull,
That thou would'st fain be soaring ?

EDITH.

Hast thou torn

Life's temple down, and now return'st to mock
Its senseless ruins ?

LAWRENCY.

Nay, I'd spare thee, love,

This most unsightly scene ; but— Knaves, there needs
No leechcraft.   Bear him in—thence, speedily,
With rites befitting, to his kindred clay.
For this mischance I will account to all
Who have the right to question.
          (GROSSVELT *and* WILHELM *remove the body.*)

Thou art pale,

Yet thou look'st gladly.

EDITH.
              Aye, my lord is safe.
Safe, and at liberty !   These cheering news
Thy murdered comrade brought me.

LAWRENCY.
                          Then he died
With falsehood on his lips.   Aye, Latymer
Escaped—that's true.   But there were hawks abroad,
And the freed pigeon circled round so oft,
Ere darting homeward, that his flight was stayed.
He'll scarce try that again.   Now, fairest cousin,—
Nay, fear me not,—*I do not love thee now.*
                          (*Leads her to a seat.*)
I would but tell thee of a thing I saw
When absent last.   Watson, thou know'st, is dead ?

EDITH.

Dead !

LAWRENCY.
      On the scaffold.   So is Clarke,—these both
Less guilty than thy lord.   I stood by them
In the last moments of their awful doom.
They were dragged forth—

EDITH.
                Spare me the tale.

LAWRENCY.
                          And hanged ;
But not to death.   Oh ! that were merciful
To what succeeded.   With clenched hands,—with throats
Black with the stifling rope, and breath that came
In short convulsive throbs, they chained them down.
(Already pale ?)   'Tis well thou could'st not hear
The last loud shriek of mortal anguish, wrung
From those whose superhuman fortitude

Up to that hideous moment stood supreme,—
Nor note the savage yell that round me rose
When the masked torturer, with his bloody hands,
Tore from their wretched bosoms life's quick source,
And hurled it in the flame!   What victim *next?*
List to the thrilling whisper of thy heart.
(*Pause.   He rises.*)
He is condemned.

EDITH (*kneeling at his feet*).
Hear me, thou bloody judge!
If thou canst fear,—hast faith in holy prayer,—
If thou believ'st there is a time when thou,
Before a wak'ning universe shalt stand
And answer the demand, " Why didst thou thus?
Where is thy brother?"—spare my perilled lord.
Or, if thou canst not, take me to him.   Let
Us meet on this side death.   We do not ask
To mar thy triumph,—to regain the peace
Thy hand has wrested from us.   We will die,—
We will both die!

LAWRENCY (*aside, irresolutely*).
Sad music!   Cease,—oh, cease!
Quick, to my aid, dark fiend, or I am lost
To my revenge, and thee! (*recovering himself.*)   Arise,
    arise!
I owe ye no such favour.   Woman, hark!
(*Seizes her arm.*)
Heard you that cry?   It is the greedy rack
Distorting his young limbs!   Look! his white cheek,
Palsied with inner anguish! his pale lips
That thou hast kissed—the hand that thou hast strained—
The breast that was thy pillow!   Hark! he cries
Aloud for death, and death is merciful.
But *thou*—thou wilt not hear!

EDITH (*starts up with sudden wildness*).
Speak—speak! canst save him?

LAWRENCY.

Aye,—so thy part be done.

EDITH.

'Tis o'er,—I yield.
Do what thou wilt.   Come, devil as thou art,
Struggle no longer for thy hellish hire.
Body and soul, destroy me !   Work thy will.
In all the outward fashion of a man
Thou dost confront me, and I hear thy voice
Fearfully tempting.   Look ! there is God's throne,
Whereto the stain of murder doth attain
Ere earth can green it o'er.   God's blessed air
Surrounds us, and is passing onward now,
Soiled with thy words of sin and treachery,
Yet harmless all to thee ; from this I know
That Heaven forsakes me.   No; he shall not die !
I'll rend mine honour first ; then, dying, sue
At his pure feet for pardon.   Live, my Dudley !
How can I leave that form of honoured life
To the rude scoffs of maddened multitudes ?
How can I give the generous heart, a prey
For human wolves to tear ?   Take life,—hope,—honour,
But save,—oh, save him !

(She falls senseless at his feet.) '

END OF ACT IV.

ACT V.

SCENE I.—*An Apartment.*

(EDITH *is seated on a couch, her head bent down
on her hands.* GIOVANNI *kneels at her feet.*)

GIOVANNI.

She hears me not ; yet for a weary hour
I kneel, and clasp this dead-cold hand, and pray
Some word or sign of consciousness. Oh ! speak,
Lady ! sweet mistress ! poor Giovanni calls.
These woes have killed her.

EDITH.
                  Had they but such power!
Life, that deserts joy's new and glittering fane,
Clings to its ruins. Boy, the hopeful die,—
The trusted,—loved,—those for whose weal, bowed
    hearts
And hands uplift, and sacrifice of tears
Are offered. Hark,—a step ! Secure the door.
Ah ! that were vain. Who comes? (*Enter* MARION.)

MARION.
                  My master, lady,
Craves pardon for his seeming negligence.
He lingers but to seal a hurried scroll
Touching the theme on which you spoke this morn,
And will attend you, madam. (*Exit* MARION.)

EDITH.
                  Then all's true ;
I did not dream. Under the peaceful wing
Of holy night the dark assassin comes
To strike at my soul's health. Giovanni, hark !

Had guilty snares beset thee,—life become
A thing unprized—which, being spent, would buy
A dearer life's salvation—what would'st do ?
Speak boldly.   Thou would'st—ha !

GIOVANNI.
Die, madam! spurn
The slavish load, and *die !*

EDITH.
Why, that's well said. (*Pauses.*)
Giovanni, thou hast loved thy mistress ?

GIOVANNI.
Aye,
Lady, my counsel proves it.

EDITH.
And wilt serve her,—
Thou wilt ; I know thee.   Canst thou call to mind
One summer's eve, Giovanni, when I sat
In yonder bower, and (quicklier to beguile
The absence of my lord) taught thee strange names
Of many curious herbs, whose deep hearts hide
The healing balm of death ?   And, idly, too,
As then I thought, showed thee a cunning mean
To draw from them their rank and inner juice,
And make them skilful ministers to hearts,
Like mine, past other cure ?

GIOVANNI.
Yes, I remember
That evening, madam ; not, I fear, the task.

EDITH.
Cull me white lilies, and the hooded flower
That in its monkish cowl at once doth bear
Both death and healing ; nightshade, with its fruit
Of royal purple ; drooping widow's flower,
To me most fitting ; swallow-wort of gold,
That lures the honey-seeker to its heart,

Then hugs the thief to death ; and last, good page,
Forget not that stout hemlock, by whose aid
The wise and honoured heathen won his way
Into the gods' embrace.

GIOVANNI.
    I'll do it, madam.   (*Exit.*)

EDITH.
Thus, tyrant, I recall the extorted pledge,
And, in its stead, give life.   May that suffice
To turn thy vengeance from that richer food
For which it hungers,—teach thee penitence,
And pity to thy kind.
    (*She moves towards a portrait, and kneels.*)
    Mother, 'tis thou
Should'st stead me in this misery ; but, oh !
It breaks my heart to look on thy sweet face,
So proudly innocent.   Though but in thought
Grown vile, that glance condemns.   Down, guilty head,
Into the dust of the impassive earth
That can no more thy dainty looks defile,
More pure than thou.   My unknown parent, if,
As I did never nestle on thy breast,
Nor in thy kind arms ready refuge weep
My infant griefs away,—so my lost soul
May miss the path to that blessed world where thou
Hast rest for aye— yet pray for me,—for one
Who, sick with sorrow and beset with snares,
Found this world's paths too rugged for her tread,
And the grave's peace too tempting.   Ha ! what light
Steals o'er thy features ?   'Tis Heaven speaks to me
In pity of this deed, and—
    (*Re-enter* GIOVANNI *with chalice.*)
    Thanks ; you have found
All my deliverers,—cool and fresh, and filled
With that rich solvent, at whose softest kiss
Life's chain drops from us.   For this service, boy,
I must be still thy debtor.

GIOVANNI.
There is more
To do.   Revenge.

EDITH.
I will not have it so.
I'll tread that path alone.   My last true friend,
Farewell.

GIOVANNI.
Farewell, sweet mistress.
(*He retires.   After a pause, a step is heard ap-
proaching.*)

EDITH (*starting to her feet*).
Ha! he comes.
Earth chides me hence, Heaven beckons, and I pause,
As there were space for question.   (*Drinks.*)   Fatal cup!
Sweet hath o'ercome thy bitter,—life thy death.
I am ready for thee.
(*Enter* LATYMER, *pale; his dress bloody.*)
Thy—thy message?   Speak!
Com'st thou, impatient of thy lonely grave,
To meet me, hastening to thee?

LATYMER.
Edith,—wife!
Calm thee,—I live.

EDITH (*in a low, troubled tone*).
My brain seems wandering.
The villain mocked me, for he could not save,
And so my sweet lord died.

LATYMER.
He lives for thee.
My loved,—my lost one!   To thy home, my heart.
Do you not know me?

EDITH.
Aye, methinks I do.

But do not trifle with me ; I have slept
And had a dream so fearful, that I see
Its phantoms round me yet.   Oh ! can it be
That I do stand beside thy living form,
Feeling thy touch, and dwelling on thy tone ?
Speak on, speak gently.   Say that woes are past,
That we shall live as in old loving days,
And all be peace again.

LATYMER.
It shall.

EDITH (*clinging frantically to him*).
Oh, come !
Why linger, then ?   Why draw one other breath
In this hot atmosphere of shame and sin ?
Oh, come—come—come !

LATYMER (*eagerly*).
It is my prayer.

EDITH (*sinking back*).
Ah, me !
This is lost labour, Dudley.   I would fly,—
Indeed I would ; but ever, when I move,
Some unseen monster seems to coil around,
And force me from your arms.

LATYMER (*drawing her towards a casement*).
Look forth, my love.
There lies our path, across the wooded glen,
Whose mazes we have trod so oft together.
Shall we essay it now ?   See how the night
From her fringed mantle flings a silvery star,
To be our guide and welcome !

EDITH.
Blessed star !
Stand in the gate of heaven, and guide me hence.

My strength begins to fail.   Oh, Lawrency !
Thy bitter vengeance !

LATYMER.
Ha ! my dungeon dream !
Thou dost not mean that— Mercy, God !

EDITH.
'Tis true.
I see you murmur to yourself.   'Twas guilt ;
Yet do not cast me from you.

LATYMER.
Edith,—Edith,
(GIOVANNI *enters and springs to her assistance.*)
Spoke I too harshly ?

GIOVANNI.
Hadst thou come this morn,
All had been well ; now, *death*.

EDITH (*reviving*).
Thy hand,—thy hand.
Be armed, dear husband ; he has spoken sooth,—
Our life of love is over.

LATYMER.
I have heard
Of strange delusions that do mock men's souls.
How changed thou art !   Thy voice is deep and stern,
That made such music as a sleepless bird
Might scatter through night's waste.   That drooping
form,
Where is its matchless majesty ?   Why grows
Thy brow so dark and wrinkled that, but now,
Fair as an angel's seemed ?

EDITH.
Dudley, I die.
Start not—grieve not, but hear.   When thou wast gone,

Came there that false betrayer,—that foul friend,
And hourly hissed into my helpless ear
Dark tales of blood and torture ; spoke of wolves,
That, shaped like men, had bloodier hearts, and yelled
And thirsted for thy life—my *husband's* life !—
Which he could save, he only ; and myself
Alone could find the ransom.   I grow faint.
Nay, spur thy fancy ; bid it leap the gulf
And roam the hell beyond.   Canst guess the price
Of thy redemption ?   Do not speak.   'Tis true ;
In your white cheek I read it.

LATYMER.

Villain—villain !

EDITH.

He talked of what was done ; the fate our friends
Had borne, their shrieks, their terrible death.   In brief,
I did consent—

LATYMER.

Ha!

EDITH (*faintly*).

Let me say all.

Though in mine agony I did consent
To be thy saviour, think not, dearest lord,
I would have lived to be thy scorn and shame.
No,—no ! I better knew myself, and thee.
Listen.   The hour was near,—the torturer bent
To claim his devilish pact.   Thus driv'n to bay,
Finding no way to freedom, love, I made one.
Yes, I have drunk, and die.   Dudley, forgive.
Sweet husband, pardon me.   (*Sinks at his feet.*)

LATYMER.

I stand and gaze,

As if some magic touch had made me stone,
Leaving no sense but vision, and that spared
For torture,—not in mercy.   Art thou, Edith,

My love and life?   My flesh begins to creep.
How came I hither?   Would this dream were o'er!

EDITH.
Dudley, come nearer.   All is darkness now,
But I can hear thy voice,—my faint heart thrills
To its accustomed echo.   Griev'st thou, Dudley?

LATYMER.
My tears speak for me.   Edith, I—   Oh, God!
I am a wretched and heart-stricken man,—
A guilty man!   Spare me this child,—this lamb
From out the world's great flock.   Oh, gentle one!
Oh, noblest heart that e'er this world did bear!
I have done this,—*I* loved thee more than Heaven,—
And jealous Heaven recalls thee to itself,
And will not heed my prayers.   Thus, hand in hand,
Cold lip to lip, and bleeding heart to heart,
We will obey the summons.
          (*Places her on a low couch, and kneels supporting
            her.*)

EDITH.
                    Welcome rest !
The day has been too long.   Nay, do you weep?
No tears.   I am your wife,—your honoured wife ;
Your—happy—wife.   Dear Dudley, will you give me
The good-night kiss?   That's well.   And now, my head
Feels weary—on thy bosom—thus—to sleep—

LATYMER.
To sleep!
          (*He lies down at her feet.   After a moment,
            GIOVANNI approaches and whispers him.*)
          What art thou, bloody counsellor ?
I know thy favour, and I heed thy words.
Oh, *you*, Giovanni !   In one breath, my boy,
How dark the world has grown !   Come,—to the work !
                    (*Rushes out.*)

SCENE II.—*A Dark Gallery.*

(*Armed servants of* LATYMER, *with* HUGH KEN-
SELL, *a prisoner.*)

FIRST SERVANT.
Finish thy tale.   He burst the outer gate,
And entered by the oriel.   Whither then ?

SECOND SERVANT.
Straight to the lady's chamber.   I, meanwhile,
Sought thee and our bold comrades here, with whom
He bade me wait his summons, to escort
The lady forth.   He swore us all to touch
No hair o' the base informer,—else—

FIRST SERVANT.
                                        Who's this?
Faith, he's no cherub !

SECOND SERVANT.
                    Sir, this cavalier
Is gaoler commonly, and, at over-hours,
Headsman, of Winchester.   Seeing him on our track,
We made free with his person.   What's his errand,
The devil, that sent him, knows ; but if he came
In chase of Master Latymer, 'twas lucky ;
For, as it seems, he's caught him.

KENSELL.
                            Fool ! you lie,—
'Tis Lawrency.

SECOND SERVANT.
            Come, sir, be civil.   Speak
The truth for once.

KENSELL.
                I do.   And were't, my friend,
Your natural tongue, you'd understand it better.
I follow Lawrency.

FIRST SERVANT.
And why?

KENSELL.
       He's lured
My daughter from me, and pretends— Good knaves,
Let me but see this man.

SECOND SERVANT.
      Perhaps you will.
Hast e'er a halter with you? You *shall* meet,—
You precious pair of rogues!

FIRST SERVANT.
       Is it not strange
We hear no summons? What's the signal?
      (*A blow is struck on the panel.*)

SECOND SERVANT.
         That!
  (*They rush out, dragging* KENSELL.)

———

SCENE THE LAST.—*A Saloon. Night. At one
side the remains of a banquet.*

(LAWRENCY *at a table covered with books, papers,
plans, etc. Lights down.*)

LAWRENCY.
Thrice have I moved those hangings, yet could swear
That their dark folds concealed some form instinct
With moving life. How yon grim portrait stares!
His eyes outgleam my cresset. S'death, he smiles!
Truce with thy ghastly merriment; I'll spoil
Thy grinning, friend, to-morrow. Sense o'ertaxed,

Plays us, in spite, strange tricks.   (*A pause; he writes.*)
                         'Tis very still,
And yet it is not.   I have seen it writ,
That on the brooding earth *no silence* dwells,
But ever there are deep mysterious sounds,
Whose source we know not, flitting to and fro,
Like shades condemned, that wander earth and heaven,
Yet nowhere find a home.   What have we here ?
                         (*Tossing over papers.*)
" Hangings for chamber in the eastern wing,
Six nobles and a mark."   " For closing in
The right of pasturage, ten marks."   " The sale
Of old Dame Gillian's tapestry brought no more
Than fourteen crowns."   Indeed !   What's this ?   " The
    plan
For building of the church you promised, when—"
'Tis nought.   Lo ! how the tongueless night doth give
Significance to every wonted sound !
'Tis time.   Who waits there ?   Julian, boy !
                         (*Enter* MARION.)
                         The hour ?

                    MARION.
Deep midnight, sir.

                      LAWRENCY.
                'Tis fitting.   Place a lamp
Without.

                    MARION (*aside.*)
           He hath not changed his purpose.   Heart,
Hold *thine.*

                    LAWRENCY,
          Away, sir ; go !

                    MARION (*approaching*).
                         My gentle lord
Is weary with much study.   I have here
A draught so soothing—

LAWRENCY.
                              Give it me.   I drink
To—   Dost thou see the devil, boy, that thus
You tremble and grow pale?   I drink to *Hate*,
And Vengeance, crowned and full!   (*Drinks.*)

MARION.
                                 The cup is drained.
There's no drop left—not one.   A worthy pledge.
Revenge,—revenge,—Oh, God !   (*Rushes out.*)

LAWRENCY.
                                 The boy hath had
His revel with the pages.   His young brain—
Why wait I here ?   My soul hath spurned aside
Its sick oppression, and triumphant sits
Upon the chariot of my hopes, which stand
Full-winged to bear me home.   Thus, Edith, *thus*
I sweep to my revenge !
            (*As he is rushing out, the door is thrown open.
            He stands petrified.*)
                                 Pale dream, that hast
No bond, nor fellowship with breathing men,
Remain, or vanish, know thy mission vain ;
Thou canst not teach me fear.   Back to thy grave,
Thou gaunt and bloody thing !
            (*While he speaks,* LATYMER *has appeared at the
            door.*)

LATYMER.
                              To summon thee,
I come.

LAWRENCY (*aside, recovering*).
"Tis he himself,—his voice,—his eye !
Whence and how cam'st thou hither?

LATYMER.
                                 I was bidden
Unto a bloodier banquet, but escaped,

And I am here.   I knew not, gentle cousin,
My seat so fairly filled.

                LAWRENCY.
                Dudley, be calm.
You need repose.   Ho, Julian!

        LATYMER (*placing himself before him*).
                        Would you quit
Your guest thus rudely?   Nay, then, I must seem
Discourteous too.   Look on this sword, and mark,—
If thou dar'st seek, by voice or sign, to raise
Thy slumbering vassals to oppose me here,
I'll set it in thy bosom.

                LAWRENCY (*aside.*)
                        Curses light
Upon those drunken villains !   He is armed,—
I helpless !   In his wild and glaring eye,
Despair and madness sit.   I am a child
Beneath his arm !   (*Looks eagerly round.*)   The flask !
                        Oh, whispering fiend !
Another step with thee?   (*Drops a ring into the chalice.*)
                        I'll walk aside ;
If he should stumble on the smiling death,
Why, 'tis no deed of mine.   (*Rises and walks forward.*)
                        Drink, cousin, drink !
We'll talk anon.   You're travel-worn and tired,—
Drink !   All shall be made clear.   You will confess
I have done cleverly and wisely.   Come,
This is a merry meeting !

                LATYMER.
                And shall be
Yet merrier ere it end.   (*Drinks.*)   There's life in that !
Aha ! how glibly through the warming veins
The red magician speeds.   Now tell me, cousin,
Hast thou done well by me?   Hast safely kept
My precious gem?   Holds honour in thy breast
Her wonted throne ?

LAWRENCY.
What's this?   Some meddling foe
(For such I have) hath soiled my fair report
In my good kinsman's mind.   Did he but know
What loving, dangerous zeal I—

LATYMER.
So I thought!
And how the knaves belied thee who presumed
To call thee—false !   Cousin, this curious ball—
This world—hath known strange habitants ; the bold,
The stealthy sinners,—murderers, courtiers, rogues,
Flatterers, and thieves,—but never one so base,
But, in some secret chamber of his heart,
There lurked a chord of mercy.   Could I think
Thou would'st not listen to that syren voice
That older villains hear ?

LAWRENCY (*aside*).
Thou'rt slow of work,
My potent minister, when most I need
Dispatch !   His cheek grows white,—he gnaws his lip !
Good, good ! (*Aloud*)   What say'st thou, Dudley ?
What dost mean ?
Mercy !   To whom ?

LATYMER (*starting up*).
To that poor lamb, which I,
Deluded fool ! hid in the he-wolf's den
For safety.   Hark ! dost hear her bleating cry ?
Thou didst not think the shepherd's ear was yet
Awake to such a sound !
(LAWRENCY, *alarmed at his increasing violence,*
starts up. LATYMER *seizes him.*)

LAWRENCY.
Take off thy hand !
She shall come hither.

LATYMER.
                She shall come, indeed !
And scare us with her beauty.   True, her cheek
Hath lost its red, her eye its fire, her look
Its scorn, that should have struck temptation dumb ;
But, in their stead, there glitters on her brow
The star of everlasting peace, beyond
Thy power to cloud it more.   You have been feasting !
Place for the queen of the revel !

> (*Dashes open the door in centre, displaying the
> corpse of* EDITH *on a couch.   The armed ser-
> vants bear it forward,* GIOVANNI *and* MARION
> *follow.*)

LAWRENCY.
                      Some wild jest,—
Some Christmas mummery?   You cannot mould
Men's fears and fancies thus.   What have ye there,
This is past fooling ?   Answer me !

> (LATYMER *lifts the covering.*)
                      Is *Death*,
So dim and corpse-like in its shape and hue,
The revel's queen ?   Ho ! stand aside.   What, sirs !
Think ye I dare not meet her eye to eye ?

> (*They stand back.*)
How this hath chanced, I know not.   Since thou hast
Paid Nature's debt, I can forgive thee mine.
Thou who didst mar my fresh and budding hopes,—
Seal up the fount of mercy in my soul,
Repel my gentler purposes,—and pay
Mine eager love with scorn.   Firm in my wrongs,
I'll look on thee again, thou proud—

> (*He lifts the veil, then dropping it, falls beside the
> couch.*)
                      Oh, God !
Look not upon me thus,—not *thus !*   Oh, Edith !
Thou know'st I am not used to meet thy smile !
Open those white lips, taunt me with my guilt,
Point thy pale finger to the abyss whose fires
Are kindling to avenge thee.   Did I say

I loved thee *not?* It was the fiend within
That vomited the lie! Hate and revenge
Snatch from this mangled heart their mask and scale,
And leave it naked to remorse. Ah! why—
Why didst thou crush the angel mercy down,
And raise instead this demon? Wherefore deal
So hardly with my blind and baffled love,
That, mad for vengeance, saw not where it struck?
Oh! art thou gone, sweet Edith? Must the world
Awake to glory and to life, and thou
Keep thy cold pillow,—the red, writhing worm
At banquet on thy beauty? Edith—cousin—
My love—my hope—my promise,—art thou gone
For ever—ever?

       LATYMER.
    Loose that lifeless hand.
Pitiless ruffian! Hast thou so much grace,
Commend thy soul to God.

      LAWRENCY.
      What do you mean?

      LATYMER.
To kill thee!

    LAWRENCY (*pointing to attendants*).
    Here are swords enough, brave cousin,
Against one naked breast!

      LATYMER.
      You will not fall
So nobly. Forward, fellow!
    (KENSELL *walks suddenly forward, and con-
    fronts him.*)

     LAWRENCY (*recoiling*).
      Kensell!

      KENSELL.
       So!

I've found you, master.   You've escaped one knot
To run your neck into a harder.   Come !

LAWRENCY (*aside*).
Has poison lost its power?   I must gain time.
 To LATYMER) You'll let me speak first?   By the kindred
   blood
That fills our veins,—you'll hear me?

LATYMER.
                    Speak.   You've gazed
Enough on that dead glory, and thy breath
Insults the parted spirit.   Say at once.
(*To* KENSELL) Fellow, prepare !

KENSELL (*gruffly*).
                    I'm ready.   Why lose time ?
He'll talk you by the hour, and 'scape at last.
Well, never mind,—he's young.

LAWRENCY (*starting to his feet*).
                    Then list to me.
With all the serpent passion of man's soul,
I hate thee, Latymer !   From infancy—
From merry childhood—*hate* thee !   Thou hast been
The shadow on my path—cloud of my air,
That shut out heaven—the reptile on whose scales
I trod, and slipped.   Ev'n from that earliest time
When, sporting in the woods, I plucked a rose,
The queen-flower of the fields, for Edith's hair,
And you—the stronger—tore the coveted prize
Away, and bade me seek if all the woods
Held such another,—from that hour thou hast
Forestalled me ever.   Who was't taught me sin ?
Who, hate ?   Who, jealousy ?   Whose influence drove
My tortured heart to wild and reckless ways,
That rooted me from out thy father's love,
And set my bark afloat in life's wide sea
With scarce a sail ?   Who took my promised bride—

My beautiful—whose fair possessions might
Have given the outcast beggar wealth and home ?
Why, *thou*—and *thou*—and *thou !* And didst thou
    dream,
Poor fool ! that I should crouch beneath thy glare,
Though stealing through the dark, defenceless night,
With murder-scowling bravoes at thy back,
To slay me on the hearth ? Hast yet to learn— ?
You called me—serpent. Dost thou feel my fangs
At work within thee ? Ha, thou dost ! Down—down !
Boy, wilt thou die unshriven ? To thy knees,
And pray !

      Latymer *(dropping his sword faintly).*
          I feel it. For this half-hour gone,
My soul hath wrestled with the coiling death ;
Now nature yields into its cold embrace,
Shuddering and stiffening. Give me light and air,—
I thirst.   *(Attendant offers wine.)*
        You proffer death. That cup,—'twas drugged.
Where lies my Edith ? My—my martyred love,
For *my* sake murdered ! Lead me to her side.
This anguish, love, is sweet ; each fiery throb
Doth pluck our souls together. I shall soon
Be with thee now. My sight fails *(feeling)*, but I know
This face,—how cold ! My Edith, it is I.
                (Falls on the couch.)

      Giovanni *(to attendants).*
What ! are ye men, yet stand and gaze as if
On deeds of daily import ?
         (They advance on Lawrency.*)*

     Lawrency *(snatching up* Latymer's *sword).*
           I will take
But one life more, that's *his* who first shall raise
His steel against me. Not to *you* I owe
Or pay this being. From some mortal cup
Proceed, I know, these scorching pangs that drink

Its fainting sources up.   Who gave't I know not.
Stand ye aside in peace, and let me die.

FIRST MAN (*to the rest*).
Draw back awhile.   'Tis true,—his livid cheek
Confirms his words.   Repent, unhappy man ;
Think on thy crimes,—thy plots,—thy treachery
Against the king.

GIOVANNI.
The woman that you loved,
In furtherance of a wild and fiendish hate,
You practised with base menace, and lewd arts,
Against her spirit's health, and, failing, slew
Her life, through wild despair.

SECOND MAN.
Your earliest friend,—
The son of him who gave your infant years
A blest and kindly shelter,—you have slain
By poison at the board.

LAWRENCY.
Speak to the dust,
Wherewith this seared, uprooted stalk of life
Shall quickly be confounded.   It will heed
As much as I.   Ye babbling fools, that still
Condemn the weeds of guilt, but never heed
What hand hath sown and fostered them, get hence
And leave me to my fate !   No word from lips
Of earth can move me more.

MARION (*coming forward*).
Art sure of that ?
The draught whose hideous, fatal functions call
Blood from thy cheek, light from thine eye. and from
Thy scarcely ripened manhood power and life,
Was given—*by me.*

LAWRENCY.
Ah ! wherefore ?
(*She discovers herself.* LAWRENCY *starts, and staggers towards her.*)

Marion !—*Thou !*
(*Falls dead.*)

THE END.

JEFFREYS;

OR,

THE WIFE'S VENGEANCE.

A Play,

IN FIVE ACTS.

PREFACE.

The character of George Jeffreys (Lord Chief Justice,
and afterwards Chancellor, of England) somewhat
roughly described by a recent writer in the 'Times,'
as the *beau idéal* of drunken justice, and condemned in
Lord Campbell's elaborate memoir to unmitigated
obloquy, offered, in my opinion, materials for a stage-
hero worth consideration. Striking incidents are, however, necessary, even for the " bringing out " a character
full of originality ; and of these the career of this
extraordinary man, though replete with political and
professional adventure, scarcely supplies one of a nature
adapted to dramatic purposes. An opportunity for
bringing the character of Jeffreys into juxtaposition with
one no less singular—that of James the Second—would
certainly have offered a powerful temptation, had it
occurred to me at an earlier moment ; and had I not,
moreover, since read a play, wherein the latter is por-
trayed with so masterly a hand as to discourage any
attempt by lesser bards to follow. I allude to that fine
tragedy, the ' Earl of Gowrie,' by a gentleman who, if
report speaks sooth, has not long to rank with the
unacted. It was needful, therefore, to present a story of
the times, and introduce the judge as an accessory,

rather than a principal therein ; an arrangement which materially detracts from the *effect* of the part, and which (combined with the author's inability to realize his own conceptions) considerably enhances the labour of the talented performer, who has kindly undertaken the personation.

An additional interest attaches, in my mind, to Jeffreys' history, from the fact that local tradition has marked the old "Mansion" at Leatherhead, in Surrey, many years in possession of my family, as the occasional residence of the Chancellor ; and pointed to a strange concealed chamber, beneath the cellarage, as a *cachette* prepared by his order, for a refuge in case of sudden danger. In our juvenile days, a terrible judicial presence certainly seemed to pervade that subterranean region :

A sense of mystery the spirit daunted,

and a threat of summoning the " Judge " was a charm to allay the wildest nursery storm.

The impossibility of placing a criminal trial—in all its solemn and somewhat tedious formality—upon the stage, is so obvious as to render needless any apology for the sketchy and imperfect character given, in the fifth act, to the memorable "red assize."

DRAMATIS PERSONÆ.

MEN.

JUDGE JEFFREYS . . . . Mr. Phelps.
POMFRET, (*a Dorsetshire Gentleman*). Mr. H. Marston
DE L'ISLE (*a Follower of Mon-
mouth's*) . . . . . Mr. H. Mellon.
MORGRAVE (*a former Suitor of Lady
Grace*) . . . . . Mr. G. Bennett.
L'ESTRANGE, (*Secretary to Jeffreys*) . Mr. Morton.
COLONEL KIRKE . . . . Mr. Knight.
LORD FEVERSHAM . . . . Mr. Warde.
TORY TOM, (*a mischievous Clown*) . Mr. Scharfe.
HODGE HOLEPEEP } *Rustics.* { Mr. Graham.
OZIAS HEMP } { Mr. C. Fenton.
Host of the Red Lion . . . Mr. Williams.
Marshal . . . . . . Mr. Lingham.
Jailor . . . . . . Mr. Doughty.
Clerk of the Court . . . . Mr. Franks.
Rider . . . . . . Mr. Josephs.
Page . . . . . . Master Newman.
Servant . . . . . . Mr. Thomas.

WOMEN.

LADY GRACE (*of great wealth*) . . Mrs. Warner.
MISTRESS ALICE (*sister to* POMFRET,
married to DE L'ISLE) . . Miss Cooper.
JULE VANE (*her Attendant*) . . Miss Stephens.

Guards, Country people, etc. etc.
Scene in Dorsetshire. Time, 1685.

ACT I.

SCENE I.—*Terrace before Pomfret house.*

(LADY GRACE *alone, seated on a rustic bench.*)

LADY GRACE.
I'll try him.   'Tis my birthday.   Now, will he
Remember that, I wonder?   Thirty-five!
Am I so old?   Alas! in truth, yes.   This,
Joined with a fading face, makes the ear quick
And jealous of time's foot-fall.   Let him pass
This one day with me—nay, let him but meet me
With the frank look of old—for that's enough
For me.   I am not of those wives who must
Have all words sauced to their love's palate!   No—
Let him do thus—and this fair morn shall be
The first of a new summer.   I will weed
All self-tormenting fancies from my brain,
Smooth every tangled thought, and henceforth deem
That thou, my young, gay mate—my dear, dear Harry!
Age-stricken as I am, canst love me.

POMFRET (*without*).
                    Quick!
A fresh horse, instantly!

LADY GRACE.
          But just returned!
          (*Enter* POMFRET—*page following.*)
I'll be indifferent too.   Ah—*now* he sees me!

POMFRET.

What, not a smile to light me forth, my Grace?
I shall ride heavily.   Take my hat, boy.   See—
The feather droops—'tis broken, is it?

LADY GRACE (*aside*).

Horse—
Feather—and—wife—'Tis well.

POMFRET.

No word, Grace?

LADY GRACE.

Yes,
Good morning—and good speed.

POMFRET.

Good morning—and—
Off with this mask, dear wife, and let me see
The bright face under it.   Nay—nay—look thus
A moment more—and I am grave as thou.

LADY GRACE.

Sir, I am sorry that my natural gloom
Shadows your mirthful humour.   Age, you know,
Is spleenful.

POMFRET.

Age!

LADY GRACE.
Is spleenful.   You have heard
Such words?

POMFRET.
And used them.   I—I could not mean—

LADY GRACE.

That they should reach me.   Know you not, ill words
Have fleeter wings than fair?   Your horses wait.
Let me not stay your pleasures.

POMFRET (*offers to take her hand*).
You ! Their source
And fountain !

LADY GRACE.
Am I ? True ; I had forgot
My gold. O shining curse ! great as thou art—
Set up in the high places of this world !—
One grain of the dank soil from whence thou'rt wrung
Is worth the total mine !

POMFRET.
Come, come, my love,
"Tis a good, sensible metal—malleable
To fair and worthy shapes. If wrong there be,
"Tis in the hand that studies not to wield
So great a weapon wisely. Come, come—psha !
What stuff is this ? Give me your finger ; since
With so much only of that dear white hand
You starve my lips when angry. Ah, sweet Grace !
Wherefore so doubting? Must I, hour by hour,
Proclaim my gratitude, and——

LADY GRACE (*scornfully*).
Gratitude !

POMFRET.
My deep affection !

LADY GRACE (*aside*).
Hypocrite !—May Heaven
Forgive me for so loving him !

POMFRET.
One kiss,
And I depart. Not on this day, my love,
Let anger rest between us !

LADY GRACE.

This day!—this!
(*Aside*) Ah! he remembers! Heav'n be praised!
Yes!

POMFRET.

Peace
Reigns in the heaven, beauty on the green earth :
I could not quarrel with my dearest foe
With God's sun cheering me.

LADY GRACE (*aside*).

Alas! the day
Hath but a common glory. Pomfret—I—
I thought—I trusted—that —— but go—go—go!
(*Bursts into a passion of tears.*)

POMFRET.

My love!—my own Grace!—what is this? Dost thou
So much desire my presence? I must seem
The more ungrateful—for I leave thee,—aye,
And fortune, governing my will, forbids
That I should tell thee wherefore. On my knee,
Sweet wife, I beg your patience, and —

LADY GRACE.

Forbear!
You do but more afflict me.   (*Exit.*)

POMFRET.

I am a fool!
'Tis love's worst policy to entreat a mood
That will not be assuaged. To every riddle
That crowds this puzzling world belongs some clue—
But *woman*! There; 'tis easier to divine
Which surface of that twirling leaf shall kiss
First the damp earth, than follow to its source
A woman's complex humour.

(TORY TOM * *enters, and stands aloof.*)

TOM.
Halloa ! sir !
You're master Pomfret,—the poor gentleman
That married the rich wife ?

POMFRET.
Well guessed, sir.

TOM.
Here,
Catch this !
(*Tosses a letter to* POMFRET, *who examines it, then
reads eagerly.*)
What answer ?

POMFRET.
None for thee, knave. Go ;
I hasten thither.   What could make her choose
So blunt a page as thou ?

TOM.
Why, sir, she said
That she liked handsome servitors, for such
Were mostly honest too.

POMFRET.
She paid you, then,
With flattery ?

TOM.
Yes, sir,—and twopence.   You
Would give the rest.

POMFRET.
Not quite so fast, my friend.
Who bade you seek me here ?   Whom saw you, sir,
As you came hither ?

* Note A.

Tom (*pointing*).
Only she.

POMFRET.
She!   Who?

Tom.
Why, she—the lady there.   She asked me what
I sought, and I said *you*, and then I showed
The note —

POMFRET.
You did!   Well —

Tom.
And she started, so—
Her face grew white—then red.   She tossed her hands
Angrily—so—burst into weeping—cried
" *There—there he is!* " and left me.

POMFRET.
Bravely done,
Most clever youth ; yet not so clever as
A moment since I thought you.   Go.   (*Exit* Tom.)
De l'Isle,
Fainting with corporal anguish—more with pain
For her who shares his peril!   Bloody Jeffreys
Commissioned here.   Fair sister, the more need
To seek thee—aye, and presently.   I am loath
To part without a word—   (*Approaches the window.*)
Hark!—Grace! to leave thee,
With anger at thy solitary side,
The worst companion.   Psha! one single word,
Might I but speak it, would renew those smiles
Whereon my heart still banquets.   Grace, I say,
The day grows while I linger—   (*Going, reluctantly.*)
Psha !—'Tis useless !
(*Exit.*)

SCENE II.—*A Room in the Mansion.*

(LADY GRACE. MORGRAVE.)

LADY GRACE.

Thanks for your pains ; and if their fruits, my friend,
Be gall to this spoiled heart, with early loves
Too lavishly o'erfed, I recognise
That self-denying zeal which will not shrink
From functions of low nature, base or hateful,
Through pity of its kind.

MORGRAVE.
Madam, what else ?

LADY GRACE (*warmly*).
No ; friendship hath no fellow.   Sure it seems
A copy of that high beneficence,
That, mingling mercy with correction, leaves
Its love but half concealed.   Thanks, heartily—
More of my husband, then.   I am prepared—
You see I am—to hear all.   Let me learn
The worst of his defection.
MORGRAVE.
To what end?
I do beseech you, force me not to bear
More witness 'gainst my friend.

LADY GRACE.
Are you not *mine?*
Man, have you led me to a strait so dismal,
But to cast off my hand?

MORGRAVE (*suddenly*).
What would you know?
Lady, your eyes look through my soul, and give
Thoughts that lie dead new birth.   Oh ! my first faith,
Trust not to mine enforced apostasy—
Lest I— Enough—I am myself again !

My heart is in your hand as ever, lady—
Dull, passionless, slave of your will.   Oh! mould it
Even to what shape you fancy.

LADY GRACE.

                  Yet what's left
To learn?   But twelve months wedded!   Now, wherein
Have I so wronged him?   But he's grateful, sir;—
He may be grateful, if not loving.   Was't not
This hand that, from the darkest haunts of the world—
Those poor, condemned corners, where proud hearts
Seek out lone spots, and perish—drew him forth
To wealth?   Nay, let that go.   How *speaks* he of me?

MORGRAVE.

Press me not there.   Oh! be content—

LADY GRACE (*passionately*).

                      I ask,
How speaks he of me?

MORGRAVE.

               As a truant flies
Scholastic thraldom, or a soft court-slave
That royal atmosphere of busy lies,
Where heart, eye, tongue, are fettered,—does your lord
Avoid your gracious presence; yielding so
For trash (blind merchant!) wares both sound and new;
Selling your sweet smiles for the drunkard's glare—
Your wise discourse for lewd and witless speech—
Your pure affections and true heart for—nay,
Not from *my* lips.   (*Half aside.*)

LADY GRACE (*faintly*).
Go on.

MORGRAVE.

               We must confess,
Wine and gay fellowship may wean some hearts
From reverence of a too-much absent tie.

There's one among them—Montford—lately bound
To a rich dame, whose womanhood, in sooth,
Steals towards its winter.   'Tis his wont to ape
His lady's mien—her palsied brow, thick speech,
And tottering gait.   " Ha !" Pomfret cries, " like mine ;
Grace, to the life !   Her glance, her vinegar smile,
Wherewith, kind soul ! she greets me in the morn
After late watching !   Here's to all old wives !
Peace to deserted pillows !"   Have I killed you ?

(She sinks down.)

Madam !   Alack, she hears not.   Grace—sweet Grace—
My love, and cruel foe—light of my hope,
Yet with a gulf between !   Oh, pardon me !
Love, pity, rage, combine within, and set
My long-held passion free.   O pardon, Grace !
Stay not for colder reasons, when this man—
By every sweet chain fettered to his troth—
Hath taught the way to break it !

LADY GRACE (with a sudden effort).

Master Morgrave,

I thank you for those words.   My fearful spirit,
By gazing too much down a dreaded height,
Had nearly fall'n below.   Your mistimed speech
Hath plucked me back.   I do mistrust thy words,
And that my happiness indeed hath grown
So deadly sick, seeing to what end you come,
And what foul remedy you dare prescribe me.
Sir, for myself, if, as you say, my years
Are grown so ripe, I thank Heav'n that, therewith,
Judgment hath ripened too.   Your last rash words
Wounded, but warned—and saved me.

MORGRAVE.

This rebuke

Is the blind spurning of a chafed, high spirit,
That knows not friends from foes.   I can give proof
Of all that I affirm.

LADY GRACE.
Thou canst ?

N

MORGRAVE.
          Enough
To satisfy the heart that hungers most
For jealousy's sharp food. That—

LADY GRACE.
         Master Morgrave,
You are foully false, or I most foully wronged :
Such is the doubt unto whose dread solution
I challenge your advance. I will have proof,
Or, by the heav'n above us—yea, by that
Once cloudless in my heart, now blurred and dim—
I will denounce your baseness.

MORGRAVE.
        How, if I prove
My truth?

LADY GRACE.
    Then shall you lack no gratitude,
Nay, nor reward.

MORGRAVE (*eagerly*).
That smile—

LADY GRACE.
        O, sir, beware
How you interpret. Yet, be sure of this,
If wronged, I will have vengeance.

MORGRAVE.
        'Tis agreed.
Encase your fair form in some coarse disguise,
And come with me. You fear not?

LADY GRACE.
        In my heart
Is room for but one terror.   (*Exit.*)

MORGRAVE.
    Pride's a dress

That ever best became her.   That which she
Calls age, hath sown but little wisdom here ;
For when, as now, I holiday my hate,
And clothe it in love's dollish frippery,
And perk it in her very face— Come, come,
No triumph yet !   As one whose debtor climbs
To sudden wealth, let me sit down, and strain
My claims—once fruitless—to their utmost.   First,
Thy coyness—ah ! for that's a costly crime
'Gainst us plain-dealers.   Secondly, that thou
Didst, for this boy, reject me.   Next, I'll rack thee
For mere delight.   In the last place, to feed
That hate which, like a growing savage, craves
Each day robuster food.   Cold spirit, disdain—
I will exorcise thee.   My wand be pain.   (*Exit.*)

END OF ACT I.

ACT II.

SCENE I.—*Evening. A wild spot of Moorland.*

(Tory Tom *enters, laughing heartily, holding a hideous mask in his hand.*)

TOM.

I've settled that youth's courage.   He'll not stop
This side of "father's" hut.   Ha, ha!—halloo!
There he runs still !   What mischief next ?   Who's here ?
Two travellers, 'faith !   They've lost their way.   Pray
    Heaven
They seek't of me.   They seem in wrath, too.   Ha !
No.   Fool !   I'm drunk—or dreaming.   Sure there's none
Like *him.* 'Tis he ! 'Tis he !
                 (*Claps his hands joyfully.*)
           Jeffreys !—black Jeffreys !
The hanging, brawling judge, that had me —*me*—
Whipped from the court for aping him.   Aha !
Thanks to that brow's black arch.   Sweet spirit of mischief,
Whom I do nought but serve, inspire me now.
What shall I do with him?   Skulk, and make sure.
Ah ! that's his voice.   (*Skulks apart.*)

(*Enter* JEFFREYS *and* L'ESTRANGE.)

JEFFREYS (*angrily.*)
      The fault was yours, L'Estrange.

L'ESTRANGE.
Nay, nay, my lord.

JEFFREYS.
I say, aye, aye—sir !   You should know the ways—

That's in your office.   But for this mishap,
We had been supping now at Dorchester.
Plague take your ignorance!   All the country stirred—
Sore as a half-healed wound too.   Here's a triumph
For disaffected souls!   My lord chief justice
Starved on a barren moor!   I say—

L'Estrange.

                                          The wheels
Are extricate ere now.   This soil—

Jeffreys.

                                    The soil
Partakes the nature of the clowns that till it.
Close—close it is—and stubborn—with a dull,
Black, and rebellious flood still bubbling through,
That yields at slight'st dependence.   Stay, l'Estrange—
Don't leave me, sir—don't leave me!   (*Grasps him.*)

L'Estrange.

                                     Nay, but—

Jeffreys.

                                         Come,
I did but jest.   Deserted as we are,
Don't quarrel.   Why, how curst a place is this!
Not one dry turf to rest the languid limb—
Not half a hedge for shelter!   Who goes there?
"Tush! 'tis an owl.

L'Estrange.
There should be—or I err—

An hostel hereabout.   Here comes a native.
                                  (*Tom appears.*)
Holloa! you clown.   Come hither.   Which of these
Cross-paths conduct us—

Tom.
Which you please.

JEFFREYS (*angrily*).
                              They bend
To every point of the compass!

TOM.
                      So they do.
But each may lead a man to the devil, and that's
Your journey's end, I take it!

L'ESTRANGE (*restraining* JEFFREYS).
              My lord, hold! (*Aside*)
I know this fellow. He's more knave than fool—
But men make light of him. Why, sir, this clown
Could hang up half the county; and, I tell you,
Could you attach him, he were worth a score
Of Kirke's rough, blundering bloodhounds.

JEFFREYS (*eagerly*).
                    Say you so?
You, fellow. Hem! my merry little man—
You've a sharp eye—an honest face. Wilt be
My servant, boy? What say you?

TOM (*surveying him from head to foot*).
                 Well—I'll take you
On trial. What's your name?

JEFFREYS.
              What's thine, my friend?
That's more to the purpose.

TOM.
Tory Tom.

JEFFREYS.
                 Then, Tom,
My politician-- know'st thou ne'er a hostel
Where we may wash our throats? None of your sheds—
Your sneaking, hedge-side, beggar-haunted dens
Of barley-broth, and ale of turnips! Show us
Where jolly fellows congregate.

TOM.
This way.
I'll show you a brave sign, sirs ; and a tapster
That never leaves a guest with parching throat
For want of good example. (*Aside*) So, my lord,
You thought I had forgot you. Wait and see.

(*Exeunt.*)

———

SCENE II.—*A Close, with a humble Cottage and Garden.*

(POMFRET. DE L'ISLE, *wounded*. ALICE.)

POMFRET.
Oh! you did well to send for me. This rumour
Took wings, and gathered round me as I rode :
No tongue but adds some terror to the tale—
No eye but frowns mistrust. L'Estrange is coming—
Kirke and his bloodhounds are already here—
And black George Jeffreys follows, breathing death.
Husband your strength, De l'Isle. Sister, hold fast
Your wonted courage. To remain is death.
You must be gone to-morrow.

DE L'ISLE.
Be it so.
They took my better arm at Sedgmoor ; but
Left legs to run, and so remove all danger
From the brave homes that shelter us.

POMFRET.
To rest.
I will arrange with Alice my design
For your departure, and new home. At night
I'll send again.

(*Exit* DE L'ISLE. POMFRET *and* ALICE *pass
to and fro conversing*. MORGRAVE *and* LADY
GRACE *enter, and stand apart*.)

MORGRAVE.
Here is a holly screen,
Made for our purpose.   Couch, and note them.
(POMFRET *and* ALICE *return.*)

POMFRET.
That
Were safe, indeed—but far too distant.   I
Would hold you ever near me.   There are spots
Ev'n in our own demesne—

ALICE.
No, Harry, no.
That must not be.   The common voice reports her
Noble and free of heart.   She must not know
How dearly we are bound.

MORGRAVE (*aside to* LADY GRACE).
Sweet hypocrite!
Are you not grateful, madam?

POMFRET.
Well, be't so.
You are right, my Alice.   She shall never know
How dear a treasure I have hoarded here,
Out of her comprehension.

LADY GRACE.
Open, earth!
Pluck me to the centre.   I can better hate
Than blush for thee, thou false one.   I'll not share
Thy guilt, by being its witness.   (*Going.*)

MORGRAVE (*detaining her*).
Pause, I pray you—
Else, in some mood of weakness, you will turn
Your anger on me, and deny the meed,
Saying, this was not so.

LADY GRACE.

I am your sport:

Let it go on.

ALICE.

It is my only prayer.

Oh ! must you leave me ?

POMFRET.

I am expected, sweet ;

Should I be sought for, some o'er-zealous foot

Might track the mazes of your labyrinth—

And that were perilous. There's one, I know,

That marvels at my absence. Come—one smile—

I'd take some comfort with me. So, farewell—

And with this kiss—

MORGRAVE (*turns suddenly*).

Come, will you go?

(*Exeunt* POMFRET *and* ALICE.)

LADY GRACE.

Go ! Whither?

Home ! home ! No, no. In love's place, by my hearth,

There sits a ribald fiend. Mine eyes dream, too—

You were but now a proper man enough,

As nature's image goes. Faith is of heaven.

What makes you look so devilish?

MORGRAVE.

All things yet

Are coloured by your just resentment, lady.

'Tis of your calmer reason I must seek

Which shows the better—mine ill-featured truth,

Or *his* fair falsehood.

LADY GRACE.

Light, that shows the sin,

Is not itself of pure source always. I,

That, with the heart he values not, bestowed

Rank, luxury, pleasures.   Why do I talk of that?
These were but mates, and idle consequents—
The gaudy, useless tints my fancy chose
To deck out love with.   Oh, my Harry!   Oh,
My heart-selected! would thou hadst ta'en my wealth—
Scattered my fortune's gifts—yea, buried them
Deeper than thought in the unfathomed sea,
So thou hadst left thy love to buoy me up
Into God's haven with thee!

               MORGRAVE.
                    Nay, be calm.
Bethink you of what course—

               LADY GRACE.
                    What course!   Advise
With *thee!*   I have counsellors.   Stand more apart.
I hate thee heartily.

               MORGRAVE.
                    And thus requite
The service you demanded!

               LADY GRACE.
                    Psha! I'll give you
What you love better—vengeance!   You can't dream
Ill more intense—revenge more exquisite
Than I will cater for thee.   Never pinch
Thy features into that love-shape.   Good faith!
They were not measured for it!   Was't for love
Of me, you did entice me hither?   No.
Love's thoughtful—patient—pitiful for love—
Is gentler in his needful surgery—
Finds remedy, not rancour.   He has broke
My heart—but you'll not gain by that.   Be sure
Those poor, poor remnants are too costly yet,
For breath of thine to sully.

               MORGRAVE.
                    I—I swear—

LADY GRACE.

That wilt thou, readily.   And so do I.
I'll use thee for revenge—and yet will be
So tender with the instrument I wield,
That angels shall not blush at my device,
Which seems, but is not, sin.   Only mark this ;
When I shall smile—or beckon—clasp thy hand—
Or seem—pah !—*fond* on thee—presume not on't :
'Tis artifice—no more.   For from this hour,
When thou seem'st nearest, stand'st thou most aloof—
Aye, man, as distant from my soul's pure gate,
As blest ones from perdition.

MORGRAVE.
                    Well—content.
(*Aside*) For all this I will have thee at my foot.
Meanwhile, these high heroics do but add
An item to the long account.   Well, patience.
                              (*Exeunt.*)

———

SCENE III.—*Before a road-side inn, the Red Lion.
    Many country people drinking.   Host bustling to and
    fro.   Behind, the moorland.   Gibbets, etc.*

HOST.
Come, sirs, be busy.   What ! a sucking babe
To-night should be your tapster.   I shall never
Be a fat host, I fear.   Let me have work,
Or else I shame my calling.

FIRST MAN.
                    Five foot round !
That's starveling measure, host !

HOST.
                    Wanting an inch—

More than an inch, I swear, sir. Ale? I've seen
But two-and-thirty winters yet.

SECOND MAN.
Thin host,
What is the score, I prithee?

HOST.
Let me see :
Two cups of cider—one, metheglin—bread—
Twelve cups of ale—sirs, a jacobus.

SECOND MAN.
Out,
You common robber ! *Twelve !* As much as thou
Hast years but two-and-thirty. Host, you count
Ale-score and age-score by a different rule.
Well—well—here comes black Jeffreys. He has a charm
Turns all men honest, but himself.

FIRST MAN.
Black fiend !
He hung my sister's son.

SECOND MAN.
And will hang thee.
Content thee, friend. We are all traitors *here*.
Host, you shall have fair company adorning
These neighbour-gibbets. Here's a hint, man, for thee.
Keep with the times. Down with thy lion there—
Put up the triple tree !
(*Sings.*)

Bustle, bustle, my Lion-host !
Tipple the ale—the mead.
Old death seeks just such a well-fed ghost
To pamper his glutton greed.
Right soon you'll hear, mid the jolly feast,
A low voice whisp'ring thee—
You must down, good host, with thy scarlet beast,
And up with the triple tree !
Chorus—You must, etc.

> Loud let the British raven croak,
>   For the Briton's faith is fled—
> Guilt elbows guilt 'neath the rich man's cloak—
>   Poor honesty goes to bed,—
> And, Lion-host, with the waist so fair,
>   The gallows creak for THEE!
> Then down with dog, ape, lion, and bear!
>   Hurrah! for the triple tree!
>   *Chorus*—Then down, etc.

Like you the carol, sirs? 'Tis mine. More ale,
Mine host of the gibbet! Ere our necks be stretched,
Here's to King Monmouth's memory! Hurrah!
A rouse! a rouse!   (*Enter* TORY TOM *hastily.*)

TOM (*eagerly*).
            Sirs, here's the man to thank you!
Don't stare—I'm sane enough, and sober—Jeffreys—
Black Jeffreys—lost—benighted—close at my heels—
You'll see! Now work your pleasures. Strangle him—
Toss him in blankets—duck him in the pool—
Only—don't hurt him. He's my master. Sit!
Keep up the fun.

HOST (*eagerly*).
            Hist! Here they come, sirs. Hist!
Plague take your drunken tongue!

SECOND MAN.
            Drunk! You must broach
A better cask first.
            (*Enter* JEFFREYS *and* L'ESTRANGE.)

JEFFREYS (*aside to* L'ESTRANGE).
            Here's as fair a knot
Of snakes as ever coiled. Landlord, a stoup
Of liquor. Come, be quick, man. Here we'll couch—
Two ferrets in a burrow. Mark, L'Estrange,
That rogue in the blue gaberdine. If e'er
I saw a rebel, he's one.
            (*They sit apart, while* TOM *hovers about at back,
            etc.*)

Tom (*observing them uneasily*).
                              I've led my lord
Into a pretty wasp's nest!   One bold spirit
To lead the way, and the whole swarm set on him—
And turn me out of service!   (*Moving about.*)
                              Hold!   What's that
Moves yonder on the moor?   His guard—I'll swear
I saw the muskets glitter.   They must come,
Or he be murdered.   And—for these—tut, tut!
Good fellows as they are—there's not a rogue
But I've a score against him.   (*Steals off.*)

L'Estrange (*to* Second Man).
                              Holloa, friend!
You seem a jovial comrade.   Taste this stuff—
Thine honest name, my friend?

                    Second Man.
                              Hodge Holepeep, sir,
That sees with half an eye.

                    Jeffreys (*aside*).
                              The parish wag—
Dispenser of small jokes.   The next?

L'Estrange (*to* First Man).
                              Your health,
Good master,—humph! your name?

                    First Man.
                              Ozias Hemp,
An't please your worship—christened by my lord
Chief Justice Jeffreys.   He that hanged my father,
Brother, and sister's son, could scarce do less
Than be my godfather.   Bless your pleasant face!
He's very like your worship!   (*To* Jeffreys.)

                    Jeffreys (*starting.*)
                              How! like *me?*

SECOND MAN.

Aye, sir, in visage—nothing else—an't like ye.
You are a temperate gentleman—he's a sot.
You are a soft and mercy-loving sir—
Jeffreys, a dark-souled monster, ever hunting
The lives that shame his own.

FIRST MAN.
A mouthing fiend—

SECOND MAN.

A brawling drunkard—

FIRST MAN.
True—a beast.

JEFFREYS (*aside to* L'ESTRANGE).
I vow
They know me! Let's begone. (*Aloud*) A beast. *What*
beast,
My merry souls?   A lion?

SECOND MAN.
That bold brute
Worries the free.   My good lord justice's game
Comes shackled to *his* lair.

JEFFREYS (*aside to* L'ESTRANGE).
The chase is up.
L'Estrange, I'm known—run—fly !   (*Rising.*)

L'ESTRANGE.
Sit, sit—my lord !
'Tis rooting their suspicions.   How now, sirs !

SECOND MAN.

A health, my masters ! fill the beakers, host ;
'Tis worth the drinking.   Three in one !   Here's health
To master Harry Pomfret.   Shout !

L'ESTRANGE (*aside to* JEFFREYS).
                              Oho !
Tenants and hinds of Pomfret manor—ha ?
There's a hint gained, at least.

                    SECOND MAN.
                              Confusion, sirs,
To those black-hearted traitors that betrayed
Sweet Monmouth's life ; and to his murderer,
George Jeffreys—present death !
                    (*Shout. He approaches* JEFFREYS *and*
                    L'ESTRANGE.)
                              How now, my masters !
Do ye refuse my pledge ?

                    L'ESTRANGE (*starting up before* JEFFREYS).
                              Fellow, stand back !
You push the jest too far.

                    SECOND MAN.
                              The jest ! Ha—ha !

                    FIRST MAN.
Gag them, and force it down their throats !

                    HOST (*behind*).
                              Take heed !
Look how he fumbles in his vest.   Your spy
Always goes armed.

                    A WOMAN (*coming close to* JEFFREYS).
                              How pale your lordship grows !

                    ANOTHER
Aye—black hearts make white faces.

                    FIRST MAN.
                              Pond or gibbet ?

SECOND MAN.

Or both !

(*They surround them menacingly.*)

JEFFREYS (*in a loud voice*).
Fools ! look behind.
(JEFFREYS' *military guard enters, guided by* TOM.)

TOM (*aside to* JEFFREYS).
My work, my lord—
If it's worth payment, keep these clowns from your
Red rascals' fingers.

JEFFREYS.
Why, what sanctified,
Prim souls are these become ! Sweet friends, I thank ye,—
I thank ye for your purposed entertainment.
Why have ye thrust the gallows on my mind,
That came disposed to mercy ? Lion-host,
Book up your scores. You'll lack some guests—for know,
My friends, that every honest visage here
Is on my memory's page as clearly writ
As, in this book, your names. Farewell. Be merry !
Drink while ye may—*to-night*. The beast, you see,
For once creeps harmless to his den.
(*Exit with* L'ESTRANGE *attended.*)

FIRST MAN.
We've done
Our business.

HOST.
Yes, and master Pomfret's too !
That's worse. *You* merit it. Beshrew ye all ! *

* Note B.

END OF ACT II.

ACT III.

SCENE I.—*In Pomfret Manor.*

*(Night. LADY GRACE is seated pensively at a table,
in pretended study*—JULE VANE *attending.)*

JULE (*approaching her*).
Will you to rest, my lady?

LADY GRACE.
                    Whither, Jule?
To rest?   I hear a voice within that tells me
I never shall sleep more.   Come hither, Jule,
Am I not patient?   Have I not borne?   And, lo!
How bitter a reward!

JULE.
You have deserved
Much, my dear lady.

LADY GRACE.
                    Much!   Oh, patience, Heaven!
How measured, girl?   How much of her lord's love
May a poor wife make bold with?   Piece? or grain?
Or drachma?   Give me no such pedlar's phrase.
Love's food is *love*.   What is the matter, Jule?—
What is the reason he has ceased to love me?
Grow I lank-visaged? white-haired? sickly-eyed?
Hath stiff age chilled my pulses?—hath wan care
Scraped furrows in my cheek?

JULE.
                    These two months gone
You have lost beauty, madam.

LADY GRACE.
                    Thanks, dear Jule:
You will not flatter, with a finical lie,
That which needs cure or death.   Were it no more,
Peace and sweet hope should redden on this cheek,
Like flowers of early spring—more welcome-fair
For the dire season gone.   Out of these knots—
These yellow snakes, that wind at their large will—
I'd weave a thousand cunning silken webs,
To snare my bird that wanders.   Nay—lost pain!
'Twould fly again, and farther.   Wo! ah, wo!
Such gall should from such rooted sweetness grow!

JULE.
Comfort, dear lady.   Speak him fair, and —

LADY GRACE (*passionately*).
                                    Fair!
Woo him, perhaps! watch for his tardy step!
Then sit at his footstool—fondle with his hand—
" Sir, prithee, *love me;* so you'll set me there,
The darkest corner of your heart I'll make
A sunny Eden!"   Hark!   (*Starts up.*)

JULE.
      'Tis he, my lady,
Accompanied ——

LADY GRACE.
The better.   (*A Servant enters.*)

SERVANT.
            Master Morgrave,
To see your ladyship.

LADY GRACE.
      'Tis well: I come.
                        (*Exit Servant.*)
Jule, not a word.   Thou lov'st me, child.   Be secret—
Be patient.   *I* am.

(They go out.—Enter at another door POMFRET
and L'ESTRANGE.)

L'ESTRANGE.
Therefore have I sought
These western shambles—this Aceldama.
Since blood must flow, it is my care to choose
That which, if left to its natural promptings, would
Grow most ungoverned, and beget worst sores
In this afflicted country.   The dull fools
Have styled me Jeffreys' jackal !   Psha ! they jeer
Their friend ; for, look you, if I give my lion
A tit-bit here and there, 'tis but to soothe
That fierce insatiate appetite, which else
Would, bones and all, devour them.

POMFRET.
By your words,
Some such especial morsel you expect
To trace among us ?

L'ESTRANGE.
To be honest—*no*
Many good fellows are in hiding here,—
Involuntary woodsmen—(I shall pounce
On some half-dozen)—but of better blood,
Nothing—no, nothing—I assure you.

POMFRET.
What
Of John de l'Isle, of late ?

L'ESTRANGE *(carelessly)*.
Why, that his head
Being valued at three thousand crowns, he has moved
The prize to safer distance.

POMFRET.
So !   He hath ?

(*Aside*)　All's well, then.　If *this* sleuth-hound miss,
　　the scent
Is cold indeed !— (*Re-enter* L. GRACE, *with* MORGRAVE.)
　　　　Dear Grace, this gentleman,
Master L'Estrange —

　　　　　　　LADY GRACE.
　　　　Your friends are welcome, sir.
　　　　　　　　(*Turns away.*)

　　　　　　　POMFRET.
Morgrave, how now ?

　　　　　　　MORGRAVE.
　　　　Ha !　At your service, madam.
(*They retire together, and sit conversing apart.*)

　　　　　POMFRET (*after a pause*).
Sir, you will pardon this chill welcome : I
Partake it, as you see.　Come, come, sit down.
To follow our discourse.　Your look, I see,
Is yonder.　Yes, yes—we must let them have
Their gossip.　So, the judge—　They are old friends,
Very old friends.　　　　(*Observing them covertly.*)

　　　　　　　L'ESTRANGE.
　　　　Indeed !

　　　　　POMFRET (*quickly*).
　　　　　　　Why should you say
Indeed ?　In truth, he—　Psha, sir ! we don't mete
Friendships by *time*.　At the first beckon, oft
Souls rush together, and their strict embrace
Scarce death shall sunder.　Then, again, we see
Natures so doubting, dwelling with such fear
On timorous question of the metal's truth,
That there's no time to use it.

　　　　　L'ESTRANGE (*smiling*).
　　　　　　　Yonder seems
The former sort.

POMFRET.
You laugh, sir!

L'ESTRANGE.
Did not *you?*

POMFRET.
I!—yes, of course.—So, sir, you think—you—think—
The coming of the lord chief justice augurs
Some lavishment of blood?   (She has made him sit
Close at her side.)   But then, sir —   (How they pore
Over that missal!   Curse him!—" *Wonderful!*
Strange colours—ha!"—Perish the hand that wrought
A veil so specious!   Doubtless, much ye think
Of it!—" *Ah! curious, quaint, and well devised!*"
Would they were scorpions, sweetheart, for thy sake!
They'd sting thee back to duty.)

LADY GRACE (*aside, watching him*).
So, my friend,
Wince you at *this?*   Your heart's not callous—nay,
I'll probe it deeper ere I've done with you.

L'ESTRANGE (*rising*).
Well, well—to-morrow —

POMFRET (*starting*).
Master Morgrave!—Death!
Pardon.   I mean—we need your counsel.   Traitors
Are stolen into our precincts.   How may we
Detect them?

MORGRAVE (*confused*).
Traitors!

LADY GRACE (*half aloud*).
Go, I pray you—go!
If he be crossed I fear—

MORGRAVE (*rising*).
Enough.

LADY GRACE.
Thanks, thanks!
He knits his brow.   I should begone.   Is't so
He means?

POMFRET (*impatiently*).
Come, master Morgrave.

LADY GRACE.
Sir, good night.
Whene'er it fits your leisure to resume
This learned and pleasant converse, here, be sure,
A willing pupil stays.—(*Half aside*)   To-morrow noon,
Come to my garden-bower.   (*Exit.*)

POMFRET (*aside*).
Mine ears are liars.
No—no ; there's nothing in the words—tut ! nothing—
Some study, doubtless—but the *look*.   Let words
Prate of things fair and wholesome, the bold eye
Betrays the bitter kernel shut within—
And that's the heart on't.   Aye, mock love and duty,
And so to prayer.
(*He strides up suddenly to* MORGRAVE.)
Morgrave, you are a villain !

MORGRAVE.
Pomfret !   Stand back.   What mean you ?

POMFRET.
Never seek
To fool me with your bland, persuasive tones,
From that I owe myself.   Hold off, L'Estrange—
I say, a villain !   I have long believed it :
Sure as a cloud brings rain, distrust and grief
Track this man's presence near my hearth.   I tell you,

If ever wretch were doomed to walk the world,
Dogged by a smiling devil swathed in rags,
Stolen from virtue, I am he ;—and *this*
My—　Back, L'Estrange !　You heard me, sir, I think,
Pronounce you—villain ?　Must I add thereto
A coward, and—

L'ESTRANGE (*restraining him*).
　　　　　　Beneath your own roof !　Nay,
If fight you must, come forth.

MORGRAVE (*retreating*).
　　　　　　　　He's mad with rage.
I will not fight—at least, not here.　Take notice,
I draw not on him.

L'ESTRANGE.
　　　　　Best begone, then.　See !
He slips my grasp.　I cannot help—away !
There will be blood !

MORGRAVE.
　　　　　I am his guest.　I lift
No hand against him.

POMFRET.
　　　　Thou, my guest ! What ?—*thou !*
Good faith !　I welcomed thee, like him who hung
A skull beside his banquet-chair, to curb
The passion of his joy !　I bore thy presence
In very scorn of fear ; beheld thee twine
In serpent-folds around mine honour's tree,
Yet crushed thee not ; for I believed its treasures
Beyond thy wit to harm.　There ; go.　L'Estrange,
You have heard all.　Not for my sake, nor for
This dog's, but hers, whose honour, if but scratched,
Must die, be mute on what has chanced.　For *thee*—
Begone, I say !　　　　　　(*Moves towards* MORGRAVE.)

MORGRAVE (*as he retires*).
You shall repent this!   (*In a loud voice.*)

POMFRET.
                              Ha !
He threatens!   Thus I spurn you—   Grace !
        (LADY GRACE, *re-entering, throws herself between
        them.*)

LADY GRACE.
                                        Alas !
You have slain my peace.   Kill not your friend.

POMFRET.
                              My friend !
Come from your shelter, sir.   Do you fear still ?
There—   (*Throws his sword at* GRACE'S *feet.*)

LADY GRACE (*taking* MORGRAVE'S *hand*).
        Master Morgrave, for my sake, withhold
Your just resentment.

POMFRET.
                For her sake ! Grace ! wife !
You know not what you do.   What, madam ! loose
That villain's hand !

LADY GRACE.
                Is truth in any shape
So hideous to thee ?   Fettered by no vow,
This friendship shames the vile and borrowed love
That scoffs at dearest duties.

POMFRET.
                Woman—wife !
What dost thou mean ? what innocent play lies hid
Beneath a mask so lewd ?   Have I deserved this ?
Didst thou endow me with thy fortune's gifts—
Thyself, far richer—but to shame me ?   Look—

I cannot rend in fury that white hand,
Nor pluck yon cowering traitor from thy skirts.
But I may take mine outraged honour hence
From this polluted home, leaving thy thoughts
My sole avengers.　Nay, thou shalt not say
That I have e'er been harsh with thee.　Once more
Let go that hand !　I pray thee, Grace, sweet Grace,
Put not thy sacred honour to such shame
As my sad love hath borne.　Stand'st thou unmov'd ?
Farewell for ever !　　(*Rushes out*, L'ESTRANGE *follows*.)

MORGRAVE.
Guilt that turns to bay
Can for the instant force as bold a front
As any.　Dearest lady—　　(*Offers to take her hand.*)

LADY GRACE (*standing bewildered*).
Gone for ever !
Did he say—*ever ?*　Who is't grasps my hand ?
Back, sir—and touch me not.　Will you insult me
Ev'n in my husband's—　Man, dost thou believe
That, on the ruins of an holy love,
I'd let thine inclination—that rank weed—
Take root and flourish ?　See, I have done all
I promised thee.　You are avenged.　I, wretched—
I am faint.　Yes, lead me in ; but then, if you've
A man's heart, quit me.　I must think—must weep.
(*Bursts into tears.　Exit.*)

———

SCENE II.—*A part of the Grounds near the Manor-house.*

(DE L'ISLE *enters*, ALICE *supporting him eagerly
along.　Sounds of pursuit.*)

DE L'ISLE.
No farther.　I—I faint.　Let go this heap
Of worthless flesh—and save thee.　Hark—their voices

Float up the wind !   Quest on.   The wounded hart's
At bay.   Fly—fly, sweet Alice—fly !

ALICE.

I leave you !
One trial more—one effort more—   See, love,
I almost bear you.—   Oh, this woman's arm !
Weak as a sapling !

DE L'ISLE (*sinks down*).

We shall rest, love, soon—
Here is my grave.   O, earth—kind mother ! open
Thy cool and dewy breast, for bitter pangs
Oppress me, and the toil of fevered life
Is heavy on my heart.
(ALICE, *wringing her hands, sinks beside him.
Enter* MORGRAVE.)

MORGRAVE.

Those tears were prophets ;
Plainer than tongues they teach me that the way
Back to her heart is open yet to him—
His patience—aye, and those fierce accessions
Which love, renewed, brings with it.   I must find
Some sharper curb to rule this skittish soul—
Else, hope-fed, she will grow too powerful,
And cast me from my—   Who's there ?   (*Starting.*)

ALICE.

One who tends
A husband sick to death.   I pray you, sir,
If you are one of nature's teaching, help—
Give succour.

MORGRAVE.
But what are ye ?

ALICE.

Gentle beggars—
Nameless and houseless.   Help if you can—if not,

Pass on—forget.　'Twas but a stretching spray
That stayed you for an instant.

MORGRAVE.
　　　　　　　　By my life,
I know—I pity you.

ALICE.
　　　　Indeed!　Find him
A refuge.　Why do you pause?

MORGRAVE.
　　　　　　　It is a risk—
A mortal hazard.

ALICE.
　　　So are deeds made noble,—
Well, sir, betray us not.

MORGRAVE.
　　　　Stay! give me time
To think.　(*Aside*)　Can I not, from this chance, sift
　　out
Advantage to my power?　What if I take them
Straight to my haughty mistress, and, resigning
Their lives into her earnest care, make that
My present meed, and their concealment hold,
Like a fell curse, above them all?　'Twill do,
I think.　(*Aloud*)　Come, trust my guidance; and
　　although
Not lord of this demesne, I may perchance
Have influence as potential.　Courage, madam,
Let me relieve your shoulder of its charge.
Sir, lean on me.

DE L'ISLE.
　　　The faintness passes.　With
My first free breath I'll thank you.

MORGRAVE.

Nay, no thanks.
Good deeds repay themselves.

DE L'ISLE.

'Tis fortunate.
This world hath ne'er a treasury, I fear,
For such disbursements.

MORGRAVE.

Follow closely, madam,
And I will show you where we may obtain
An entrance unperceived.   Come, lean on me. (*Exeunt.*)

SCENE III.—*Another part of the Grounds close to the Mansion.*

(*Enter* POMFRET *and* L'ESTRANGE.)

L'ESTRANGE.

Come, come ; you're cooler ; now return.

POMFRET.

Return !
I was a soldier when I wooed, sir.   All
My wealth hung at my side ; and when I wrapped
My ragged cloak over a heart as worn,
And even in such guise, won her—she that was
My love, clothed on with gratitude, became
Mine angel.   But that's past.   This wrong of hers
Exalts mine honest poverty above
That mount of gold she sits on.   We have now
Changed places.   She, proud heart, shall sue to me—
Aye, kneeling, shall she woo her beggar-lord

Or ere he cross that threshold.   Do you smile ?
What do you mean ?   'Tis folly, sir,—not guilt—
She has to answer.   Please her, for awhile,
To toy and prate with any mincing fool—
Dare you affirm that——

L'ESTRANGE.
I !—No,—Heaven forbid.

I affirm nothing.   (*Pressing him towards the house.*)

POMFRET.
Withered be the foot,
That brings me nearer to that threshold, till
Her penitence adjures me.

L'ESTRANGE
Yet reflect—

Her wealth.

POMFRET.
What's that ?   I love her, man !   'Tis so.
Smile as you will your cool, superior scorn—
Your curst pretence of pity.   'Tis most true.
Sleep had no silent vision, thought no world,
That for its sun and centre did not choose
Her darling life.   And this was mine—this *was* !
Won—purchased—for a moment.   Ah ! that death
Had gathered home our love's sweet harvest then,
Not left the ears to wither !

L'ESTRANGE.
You shall reap
Many such harvests yet.

POMFRET.
No—none.   Farewell,
L'Estrange.   I am for the wars—less soldier far
Than pilgrim—for that hopeful sap is dry
That gives us heart-strength.

L'ESTRANGE.

If she knew that— Stay,
Pomfret, come hither.   Quick ! what chamber's that—
There—whence the light bursts ?

POMFRET.

'Tis her oratory.

L'ESTRANGE.

Ah ! she is praying.   Hold ! what shadow glooms
Along the wall ?

POMFRET (*eagerly*).
Why, hers.

L'ESTRANGE.

And those dark plumes
That crown it ?   (*Pulls* POMFRET *away suddenly.*)
Let's begone.

POMFRET (*eagerly*).
Stand still.   My sight
Was for a moment dim.   'Tis clear again.
Stand.   I invite you to a mystery.
We'll call it—eh, L'Estrange !—The Honest Wife—
A tale of truth.   Ha, ha !   And lo ! there stands
The villain of the play.   What doth he there ?
There, in a spot held consecrate to peace
And pious meditation ?   Ah, my love !
Awake ; the serpent's in thy paradise
Stinging thy soul !

L'ESTRANGE.

Why, as you say, 'tis strange.
Look how the infinite coxcomb bears himself,
Tossing his feathered pate, and leaning down,
Not with a wooing diffidence, but rather
Claiming, as 'twere, some boon—some promise—some
Intent, impatiently foregone.

POMFRET (*starting*).
L'Estrange,
Your sword !   (*Seizes it.*)   Lend it, I say !

L'ESTRANGE.

                 Tut ! what's the good ?
His is a knave's trick ; but what's *hers ?*   No, no,
I've better counsel.   As your wrongs are great,
So magnify your vengeance.   Pomfret, listen !
I say you shall have vengeance.   Will you hear ?

POMFRET (*still gazing*).

Yes—yes, L'Estrange, I hear thee.   I am watching
The sinking of mine argosy.   I stand
Upon the hither shore.   I cannot move
To rescue, but, Prometheus-like, am bound,
Clutching at air, the while a monstrous thing
Gnaws at my vitals.   Stab me, good L'Estrange.

L'ESTRANGE.

Nay, listen.   Not around that spot of light
Is gathered all the evil.   Traitors, Pomfret,
Are sheltered 'neath that roof.

POMFRET.
               Traitors !

L'ESTRANGE.

                     I told you
Morgrave came forth.   It was but to seek out
Dark spirits like his own.   By heaven, it seems
Fortune herself entwines this knot of snakes
And casts them down before you.   Haste, my friend,
Denounce them, one and all, or linger here,
Perhaps to—

POMFRET.
     Hold !

L'ESTRANGE.
     To Jeffreys !

POMFRET.
               And the end ?

L'ESTRANGE.

For *him*,—the dog's death he has earned.   For *her*,—
Should the law touch her life, she has wealth—you'll find
The judge not difficult of access.   Thus,
Guilty or innocent, you may work your will.

POMFRET.

I am your instrument.   From my strings you charm
What music pleases you.

L'ESTRANGE.
   At once, then, come.
    (*Pulling him away.   Exeunt.*)

END OF ACT III.

ACT IV.

SCENE I.—*Room in the Sessions-house, Dorchester.
Night.*

(KIRKE, L'ESTRANGE, *and* LORD FEVERSHAM
at a table.)

KIRKE.
Good.   A fair total.   Be it writ henceforth,
In Dorset rolls, if treason hath long claws,
Justice hath longer.   What with hangings, fines,
The scourge, and fear—'tis like our busy friends
Here in the west shall, for a century, lead
Patterns of Christian lives.   Lord Feversham,
Our learned judge is malcontent.   He swears
Your lordship spoiled his harvest.

FEVERSHAM.
                    I !

L'ESTRANGE.
                        Nay spare
Feversham's blushes.   He has a virtuous dread
Of being thought humane.

KIRKE.
                    I never meant
So gross an imputation.   My good lord,
You but abolished that dull hindrance, called
Trial by jury.

FEVERSHAM (*laughing*).
How should I discern

At what fine point the soldier's duty gave
Place to the hangman's ?   I am never good
At nice distinctions.   Hark !   'Tis Jeffreys !

JEFFREYS (*within*).
Knaves !
Had ye no whips ?   Must I be followed still ?
Beset at bed and board ?   May every rogue
That owns a rebel kinsman, fray me thus—
Clutch at my skirts, and clog my carriage-wheels
As I pass to and fro ?   (*Enters, his guard following.*)
Good even, colonel.
Well, my good lord !   L'Estrange, I want you.   Hark !

L'ESTRANGE (*after whispering*).
I will, my lord.   (*Exit.*)

JEFFREYS (*pacing about*).
They think all's over—ha !
Good souls—they think so.   When the storm seems past,
The game peeps from the covert.   They shall find
The sharpest arrow's in the quiver yet—
And that the red assize—(so, gentlemen,
The scurrilous rogues christen our noble court)—
Hath yet some terror.

FEVERSHAM.
What hath chanced, my lord ?

JEFFREYS.
I'll tell ye both a secret.   These—Away, sirs !
We are at council.   (*Exeunt the guard.*)
These stout Dorset folk—
Bold, resolute souls, with not a doit to lose—
Are not our men.   At Taunton,* t'other day,
I sent a knave to the gallows—one, I thought,
Would howl, and cringe, and fright the honest loons
That gathered round in thousands—(for, it seems,

* Note D.

He was well-neighboured 'mong them).   But the dog's
Pale face deceived me.   "*Ho!*" quoth he—and laughed—
"*A populous place, God bless it!*"   Now, I tell you,
Example's lost on such, and we must spare
These low-sprung weeds that fall and leave no gap,
Whose poisonous essence would not else work harm,
And turn the scythe to loftier.   I am chid
For showing favour.   Give me one high head—
Gracious or gifted—noble—lovely—young—
Mark how I'll deal therewith !

KIRKE.
                     There's one—but, 'faith,
'Tis hard to come by.

JEFFREYS (*eagerly*).
          Ha ! his name ?

KIRKE.
                         De l'Isle !

JEFFREYS.
De l'Isle.   De l'Isle.   Of kin to old dame Alice,*
That Presbyterian, canting witch ?

KIRKE.
                    My lord,
Her brother's child.   Twice has he baffled me—
This very night, two of my trusty lambs
Pounced on his haunt.   The nest was warm.   He'd fled
To Pomfret.

JEFFREYS (*eagerly*).
          Pomfret ?   Colonel, I am bold
To doubt your wood-craft—but, for once—no—no—
'Tis not so lucky, sure !
                         (*Enter an Officer.*)

* Note E.

OFFICER.
A man, my lord,
Stands muffled here without, and boldly seeks
Admission to your presence.

KIRKE (*carelessly*).
Some poor devil
Come to the mercy-market.

OFFICER.
'Faith, sir—hardly.

JEFFREYS.
No? I'll sit here then. Now, admit him. You
Are armed— (*Enter* POMFRET.)
Now, most importunate sir, we trust
The pith of this affair will recompense
Its outward husk and roughness. 'Faith! you're right.
(*Aside to* KIRKE) He trembles. Mark him.
Well, sir, let us hear
What you've to say; yet take this with you—'tis
No fitting time for mercy.

POMFRET.
I am here
Not to deliver, but betray. You choose
To hear me?

JEFFREYS (*quickly*).
O my good young gentleman,
Your pardon. Welcome to our council. 'Slife!
We are so pestered here with prayers—so stayed
In our dread office by distressful plaints—
'Tis little marvel each new visage wears
The aspect of a suppliant. Ho! there—sirs!
A chair for—master—eh?

POMFRET.
Pomfret!

JEFFREYS (*glancing at* KIRKE).
                              A name
Sacred to loyalty.

KIRKE (*with a rough laugh*).
Ha—ha!

JEFFREYS.
                    But, come!
Out with your history.   Give us who and where—
No prefacing, beseech you.   Among friends,
Short counsels ever!   Do you drink?

POMFRET.
                              My lord,
Since I demand no meed for taking on me
This devil's office—shall my prayer have weight
Against the extreme judgment?

JEFFREYS.
                    Mercy's fount
Dwells not in us, but doubtless the good word
Of master Pomfret (in so far as his
Known loyalty responds) shall have its weight.

POMFRET.
It should, in truth—else honour, love, and faith,
Are sacrificed unto a bloody end.

KIRKE (*half aside*).
My charger to a squirrel, he'll impeach
His wife!

JEFFREYS (*coolly*).
Well, where's the marvel?

POMFRET (*suddenly*).
                              Hark ye, sirs!
To you, lord justice, whose great boast it was
That upon certain witness you'd not pause

To hang up her that bore you—you, brave sir,
Who now wring English necks as gleefully
As at Tangier you trampled Moorish heads
Like acorns ; you, Lord Feversham, whose zeal
Hath saved the law some labour, I denounce
Four victims ! Does that please ? To men like you
Fond ties are spider's meshes. You want blood—
I put it to your lips.

KIRKE (*starting up*).
That's more the tune.
Your lordship's guard waits—shall I—

JEFFREYS (*gently*).
Fair and softly.
You spoke of *four*, I think, sir. Will you name me
This knot of pestilent rogues ?

POMFRET.
Two of the four
I know not. They are traitors. That's enough
For you.

JEFFREYS (*writing*).
The third, then ?

POMFRET.
William Morgrave.

JEFFREYS.
Ha !
Morgrave of Ivyburn ! What—snared at last,
Dear William ? Will, the slippery ! (*Reads tablets.*)
Here's his name—
Red cross—suspected. Come, we'll make him sure—
The fourth remains.

KIRKE (*impatiently*).
Come, sir, the fourth. My lord

Requires you name the fourth.
> (POMFRET *turns fiercely upon him, but checks
> himself. After a pause—*)

POMFRET.
> My wife!
> (*Sinks back, concealing his face.*)

KIRKE.
> By Heaven!
'Tis as I said.

JEFFREYS.
Hark, colonel!
> (*Whispers* KIRKE, *who goes out*, FEVERSHAM
> *following.*)
> Master Pomfret,
You have done well.   See that you do not choose
Another scolding mate.

POMFRET.
 What do you mean?

JEFFREYS.
To hold a court to-morrow.   As we shall
Require your presence, you had best stay here.
The wine's indifferent good.   We'll sup at eight.
(*Yawning*) Do you play brag?

POMFRET.
> The game of death I play—
And souls are forfeit.   There's a scent of blood—
Let me go forth.   I sicken.

JEFFREYS.
> No—no—no.
I may not trust you.   You are young, sir; it
Becomes mine age and office to preserve
Youth from temptation.   Ah, I once was young
And tender—very tender—till the rubs

Of the hard world, and rude, unchristian men,
Made my veins iron. But, as I said, being young,
I know what power dwells in a woman's eye—
A wife's especially. No, sweet master Pomfret,
To-night we part not.

POMFRET.
Do you doubt me, then?

JEFFREYS.
Marry, the heavens forbid! So frank a youth
Mistrusted! Hark you, master. I can guess—
Aye, without magic—that your loyalty
Moves but a finger here, while deeper views
Labour like hinds. But one attainted life
Stands between you and fortune—in my hand
The issue. Am I plain? The shears of justice,
Grown dull of late, perchance, if edged with gold,
Might clip the surer.

POMFRET (*passionately*).
            Tiger, and man of blood!
Into whose snare—brief-sighted fool!—I have
Betrayed mine innocent lamb—thou dost, indeed,
As thou hast said, instruct me. In your eyes
I read the monstrous image of my guilt,
And sink before it. What hath my fury done?
Slay and divide the spoil? Laughest thou, fiend?
My wife—my Grace!   (*Falls back.*)

JEFFREYS.
Irresolute fool !
(*Rings a handbell. Guard enter.*)
                        Poor youth !
Prepare a room within, sirs. My young friend
Hath a vertigo—eye-sickness—or some
Such soft distemper. 'Twill subside, I think—
Look to him. There ! begone.   (POMFRET *is led out.*)
                        I thought I saw

More resolution in his features.   Idiot !
Was ever chance so wasted ? *   (*Exit.*)

SCENE II.—*In the Mansion.*

(LADY GRACE *enters, cautiously guiding* ALICE
and DE L'ISLE, *both disguised.*)

LADY GRACE.
A chamber lies beyond, safer by far
Than that from which I bring you, to strange eyes
Scarce notable.   Heed not this gloom,—the best
Assurance of your safety ; and, for comfort,
Think, in this world, how oft the darkest ways
Conduct to light and peace.

ALICE.
　　　　　　　With thankful hearts,
Thankful as confident, we follow.

LADY GRACE.
　　　　　　　　　Then
Behold your refuge.   (*Opens a secret door.*)
　　　　　　　Sacred once to prayer,
'Twill but renew its holy purpose, thus
Calming poor nature's fears.

DE L'ISLE (*feebly*).
　　　　　　　Thanks, dearest lady.
Here is a tongue that shall with better grace
Rehearse our gratitude.   I faint with pain,—
Your shoulder, love.
　　　　　　(ALICE *supports him in, and returns.*)

* Note F.

ALICE.
Some strength-restoring sleep
Shall by to-morrow eve give power to move
Our dangerous presence farther.   Dearest lady,
May we then know you by no other name
Than friend and benefactor ?

LADY GRACE.
Rather say,
Grace Pomfret. Ah ! do you start ?   Why, now my
    pulse
Begins to leap too !   Heaven ! the form agrees,—
Her movements—stature !   Madam, I would see
Your face.   Do you pause ?
(Catches her hood, which falls back.)

ALICE.
Am I Medusa, lady ?
My snakes are stingless.

LADY GRACE.
Would thyself were so !
Thou fiend, so gloriously incarnate !   Thou
Lost thing, whose melancholy beauty thus
Dazzles and sears mine eyesight !   Leave me—go !

ALICE.
Is this distraction, madam ?

LADY GRACE.
If despair
Be madness,—aye.   Dost thou not see how much
Thou art mine enemy ?   Know, fell sorceress !
Your spring hath trod upon my winter's heels,
While yet some flowers were left me. Your smooth
    cheek
Ploughs furrows *here*.   The love of your sweet eyes
Hath taught mine tears.   Ah ! had you coveted
But wealth, I would have so dealt with you, that

You might have trampled gold, and haply spared
The first great bond of nature.

ALICE (*eagerly*).
                    Hear me—hear!

LADY GRACE.
You did not sin in ignorance.   I could else
Search my own soul, and pardon, but you knew
The prize you played for was another's, and,
Using your budding sweetnesses to make
More dark my front of gloom, you selfishly
Plucked from this breast, its honourable home,
A gem you cannot wear.   (*Noise within.*)

ALICE (*starting*).
                    Ah,—listen !

LADY GRACE.
                                        Yes,—
We are traced.   I thank you.   *Now* you feel. Oh,
    woman !
Have you no plea,—no palliation,—no
Grief for your fatal mischief?   Oh, I pray you !
Devise some specious cause to justify
My mercy—I would save you.

ALICE.
                    For myself
I care not ; but for *him*,—oh, save !   (*Noise.*)

LADY GRACE.
                                        Infatuate
Not less than guilty ?   To your refuge—go,
Repent !
            (*Alarm.   ALICE disappears through the secret
            door.   Enter COLONEL KIRKE.*)

KIRKE.
        All's well.   Madam, your ladyship's
Obedient servant.

LADY GRACE.
What means this?

KIRKE.
Come in,
My lambs (*guard enter*).   These rough but worthy souls,
    fair lady,
Have a small duty to perform.

LADY GRACE.
This outrage
Is worthy of its leader, else report,
Widely corroborate, to Colonel Kirke
Owes deep amends.

KIRKE.
Report may split its tongue,—
And you, fair madam, learn to govern yours.
I search for traitors here, and, if I err not,
Find one already.

LADY GRACE.
Search then, and begone!
Aye, sir, no wiser than you came, steal back
To those whose tool you are.   But haste ; day comes,
And men may be abroad.

KIRKE.
Aye, search I will,—
Even to this napkin—to this pouncet box.
Here in this cabinet's a likely drawer.
Who stuffed this damask ?   Nothing here, nor here ?
                    (*Runs his sword through cushions, et*
Throw back those tables.   Sound the panels, sirs.
Is that a crevice 'neath the tapestry ?   Death !
Where is the traitor, madam ?   Where's De l'Isle ?
            (*Seizes her rudely by the arm ; she cries out.*
            DE L'ISLE *throws open the door, and appears*
            with ALICE.)

DE L'ISLE.

Hold! I am here.   Release the noble lady.
By heaven! she knew not to what hunted lives
She did vouchsafe a refuge.

LADY GRACE (*springing forward*).
                    Ah! De l'Isle!
And *thou?*

ALICE (*embracing her*).
Your Harry's sister.

LADY GRACE.
                    Mine!   Oh, Alice!
Why did you hide this from me?

ALICE.
                    To prevent
This sad self-sacrifice.   We feared that—

KIRKE (*advancing*).
                                        Come,
Remove the prisoners.

DE L'ISLE.
                    I am ready.   How!
You will not, surely—
                    (*Pointing to* LADY GRACE *and* ALICE.)

KIRKE.
                    Sir, I know my duty
Better than you can teach me.

DE L'ISLE.
                                        This is my wife,—
Guilty alone in her unwavering faith
To my dark fortunes.   This most generous lady
Knew not my name or station,—scarce the cause
Wherefore I sought concealment.   Do not harm them;
Take my own life, and be content.

Kirke.
> Not worth
A splinter from my falchion.   For such wares
You must bid higher, when my good lord justice
Stands in the mart, your rival.   In your ear—
Look for no mercy, comrade.

De l'Isle (*gazing on him*).
> Colonel Kirke,
We are not strangers.

Kirke (*carelessly*).
> Strangers! no.   We fought
At Medj' together; and right soldierly
You bore yourself, De l'Isle.   You should have died
    there;
'Twas in your mind, I think.

De l'Isle.
> Then, for the memory
Of those old soldier-days, I—

Kirke (*turning from him*).
> Sir, I see you
But through the medium of my duty, which
Colours all men alike.   Back, comrade, tut!
I'm an old mastiff, madam; rage and wheedling
Alike are lost upon me.   (*Shot and alarm within.*)
> Well!   What now,—
A rescue?   Stand, men.   Serves me right, i'faith,
For babbling here.
> (*The doors are burst open, and a body of depend-
> ants, etc., armed, and headed by* Gabriel, *rush
> in.*)
> Let one among you raise
His finger.   (*They pause.*)

Gabriel (*furiously*).
> Cowards, where is your courage?   Stayed it
Without the door?

KIRKE.
          Body o' me!   This cock
Crows shrilly for a fowl so ancient.

GABRIEL.
                              Madam,
Our gracious mistress, hither are we come
With strength and will to guard you.   Speak one word,
Wave your hand thus, and these marauding thieves
Shall, head first, plumb the moat.

LADY GRACE.
                         Your zeal afflicts me;
I need no strength, but innocence,—no shield,
But from my country's justice.   If both fail,
There is a greater law shall one day work
More vengeance than your swords—whereto, meanwhile,
Humbly to bend is glory.   Shed no blood
For me or mine.   Come, kind old Gabriel,
Obey me.   See, your mistress, none beside,
Disarms this faithful hand.
                         (*She takes the halberd from him.*)

GABRIEL (*hesitating*).
                         Still, if I thought—

LADY GRACE.
Think nothing, but obey.   Oh, Gabriel!
This truth of thine, unsworn, may put to shame
Their plighted faith, who, to preserve it, had
A thousand times thy cause.   Away, my friends!
Thanks, and farewell.   (*They reluctantly retire.*)

KIRKE.
          'Tis prudently resolved;
Lead them away.

DE L'ISLE.
          Stay, sir!   You cannot.   How!
This instant,—so attended!

LADY GRACE.
                    Sir, I pray you
Respect our sex,—our innocence, as yet,
Not legally attainted. My—my lord
Is absent, as you doubtless knew before
You led your ruffian band to desecrate,
By night, his English home.

KIRKE.
                    Your husband, eh?
                        (*Signs to the guard.*)

LADY GRACE.
That mocking smile,—what doth it bode? Oh, Heaven!
Pomfret is innocent.   He was from home—
He cannot share this trouble.

KIRKE (*coolly*).
                    I perceive
A curious scene awaits us.

LADY GRACE (*distractedly*).
                    Gracious Heaven !
Entreat him, some one.   Sir, in mercy tell me
What hath befallen.   Hath Pomfret—   Ah, you smile
Again,—he is safe.   One word,—oh, answer !

KIRKE.
Patience.   (*Exeunt.*)

END OF ACT IV.

ACT V.

SCENE I.—*Judges' chamber in the Sessions-house.*

(JEFFREYS. L'ESTRANGE.)

JEFFREYS.

He said so, did he ?   If the seventh cup
Had passed, why then I pardon him.   Who cares
Then ?   The imagination, sir, becomes
So over-fruitful, that men scorn it.   'Faith,
'Twould puzzle the man sober to make good
Half the man drunk affirms.   Tut—I've been drunk,
And know it.

L'ESTRANGE.

He had drunk, sir, but was still
Sober as a—(*checks himself*)—as, in fact, *any* man,
Who doesn't drink.   Once and again he swore
That, in the matter of Dame Alice, you
Had sorely wronged and cheated him.   Moreover,
Young Felthorp's ransom, ere it reached his hand,
Suffered strange diminution.   And that now,
When the due working of this Pomfret mine
Might pay for all—you heed not, but would take
Three paltry lives instead.

JEFFREYS.

I ever knew
Lord Feversham an ass, and therefore used him,
Chiefly, as men employ such brutes, to drag
The more disgusting burdens.   What beside ?

L'ESTRANGE.
He said no more, my lord.

JEFFREYS.
My compliments
Unto his discontented lordship. Tell him
That, Heaven permitting, on the third day hence,
He will be present in his duty, aiding
To hang this worthy three.

L'ESTRANGE (*hastily*).
My lord!

JEFFREYS (*showing his hand*).
See here!

L'ESTRANGE.
A bloodstone—is't not ? *

JEFFREYS.
By our gracious king
Thrust on my finger when I last took leave.
I tell you 'tis my memory, L'Estrange—
My much-neglected memory. Well, there's time
To heed its precepts. You have seen me play,
Worthy L'Estrange, the gracious English judge—

L'ESTRANGE (*aside*).
Yes—being paid for't.

JEFFREYS.
Now, sir, I'll enact
The Roman. Yes, though baffled Feversham
Howl like a satyr—though the whole land join
In cries of mercy—these shall die—shall die.
Traitors, or traitors' friends, their race is run—
I have said. They die!

L'ESTRANGE.
But if—

* Note G.

JEFFREYS (*turning suddenly upon him*).
      How dare you, sir,
Stand in the path of justice?   Now I think on't,
Master L'Estrange, you shall to Bristol.   Look
To that affair we spoke of.   'Gainst these rebels
We shall not need your witness.   William Morgrave
Lends us his tongue, and saves his neck.   Away.
I follow soon.   Farewell.   (*Exit* L'ESTRANGE.)
      So much for him.
He's got the pity-fever, and must hence
Ere the contagion— Well, sagacious sir,
       (*Enter* TORY TOM.)
What seeks your wisdom here?   You must be whipped,
And know your station better.   To your kennel.
Did you not hear me, brute?

TOM.
      Come—don't hit me.
You! *you* a judge!   You'd make a brave swash-buckler,
To brawl at fairs—or cudgel-play i' the ring
For greasy halfpence. (*Evading him*) So, you thought
 you had me!

JEFFREYS.
You pestilent hound—you maggot—you poor fly—
Still in the chrysalis—and never doomed
To burst! I am glad to own thy carcase—there
To vent the spleen that stifles me.

TOM.
      Ho!—ho!
So fierce?   See how I'll tame this bitter mood
With honey-tidings.

JEFFREYS.
 Thou! A crack-brained herald
Sent from the court of Folly!

TOM.
      Yes—to greet

Madness—his elder brother.   Not a man
Of your brave guard could pluck up heart to tell you,
And so they sent the fool.

JEFFREYS (*turns suddenly and seizes him*).
How, sir !—what said they ?

TOM.
Don't strangle me.   Already the rogues say
You hang with half a trial—and—your name
Cannot bear slander.   Ah—let go.   'Tis well—
You've saved your learned fingers.   Morgrave's gone.

JEFFREYS
Morgrave ! escaped !   (*Rings furiously.   Officers enter.*)
Sirs—tell me—does this—thing—
This idiot lie ?

OFFICER.
I fear, my lord—

JEFFREYS.
You fear !
I am answered.   Go.   True coward !   He mistrusts
Even his friends.   Go—send L'Estrange.

OFFICER.
My lord,
He too is gone.

JEFFREYS.
True—that's *my* doing (*Musing.*)   All
So far conspires to save them.   They may yet
Evade—no—no—*that* way remains—and yet
Could it be managed otherwise—I hate
Such scenes—no—Pomfret must—   (*Enter Marshal.*)
They are arraigned ?
Open the doors.   Make proclamation, sir—
I come.   (*Exeunt.*)

———

SCENE II.—*Great Court-room of the Sessions-house. It is hung entirely with red.* Judges seated. A Military Guard under* COLONEL KIRKE. *Jury and Officials.* LADY GRACE, DE L'ISLE, *and* ALICE *at the Bar. Many persons below it.* JEFFREYS *enters and takes his place.*

JEFFREYS (*after a pause*).

† Sirs, we are come to this good, loyal town—
Meaning to make short work.   Not to indulge,
As some, I see, expect—in fair, set speech
And formal declamation ; not to follow
A brace of puffing trumpeters ;—for, psha !
We have seen these things twenty times before—
We come to do some business for the king !
I know such visits are unwonted !   'Faith !
Your very women storm at us—for fear
We should invade their rights—for, gentlemen,
I hear 'tis in your city much the fashion
For women to bear sway.   I say to you,
My prating madams, justice is a jade
That if she rails not, *bites*—and never stays
For compliment of sex.   (*Pauses, then resumes.*)
                    Now, hark ye, sirs—
All you who love your king, or hold in heart
The memory of the crownèd martyr—prompt
As you must be, to vengeance—yet remember
Justice must point the way.   For John de l'Isle—
Yon bold, notorious traitor—let him turn
His thinkings heavenward—

KIRKE (*aside*).
            Now it comes !

JEFFREYS.
                    For he
Hath writ his name in English blood, and waved it

* Note II.   † Note I.

Aloft before men's eyes.   An infant's cry
Shall, with the accusing angel's thunder-tone,
Call *him* to death.   His wretched partner—

ALICE.
                                        Sir,
Waste not your words on me, who scorn alike
Your wrath and pity.   If my lord be guilty,
What then am I, who from the first have been
His spur and counsellor ?

JEFFREYS.
                    'Tis well avouched—
Your turn will come, fair lady.   Now, sirs, mark me—
Here stands a third respondent, challenging
Your sad but needful duty.   Be it your task
Closely to sift unwilling witness—mine
To guard the majesty of English law
Inviolate.
          (POMFRET *here enters slowly, places himself by*
              KIRKE, *his head drooping and face concealed.*
              KIRKE *draws the guard about him.*)

CLERK (*rising*).
Call William Morgrave.

JEFFREYS.
                    Do—
And get no answer.   Spare your lungs, sir.   William
Hath left us in the lurch.

POMFRET (*starting*).
                    Gone—say they ?   Gone !—
Then Heaven forgive me—I have slain my lamb
And let the wolf go free !

JEFFREYS.
                    Sirs, I might call
This man—or that—but, to say truth, I hate

Such patchwork dealing.   In this court stands one
May spare us all the labour.
                              (*Pauses, glancing at* POMFRET.)

                KIRKE (*aside to* POMFRET).
                              Now, then—up !
Speak, man—denounce them.   Be a ready witness—
So make the judge your friend.

                POMFRET (*raising his head*).
                              Well may he deem
No better, than that these stained lips should turn
Deftly to their foul office.   But he is wrong.
Enough, I have dragged her to the scaffold's edge—
Let others strike.   Call on your bloodhound gang
That tracked them down—your spies—your messengers—
There's proof enough.

                KIRKE.
                Not for the guilty knowledge—
But see—his eyebrows shake.   He'll speak—

                JEFFREYS.
                              'Tis known—
That justice, like a river, if it run
Smooth and unchecked, spreads out and wastes itself
In wide yet harmless shallows ; but, opposed,
Crests up and overwhelms ye.   Look you, sirs ;
You know my mind now.   'Tis a short step hence
To execution—ha ?   (*Glaring at* POMFRET.)
                Alack-a-day !
Doth no man answer ?   Yet, I thought but now
I spied an honest face.

                KIRKE (*aside*).
                Now note the tiger
Lashing itself to fury.   Let him spring,
All's lost.

POMFRET.

I cannot speak.   Yet—yet, to save her—
Hold—looks she hither ?   But 'tis vain.   As well
Hurl ashes toward the weltering source of day,
As with the venom of my traitorous lips
Taint her white robe of innocence !   They'd not,
For shame, believe me.

JEFFREYS (*impatiently*).
                    Reason, then, and pity
Alike are lost upon ye.   (*Starts up.*)   *Who denounced
These three to justice ?*

KIRKE (*eagerly*).
                    Speak—speak—speak !

POMFRET (*starting forward*).
                              '*Twas I !*
(LADY GRACE *looks wildly round, and stretching
    out her arms, falls forward.   Murmurs of
    amazement and   horror   pass   through   the
    assembly.*)

DE L'ISLE.

Pomfret !

POMFRET (*starting round, recognizes him*).
Thou too— My sister—

ALICE (*stretching her arms towards him*).
                                        Here.
POMFRET (*clasping his eyes.*)
                              And *thou !*
Villain—L'Estrange—I'll have thy blood for this,—
Aye, glare on me—'twas I !

JEFFREYS.
                    Crier, make silence ;
You, madam, stay your tears.   Shall I be bantered

With such sham stuff as this ?   What know you, sir,
Of the foul crime whereof the prisoners stand
Accused ?

POMFRET.
I will not answer.

JEFFREYS (*smiling*).
Wilt thou not ?
Nay, but thou wilt, I think.   Alack-a-day !
We needs must have it.   Come.

POMFRET.
They are my kin.

JEFFREYS.
Rebels are kin to none.   Hark, we are bent,
As yet, to mercy.   Show ye obstinate,
Thwart us with closeness or reluctancy,
And I will sound a trumpet here i' the west,
Shall make the ears of every hearer tingle
For fifty years to come.

KIRKE (*aside*).
Do you mark that ?
Now, you are launched—set forth.   All's well, I tell you.

POMFRET (*in a low voice*).
What would you know ?

JEFFREYS (*showing* DE L'ISLE).
You recognise in him
A fugitive of Monmouth's?

POMFRET.
Aye.

JEFFREYS.
L'Estrange
Told you he saw them welcomed—comforted—

And—yourself absent—by your wretched wife
Housed in your mansion, ever till that hour
Sacred from rebel footsteps?   You conceive,
Nay, more, are rooted in a firm belief
That, in full sense of her disloyalty,
Your lady did this deed, which you, denouncing,
In every land where honesty is praise,
Have built yourself a name.   How say you, sir,
Is this—is all not true ?

POMFRET.
It is all true.

JEFFREYS.
I'm satisfied.   O me ! 'tis marvellous
From what tough roots the great, the mighty truth,
Shoots forth apparent !   Look you, master Pomfret ;
Needs must we had your witness—wanting which,
These might have 'scaped ; but, for it hath been given
With such an ill, disloyal grace,—stand by,
And see the end on't.   Let the trial proceed ;
God send ye good deliverance*—for if I
Read honest faces right, you have it not
Of men.

POMFRET (*starting franticly forward*).
Why, is this possible ? thou vile
And treacherous deceiver ! hast thou led me
To *this ?* didst thou not promise—Pah ! to talk
Of faith, to such as thee !

JEFFREYS.
Hey ! hey ! what now ?
What is the matter with this gentleman ?
Nay—stay him not—I'm clamour proof.   I know
My duty.

POMFRET.
And I *thee !*   To the black heart

* Note I.

I know thee, monster! and 'twere poor amends
To speak it; but that the despairing cry
Of injured lips, in place of present strength,
Hath prophecy.   Therefore, thou bold avenger,
That strik'st where God would suffer—merchant-fiend,
That sell'st thy victims ere thou slay'st them—here.
(Crosses down.)
Standing among thy trophies newliest-won,
Aye, even from their lost side—I SENTENCE THEE.
Vengeance shall haunt thee, and posterity
Howl curses on thy name.   Nay, from this heart
A living spirit cries that, even now,
Sharp retribution dogs that path, up which
Thou climb'st in thought to honour.   In that hour
When thou shalt drag thy hat upon thy brows,
For dread of each man's eye—when hopes and friends
Hourly drop from thee—think on *us*—and so
Cringe to thy fate—spurned—buffeted—a dog
Not worth a rope—flung in some headlong cell
To die! *   (*Sinks back exhausted with passion.*)

JEFFREYS (coolly).
Remove that maniac.   Come, proceed.
(Scene closes.)

———

SCENE III.—Gallery without.

(Enter LORD FEVERSHAM and TORY TOM.)

FEVERSHAM.
So loath to save his neck?

TOM.
He said, my lord,

* Note K.

Since Jeffreys swore he would respect his life,
Where was the need to fly?   Quoth I, " Sir, hope
Is but the meat wherewith my good lord justice
Fattens his beasts for slaughter."   That sufficed.
He vanished.

FEVERSHAM.
              Good : but lest this wolf obtain
The blood he covets, should they be convict,
I'll to the king, and—I have a means to win
Pardon for twenty.   Tom, thine idiotcy
Is worth a senate's wisdom.   Serve with me.
I'll make thy fortunes grow.   How goes the work
              (*Enter several Clerks and others.*)
Within?

CLERK.
       As looked for.   Thrice, my lord, he chid
The jury back, till their reluctant word
Squared with his bloody will.   O Magna Charta!

FEVERSHAM.
They are condemned, then ?

CLERK.
                  Truly, yes.   All three
To die on Wednesday.   (*Exeunt Clerks, etc.*)

FEVERSHAM.
              Ha ! so soon?   Away, boy !
                          (*Exit hastily.*)

TOM.
Not yet.   I must give warning.   Now, to knock
Their lordly heads together !
                  (*Enter JEFFREYS attended.*)

JEFFREYS (*yawning*).
                  So—that's done.
Kick out that fool.   He's growing wise.

TOM.
                              You'd best
Learn of his folly.   Hark ye: Feversham's
Gone to the king.   He creeps beneath the table—
Then, where's your house of cards?   Wise as you are,
You'd be a fool without me.

JEFFREYS.
                    To the king!
He has been bought then.   To the king—that's Oxford—
He'll win my prisoners, will he?   Let him.   Come—
At least we'll have a run for't.   Clerk, the warrant.
                                        (*Writes.*)
At noon—*to-morrow*—be it execute.
Check-mate, my lord!   (*Exit.*)

TOM.
                    Kick out that judge.   He grows

A deal too merciful.

        (*An officer re-enters.   Exit* TOM.)

———

SCENE IV.—*A Gloomy Cell in the Prison.*

                        (LADY GRACE.   ALICE.)

ALICE.
Farewell, dear Grace.

        LADY GRACE (*embracing her*).
                    And fare *thou* well, sweet Alice,
My three-days' sister.   May the world we leave
Ne'er suffer worse heart-sickness than results
From partings, brief as ours!

ALICE.
              Amen.   With me
Life hangs like slumber on a weary brow,
That nods and droops to meet it.   I ne'er knew
Tranquillity ; and yet 'tis comfort now,
When all life owns of terror hath gone by,
That I have ever been with *him*—albeit,
As 'twere, entrusted with two precious lives,
And but one woman's heart, to fear for them !
Your lot was different.   But for my—

LADY GRACE
                Forbear !
I warned you.

ALICE.
Grace, I am your murderer !
You, for revenge, but opened your great heart,
And took me to its shelter.   Oh ! complete
The good.   Forgive him, too, whose hand hath struck
This love's dear temple down ; for, on my soul,
You were his world.

LADY GRACE (*gasping*).
       Entreat me not.   I—I—
Have pardoned.   Go, dear Alice—go.
            (ALICE *embraces her and exit*.)

GAOLER (*entering*).
              A person,
With the lord justice's pass, attends without
To see your ladyship.

LADY GRACE.
       My holy guide !
Pray him to enter.   (POMFRET *enters, disguised*.)
      Welcome, sir.   Hold—(*takes his hand*)—Here,
You may well claim my service.   Come you not
To speed my faint feet to that fairer shore

Where no night lives ?   Most welcome.
(Leads him to a seat.)
There's no need
To urge me now to pardon.   One by one
Each bitter thought hath parted from my soul.
And, for my poor betrayer—Harry—Harry—
Must I so name thee ?   O my worthiest friend,
See him, I pray you.   Say I forgave.   For him
Keep all your consolations ; yes—for he
Hath greater need, believe me.   Bid him recall
Our few and fleeting hours of happiness,
And shrine them in his heart, as men preserve
Some wondrous herb of healing ; for, I fear,
A voice that never rests may sometimes mix
With his life's music mournful knells, and so
The memory of those pleasant days shall be,
Perchance, a comfort to him—for I think
He loved me—once.

POMFRET (*discovering himself*).
Once, and for ever, Grace !
Yes, you may start from me—you cannot now
Unsay those gracious words.   For them alone
I lived.   What, would'st thou clasp my bloodstained
    hand—
Grow to the breast from which I spurned you ?   No—
I am no more your lord.
(Sits at her feet.)

LADY GRACE.
Harry, dear Harry !

POMFRET.
True.   A dear husband have I been, sweet Grace.
Blind, doting idiot !   I mistrusted you—
Aye, fooled and spell-bound by a glimmering lie,
Saw not the truth that sun-like blazed beyond ;
And, lest another eye should share its light,
Quenched all my glorious day !

LADY GRACE.
Alas ! alas !

We sought for vengeance on each other's pride,
And have but mocked ourselves.   We have made war,
Like traitors, 'gainst love's sacred majesty
And high selected throne ; scoffed at his gifts—
Made poison of his sweet, his wholesome fruit—
Turned all his good to wrong.   We merit not
His knowledge—the more blest that we, for this
Brief moment, may enjoy his free delight,
Better, far better than a thousand lives,
Tortured by frigid fear !

POMFRET.
　　　　　It should be precious :
Know'st thou the price, my love ?

LADY GRACE (*eagerly*).
　　　　　But that mine hours
Are told, how sweet the travail were to bring
This late-found knowledge to its full fruition !
How happy—were it not ?—to note each cloud
Die from our heaven, and things of monstrous mien
Cower and dissolve beneath the simple spell
Of frank interrogation !   Why that deed ?
That glance of unbelief? or that cold word ?
Or that long absent day ?   So should love glean
Out of its former weakness, strength to live—
Aye, grow immortally.   O phantom bliss !
A new, bright world is born into my view,
And death leaps up between !

POMFRET.
　　　　　What—didst thou think
I came for this ?   To picture forth the joys
Thou shalt not taste ?   To snatch a short farewell,
And from thy martyr-scaffold bear my shame
Back to the world—a vile and loathed thing—
Who for a puny spite, not worth the name—
Nor with the spur—of vengeance, and to draw
In selfish age, a sick abhorred breath,

Betrayed your summer life ?   No, no, my Grace—
I had a nobler task.   My mission is
Of life !

LADY GRACE.
Of life ! Ah, Harry.   To retread
Our erring footsteps !

POMFRET (*eagerly*).
Life hath many bonds.

LADY GRACE.
Greater than love ?

POMFRET.
Yes, in endurance, sweet.
Love pays the price of contact with the world,
And so must perish with the perishing clay
That did inspire it.   If its great hope lives,
'Tis worship, reverence—but not love.

LADY GRACE (*falls on his breast*).
Love here,
And hope hereafter !   Who would more ?

POMFRET (*suddenly*).
God help me
I must not trifle longer.   Hark ! my Grace ;
Believe you I could ransom your sweet life
With gold ?   No, no !   Yon fiendish judge, I tell you
He is a tiger— thou, too dear a prey
To rend from out his closing fangs, without
A price most fearful.   Prayers he met with sneers.
I proffered riches,—he asked blood.   " 'Tis vain,
Examples were required.   Give him a prisoner,
Thy mate in birth, in name,—thou'rt free."   I grasped
The bloody terms—

LADY GRACE (*recoiling*).
Man ! and the victim ?

POMFRET (*falls at her feet*).

Here!

LADY GRACE (*staggers towards the door*).
And you believe that—never—

POMFRET.
It is too late.
Thank God, too late ! I was arraigned—was tried—
Witnesses called—my own confession heard—
All the scant needs of law were fully met
And satisfied. Without a pause, condemned,
I passed, as 'twere from life to death. But lo !
I have gained the prize I sought for, and my blood
Throws wide thy prison-gates. Look, dearest wife,—
(*Shows a parchment.*)
The judge kept faith with me ; moreover, made
Myself the bearer of this joy. All's well !
I am the prisoner now, and you are free !
Dost thou not understand me yet ? Come, love,
I wait to read in those mild eyes, that yet
They hold me worth regard. I do not now
Refuse thy pardon. Fold thine arms about me,—
Forgive me ; dost thou, Grace ?
(*She leans upon his breast.*)
It is enough.
Ho, there ! come forth, thou janitor, and set
This noble prisoner free.   (*Gaoler enters.*)
Let fall thy bars.
What dost thou stay for ? Ah, the warrant ! Hold !
Not yet content ? I am thy captive, man ;
But this—this lady—

GAOLER.
Madam, I am grieved
If the stern purport of this parchment comes

R 2

Indeed unlooked for.   You are *both* to die,—
And on the coming morn.

LADY GRACE.

All's well, my Harry.
(*Scene closes.*)

———

SCENE V.—*Night.   Exterior of the Prison.*

(MORGRAVE *enters, wandering to and fro.*)

MORGRAVE.

Is that the dawn?   Not yet.   And thou art caged,
My bird that sung so proudly !   Why, what change
A three days' prison sojourn must have wrought
In your triumphant modulations !   Thou,
Coy darling ! wouldst not brook this loving hand
About thy waist, and lo ! a brutal hangman
Girds thee with chains.   You barred against me, once,
Your sumptuous gates ; and now, ten feet of stone
Is all thy palace.   You disdained my clasp,—
Fire shall embrace thee.   Grace, mine enemy,
Proud as thou wert—poor wench,—I pity thee !
Thou lov'dst, I think, this being.   It grows chill.
(*Wraps his cloak round him, and cowers down.*)
Will the day never come ?   From tower to tower
A gleam skips stealthily,—some truant, crept
Abroad before its time.   She's wakening now
From dream-afflicted slumber, and recoils
As the grim spectre grows to life, and now
Stands weltering in her view.   She shrieks.   Ah, ha !
Pet child of fortune, delicately nursed,
How like you the new wooer ?   Come, 'tis time.

How quick the day grows!—brightly too.   The guests
Draw toward the bridal banquet.   I'll be one.   (*Exit.*)

———

SCENE THE LAST.—*Approach to the Market-place,*
Dorchester.

> (*Crowds pass towards the place of execution.*
> *Guards and Officials, who are saluted with*
> *jeers and laughter; during which* KIRKE
> *enters with his guard.* TOM *is sauntering*
> *about as usual.*)

KIRKE (*dashing them roughly back*).
Come, sirs, enough of Dorset wit.   Stand back,
You that have tender brows.   Some chance may knock
    them
Against our halberts, look ye—

A MAN (*sulkily*).
                    Mayn't one speak?

KIRKE.
I've brained a better skull than yours, my friend,
For less.

ANOTHER.
Who's that, sir?

TOM (*carelessly*).
                    Not the cock you'd think.
A workman.

MAN.
Workman!

TOM.

　　　　　　　Aye, indeed, sir; driving
A dirty, spattering, and unwholesome trade.
That's Jeffreys' butcher.　　　　　　　　　*(Shout.)*
　　　　　　　Stand—uncover—see !
　　　　　　　(DE L'ISLE *and* ALICE *pass.*)

MAN.

How slow they tread !

TOM.

　　　　　　　Aye, sir.　'Tis feared he'll die
Untimely.　Here's more dainty feeding still!
　　　　　　　(POMFRET *and* LADY GRACE *enter.*)

MAN.

They bear a noble countenance; and yet
The sun shines fairly.　Should I e'er be hanged,
Give me a storm.　She smiles, too.　Nay, sir, surely
She is reprieved!

TOM.

　　　　　　　Right, sir; reprieved she is—
Out of this bloody world.　I think—　Nay, pass;
　　　　　(*To* MORGRAVE, *who enters, and attempts to pass.*)
Here's room.　Ha, carrion-bird !

MORGRAVE (*grasping his arm*).
　　　　　　　　　　　Would you betray me ?
Be silent, Tom—dear fool.　I'll pay thee.　Yes,
If I have beaten thee, 'twas but in sport,
And I'll repay thee.　Though I look so poor,
These rags may cover gold.　I never yet
Saw one I hated die!

POMFRET.
　　　　　　　Sweet,—courage.　We
Leave fear behind !

LADY GRACE (*clinging to him*).
　　　　　　　It is not fear.　But, look !

That face—that fiendish face!—I thought I had
Forgiven all; but I—I—

POMFRET (*to* MORGRAVE).
      Poor, base wretch!
Thy presence scarce hath power to kindle scorn.
Rage is not for the dying, and revenge
Is God's.   Your hate a moment hath prevailed,
Only in mightier and eternal bonds,
To knit our souls together.   Live!   Thank God,
E'en *that* we share not with thee!

MORGRAVE (*choking with rage*).
       There—*to death!*
   (*Enter* JEFFREYS, *escorted as usual.*)

JEFFREYS.
How now, sirs?   What delay is this?   Pass on,—
Force a clear passage.   Knock me down that knave
That strives—   Why, may I ne'er taste bread if that
Is not my friend—mine ancient—truant William,—
William the slippery!   Ho, Master Marshal!
Arrest that man.   Away there!
   (MORGRAVE *is dragged off.   Enter Officer, with
    messenger.*)
       Well, sir, now?

OFFICER.
One from Lord Feversham, my lord, sent in
To stay the execution.   He demands—

JEFFREYS.
He doth!   Upon your word?   Stand by; let's see
This asking gentleman.   Your letters.   None?
Put him aside.   (*Another messenger.*)

MARSHAL.
    My lord, a second, wearing
The badge of Feversham.

JEFFREYS.
                    My noble friend!
I do respect his lordship much; but here's
A higher call than courtesy.   Put him
Aside too.   Have they reached—

MARSHAL.
                    Another rider,—
The king's, my lord.   See, they fall back.   My lord,
The king's—

JEFFREYS.
Why, man, I see him not.

MARSHAL.
                                        My lord,
This way!   (*Loud shouts.*)

JEFFREYS.
          Foiled—foiled!   What meddling fiend hath lent
Him wings?
          (*Enter* LORD FEVERSHAM *with a King's Cou-
                    rier.   Prisoners guarded as before, crowd fol-
                    lowing.*)

FEVERSHAM.
          Your lordship's incredulity
Had nearly wrought a murder.   Will you read
This missive?

JEFFREYS.
          Tell us first, my lord, what witch
Gave you her broomstick hither?

FEVERSHAM.

                    By your leave,
The pardon first.   'Tis here.   Now mark him, sirs;
Mark him, I tell you.   Here's a curious study,—
The tiger baulked of blood.   He grinds his teeth,—

Puckers his terrible brow—   Why, lo ! he smiles !
What ! have I wronged this man ?   Can pity touch
That soul of adamant ?   Hark

JEFFREYS.

Master Marshal, (*writes on a paper.*)
Hang these fifteen to-morrow ; twelve o' Wednesday,—
And the last score on Friday noon.   Now, sirs,
For Bristol.

(*Exeunt* JEFFREYS *and train.   Curtain falls.*)

THE END.

NOTES.

Note A. Page 173. Tory Tom.

A Dorsetshire clown, known by this appellation, has been honoured with a place in the records of those times. His character—as far as history (which, as in the case of greater men, has been rather sketchy in its portraiture) has depicted it—seems to have been a mixture of cunning and boldness; for the latter of which qualities, at least, the Dorset folk are remarkable.

Note B. Page 193.

Indisposed as Jeffreys already was to mercy, an incident which occurred during his western progress had like to have driven away its veriest shade. A riot and alarm arising, in which the judge was, or believed himself to be, in some personal peril, he declared at parting that "not a man of all those parishes that were of that vicinitude, if found guilty, should escape."—WOOLRYCH.

Note C. Page 196.

" He (Jeffreys) made all the west an Aceldama, some places quite depopulated, and nothing to be seen in them but forsaken walls, unlucky gibbets, and ghostly carcases. The trees were loaden almost as thick with quarters as leaves; the houses and steeples covered as close with heads as at other times frequently in that country with crows or ravens.

Nothing could be liker hell than all those parts; nothing so like the devil as he. Caldrons hissing, carcases boiling, pitch and tar sparkling and glowing, blood and limbs boiling, and tearing, and mangling; and he the great director of all, and, in a word, discharging his place who sent him, the best deserving to be the king's late chief justice then, and chancellor after, of any man that breathed since Cain or Judas."—RALPH.

NOTE D. Page 211.

William Gatchell, a constable, had been compelled to execute a warrant for bringing provisions to Monmouth's army, on pain of having his house destroyed, etc., and was sent to gaol as an accomplice! "Unfortunately," as the historian says, " he had the courage to plead ' not guilty ' " *Of course,* the jury convicted him, and he, with another, equally innocent, was hanged the following day. Gatchell was a "very decided character,"—for, as he went to execution, he looked upon the Taunton men very calmly, and said, " *A populous town, God bless it !*"

NOTE E. Page 212.

The Lady Alicia de l'Isle was judicially murdered, at the age of seventy, in the manner recorded in the State Trials, vol. xi.

Jeffreys' whole conduct and demeanour throughout this proceeding (trial it was not) are excellently characteristic of the man.

Having obtained a verdict (alike unwarranted by law or by the evidence adduced) from a timid jury—" If I had been among you, and she had been *my own mother !*" exclaimed Jeffreys, "I would have found her guilty ; " and he ordered her to be burned the same afternoon.

In conformity, however, with a broad hint from the judge, a certain mode of application for a respite was successful, during which brief interval the sentence was changed to decapitation. One thousand pounds had been offered to Lord Feversham if he should succeed in saving the aged prisoner.

NOTE F. Page 218.

" It must be confessed that he (Jeffreys) began a system of corruption on this circuit, to say the least, and being himself originally without an estate, now spared no means of acquiring one."—WOOLRYCH.

NOTE G. Page 227.

" Having plotted that the king should give some token of acceptance in respect of his services—[qy. *to come.*]—on the morning of his expedition, he had a ring fresh from the royal finger. . . . This ring was called the *bloodstone.*"—WOOLRYCH.

Note H.   Page 230.

The court was hung entirely with scarlet cloth ; "a colour," says a writer, " suitable to such a succeeding bloody tragedy."

Note I.   Page 230.

" Gentlemen,—I am, by the mercy of God, come to this great and populous city. . . . I find here are a great many auditors who are very intent, as if they expected some formal or prepared speech ; but, assure yourselves, we come not to make neither set speeches nor formal declamations, nor to follow a couple of puffing trumpeters; for, Lord! we have seen these things twenty times before; no—we come to do the king's business. . . . But I find a special commission is an unusual thing here, and relishes very ill,—nay, the very women storm at it, for fear we should take the upper hand of them too; for, by the bye, gentlemen, *I hear it is much in fashion in this city for the women to govern and bear sway."—Charge to Bristol jury.*

Note K.   Page 236.

The story of Jeffreys' attempted escape, his seizure, and subsequent death in the tower, at the early age of forty-one, are matters of history. *Some* portion, at least, of the censure which has been bestowed upon the vice and cruelty which marked his career, should attach to the harsh and profligate temper of his times.

THE

WITCH-WIFE:

A TALE OF MALKIN TOWER.

𝔄 Drama,

IN FIVE ACTS:

*(As produced at the Theatre Royal, Marylebone, May 1849,
under the direction of Mr. Ellis, Stage-manager.)*

PREFACE.

The 'Witch-Wife,' though including one or two characters of some notoriety, is based upon no circumstances of actual occurrence ; neither was it suggested,
as has been alleged, by my friend Mr. Ainsworth's
'Lancashire Witches,'—a work I had purposely denied
myself the pleasure of perusing, lest the stirring scenes it
could not fail to embody should exercise an influence
destructive, at least, of the originality, however bene-
ficial to the dramatic interests of the piece.

To any who desire a further acquaintance with the
notorious Matthew Hopkins, or insight into the grotesque
horrors practised at the period of the witch persecutions,
the State Trials and Somers' Tracts will afford abundant
information, and at the same time prove that nothing in
the following pages is unjustifiably farcical.

DRAMATIS PERSONÆ.

SIR GERALD MOLE (*a Country Knight*) . . . . Mr. J. H. RAY.
MARCHMONT NEEDHAM . . Mr. DAVENPORT.
ANTONY GABB, ⎫
HARRY MARTYN, ⎬ *Country Gentlemen* ⎰ Mr. CRAVEN.
VAUGHAN, ⎭ ⎱ Mr. WHEATLEIGH. / Mr. MORRIS.
MATTHEW HOPKINS (*the Witch-finder*) . . . . . Mr. J. JOHNSTONE.
STERN (*his Follower*) . . . Mr. MORRISON.
GAYRE, ⎫ *Judges* . . ⎰ Mr. TINDELL.
HOWLETT, ⎭ ⎱ Mr. H. LEE.
CONSTABLE . . . . . Mr. MORLAND.
OFFICER . . . . . Mr. MAURICE.
COUNTRYMAN . . . . Mr. HANCE.
GAOLER . . . . . Mr. BOWEN.

CECIL HOWARD (*Niece of* SIR GERALD) . . . . Mrs. MOWATT.
MISTRESS FRILL (*her Governess*) . Mrs. E. YOUNG.
ALISON DEVISE . . . . Mrs. J. JOHNSTONE.
MAGGIE . . . . . MISS FEIST.

Country People, Officers, etc.

A.D. 1634.

ACT I.

SCENE I.—*Library in Pendell Manor.* Sir Gerald
Mole *at a table covered with books, etc. A large black
board is suspended on the wall, with geometrical
figures, etc. A crowd of rustics at the lower end of
the room, among whom is seen* Alison Devise, *as a
prisoner in charge of* Stern *and another.* Sir
Gerald *appears absorbed in study.*

Constable (*aside to* Stern).
Come, this won't do. Accost him, Master Stern ;
Assault him with your wonted eloquence ;
Make a speech, Master Stern.

Stern (*slowly and gravely*).
Ahem !

Sir Gerald (*abstracted*).
From A
To B C D, draw three straight lines—

Constable (*aside*).
Old dunce !
He's still at his alphabet.

Stern (*loudly*).
Ahem !

Sir Gerald (*starting*).
Who's there ?
Heav'n give me patience ! There's the thread o' the work
For the fifth time snapt short. Will nothing, sirs,
Deserve of ye some daily hours of peace ?
Go, patch your quarrels in the buttery :

I ne'er knew village feud that would not yield
To the mild persuasion of a can of ale.
Ho! there, the cellarer.

STERN.
Stop.

SIR GERALD.
Well, man, speak.

CONSTABLE (*bustling forward*).
An't please your worship, *I* will.   Master Stern
Has been at school, and learned the worth of words;
He's like a ship provisioned with parched peas
Doled singly by the niggard steward.   This
Old dame's charged, on suspicion, with bewitching
Dame Pepper's old dun cow.

SIR GERALD (*studying*).
' *Which is absurd—*'
But if, as was proposed, the angle B—

CONSTABLE (*hastily*).
Sir, if your worship—

SIR GERALD.
Oh, aye!   Well, old woman,
Can you rebut this evidence?   Go, sirrah,
Call Master Marchmont Needham.   He's a scholar,
Learned in the law.   Aye, there's more sense, I tell'you,
Under his curling love-locks than resides
In twenty ermined frizzle-wigs.   He's here.
(*Enter* MARCHMONT NEEDHAM.)
Marchmont, good day.

NEEDHAM.
Good morrow, my good friend.
News reached me that our village casuists
Had broached a theory of more painful proof
Than those which in this learned page you know

So well to deal with, and I hastened on
To offer aid.

SIR GERALD.
Thanks! thanks!
(*Returns eagerly to study.*)

NEEDHAM.
The matter, friends?

CONSTABLE (*aside to* STERN).
Speak, speak, man!

STERN.
Witches—

NEEDHAM (*impatiently*).
Nonsense!

STERN.

Law—

NEEDHAM (*sits*).
We'll hear
The case, then.   Who complains?
(*Countryman steps forward.*)
What, Master Phinn!
You don't seem pinched or withered in the flesh.
What have *you* suffered?

COUNTRYMAN (*scratching his head*).
Nawthing.

NEEDHAM (*frowning.*)
What do you charge
'Gainst this poor woman?   Out with it.

COUNTRYMAN (*with much hesitation*).
Well, master,
She squints—God sain us!

Needham.

           Master Phinn, amen!
And put some brains in that disfurnished hut,
Thy noddle. Get you gone. But, in Heav'n's name,
Is not this monstrous? Some one hath a sheep
Sick of the giddies, or a hog of the mumps,—
A girl of the sullens, or a boy of the school,
And the first grandame that comes halting by,
Hath done't of fiendish mischief! Where's your proof,
Or witness?

Stern.

    Ducking?

Needham.

       Out, you ruffian!

Sir Gerald (*looking up*).

                         Stay.
Marchmont, this must be looked to; let's proceed
With caution. I'm a justice of the peace,
And sworn to thwart the devil. Master Stern,
Your charge?

Needham (*to* Stern).

      Well, sir? If she's a witch, *you* seem
Possessed by a dumb devil. Where's your tongue?

Stern (*producing a letter*).

There!

Needham (*examining it*).

     'Tis a scroll, Sir Gerald, to say truth,
Nor over clean nor clerkly; but withal
Scratched in a bold, black, earnest hand enough,
And superscribed to you.

Sir Gerald.

      Ha! read it, Marchmont.

NEEDHAM (*reads*).
" My service to your worship presented. I have this
day received a letter to come to a place called Pendell
Forest, to search for evil-disposed persons called witches.
I much marvel such evil members should have any to
take their parts—"

SIR GERALD (*uneasily*).
Who takes their parts ?   Not I.

NEEDHAM.
Shall I conclude ?
" I intend to give your precinct a visit suddenly; for I
would certainly know whether it affords many sticklers
for such cattle, or willing to give us good welcome and
entertainment : for so shall we work without control, and
likewise with thanks and recompense. So I humbly take
my leave, and rest your worship's servant to command.—
MATTHEW HOPKINS."

(*As he reads the name, a movement of terror
among the country people.*)

SIR GERALD.
Ha! Is *he* coming? Then I warn ye'all,
Burn every broomstick, say your prayers straightforward,
And get to bed betimes.   He'll find you out,
If there's a witch among ye.

NEEDHAM.
And if not,
He'll make one.

SIR GERALD (*doubtingly*).
Marchmont, 'tis a gifted man.
He comes not purposeless.   I think—I—eh—
We must commit this prisoner ?

NEEDHAM.
You will hear
The charge first ?

SIR GERALD.
Aye, that's fair.

NEEDHAM (*aside to a villager*).
Hark, little Maggie!
Seek Mistress Cecil.   (*Exit* MAGGIE.)
Master Stern, your speech,
Condensed and pithy though it be, scarce guides
Judgments not preinformed.   A trifle more
Detail, sir.

STERN (*points to a coffer held by* CONSTABLE.)
There !   (*Enter* CECIL, *running.*)

CECIL.
O, what a race !   Dear uncle,
Lend me your watch.   Quick !   I gave Mistress Frill
Once round the pleasance, where we walked, to *you,*
And beat her by—a minute.   Here she comes !
Dear lady !   Tired, ma'am ?
(*Offers chair to* MISTRESS FRILL, *who enters
panting and disordered.*)

MISTRESS FRILL.
Ah—oh—fie—girl !

SIR GERALD.
Cecil!

CECIL.
Don't knit your brows.   You know I hate it.   Come !
I've told you that before.

MISTRESS FRILL (*lifting her hands*).
Miss Cecil—child !
You make my blood run cold.

CECIL (*aside*).
It never did
Aught else.

Mistress Frill.
    Is this my teaching?   Lack-a-day !
Go stand in the corner till you've learned to give
Your elders reverence.

Sir Gerald.
        Come, come, Mistress Frill !
She's not a child, good lady.   Here, wild thing,
Sit down by me.   We'll make a pretty twain—
Justice and Mercy.   How shall we dispose
These evil-doors ?

Cecil.
    Give them a crown apiece,
And send them home.

Sir Gerald.
Nay—but—

Cecil.
        Another word,
And Mercy quits the bench.   You'll be my clerk,
Good Master Needham.   (*To* Sir Gerald.)
    You, sir, will be dumb ;
For Justice acts, not chatters.

Stern.
    Hold !

Cecil.
        Heyday !
Pray who are you ?

Stern.
Stern.

Cecil.
    Mercy will be sterner,
If you don't find your tongue.

CONSTABLE (*sulkily*).
        Madam, my lady!
(Since 't is his worship's pleasure you should hear)—
We've brought a witch for judgment.

CECIL.
        Witch! What? Where?
Old? bearded? bent? with imp and broomstick, all
Complete?

CONSTABLE (*to* ALISON).
      Stand forth there, prisoner. You, young lady,
Beware her evil eye.

CECIL (*starting up*).
       I'll risk the—*That!*
Why, that's my nurse, man, Alison Devise!
Good, patient, loving, dear old Alison!
Man, ere her years had half attained to thine,
More deeds of love and Christian charity
Stood to her count, than there are white hairs now
On her poor forehead. Alison, a witch?
Then I'm a witchling!

SIR GERALD.
       Eh! why,—eh! 'tis she.
That's certain—isn't it? For they tell us that
Witches sometimes change feature. Well, well, well—
Why didn't you speak, old woman?

ALISON (*curtseying*).
       There was nought
To answer, please you. These good gentlemen
Were so resolved, I feared, sir, I might be
A witch, and didn't know it.

CONSTABLE.
       That won't do.
Produce the image, Master Stern. We kept
One horrid witness back, hoping to spare

Your worship's tender heart, and this poor lady,
Whom—shame to yonder evil-hearted hag!—
It doth affect more nearly.   'Tis a form
In wax, shaped like the lady Cecil, doomed
To devilish tortures, which, by wizard arts,
Reach to the living copy.   First we lit

(Opens the coffer.)

On these.   Item, one broom, one kitten (lame),
Sundry glass beads, six ringlets of fine hair,
And fifteen pins, some crooked.   Next we came
To this most terrible object.   (Produces an image.)

CECIL.

Ha! ha! ha!

Dear Master Constable, I thank your zeal,
That, from this good old creature's drawer of treasures,
Has rummaged—my first doll!

ALISON.

And 'tis as like

Your little cherub face, at three years old,
As sister-peas.   God bless ye both!   That's why
I kept it.

NEEDHAM (*rising*).
Master Stern and constables,
'Gainst this poor soul three things are proven.   First,
She squints; second, loved babes; third, hath a kitten
Goes on three legs.   She is discharged.

SIR GERALD.

But stay;

To make all sure, we will impound the doll,
And pop the cat i' the cistern.   So, be off;
And, all whose conscience tingles, mend your doings,
For hither comes Mat Hopkins, Satan's foe;
One who has brought more witches to the pyre
Than I have tongue to number.   Some of ye
See the poor woman to her home in safety;
And—   (*All shrink from her.*)
        How's this?   All afraid?

CECIL.
                    I'll guard her, uncle.
Come Alise, lean on me.   Do as I bid you.
Lean all your weight.   Aye, so.

NEEDHAM (*aside*).
                    Heaven bless thee, child!
Lovely thou art, but glorious charity,
With skill surpassing nature, paints thee now
With tints of heavenly origin : I'll not
Spoil thy good deed by sharing ; yet I may
Humbly precede, and smoothe the hallowed way.
                    (*Exeunt.*)

CONSTABLE (*as they go out*).
Well, what says Master Stern, the magpie ?

STERN.
                    Wait.
                    (*Exeunt.*)

———

SCENE II.—*A glade in Pendell Forest.   Evening.*

(*Enter* ANTHONY GABB, MARTYN *and* VAUGHAN.

GABB.
I tell you, we're too many.   What the deuce
Brought you *both* poking hither ?

MARTYN (*laughing*).
        This ! (*waving a paper*).   No pheasant
Was ever snared with verse.   If you're in love,
Don't be ashamed on't !   Tell us, like a man ;
'Tis but a young disorder, like the chin-cough,

Best early caught, and done with ; but delayed—
As I live, here's another !
            (*Runs to a tree and snatches off a paper which
            GABB tries in vain to obtain.*)

                VAUGHAN.
                    And besides,
Some dogs hunt best in couples.   Here is Martyn !
Now, were not *I*—a sober gentleman,
Of staid and shrivelled reputation, by,
To check his frolic-passion—

                MARTYN.
                    What you promise,
Might have brought half the county.   Hem !   Let's see.
                            (*Reads.*)

        Glances that, if they did not please,
            Would sure with terror fray us—
        Fair suns—or blue-cold spheres that freeze ;
            Comets flashed fresh from chaos.

                VAUGHAN.
Right—your stale comet's not worth a bulrush.   On—

                MARTYN (*reads*).

        Lips like a rosebud, newly cleft—
            Ripe as an autumn plum—
        Whereon some lovesick bee has left
            Its honey and its hum.

                VAUGHAN.
Its *hum ?*   What, does she buzz ?

                GABB.
                    No—to say truth,
I lacked a rhyme.

                    MARTYN.
            B   "*hum ?*"   Critics might say
had a bee in her b   .net.   Sir, that hum's

A humbug—cut it out.   So, then, 'tis here
The spirit wanders ?

GABB.
Sometimes two.

MARTYN.
Eh !   *Two ?*
In ghosts and women, all the interest
Ends with the individuality.
I'm off.

GABB.
I see a shadow.   Steal apart !
Disperse—disperse !
(*They retire aside, as* MARCH. NEEDHAM *enters.*)

NEEDHAM.
All's clear enough.   Poor souls
The very name of Matthew Hopkins scares them
Like conies to their burrows.   I'll watch here
Till she has passed—then follow.
(*Retires.* GABB *advances, and stealing round
grasps him.*)

GABB.
Stalking deer ?
What sport, sir ?

NEEDHAM.
Master Gabb !   What do *you* here,
Alone ?   Indulgence in great thoughts, not doomed
To find their issue in heroic deeds,
Is robbery of the world, sir.   You're a thief—
I apprehend you.   Come with me.

GABB.
First tell me
What is *your* object here ?

NEEDHAM.
I, sir, attend
Sweet nature's vespers.

GABB.
So do the frogs.   I hear them!

NEEDHAM.
And, lingering in these dells, could dream—

GABB.
No doubt.
But *I*, most learned and poetic Marchmont,
Am very much awake.   Never tell me—
You care as much for vistas, towers, and trees,
As donkeys do for diamonds.   What's the matter?
Who's that parting the boughs?

NEEDHAM.
By Heaven, 'tis he!
'Tis the witch-finder, Hopkins—a bold knave,
Bankrupt in virtue as in wealth; and apt
For any deed—as who can nothing lose
In either.

GABB.
Savage brute!   He treads as though
He'd grind the very turf to powder—ugh!
(*Enter* MATTHEW HOPKINS *and two followers.*)

HOPKINS.
This path, they told us, led to the old squire's den;
But I don't—   Soft you, here are natives.   Well,
Masters, what's stirring hereabouts?

GABB (*aside to* NEEDHAM).
That's cool.

NEEDHAM.
A squirrel on that bough, sir, cracked just now

Afilbert—that proved sour. By yonder stile
There lies a weasel, simulating slumber;
But he's a cheat, I take it.

HOPKINS.
                    Sir, you're pleased
To be facetious. I demand what's new
In these wood-ways?

NEEDHAM.
                    Why, nothing, sir. That is,
The devil writes farces, and mankind enact them.
As for ourselves, we kneel, and, in bright eyes,
See future fertile acres—buy and sell
Pigs, oxen, and each other—backbite, jest,
Get drunk, and sober. 'Tis, in truth, the world's
Accustomed chaos—needing one rogue more,
With good, bold vices, to bind in the whole—
And that want's furnished. (*Aside.*)

HOPKINS.
                              Will this present path
Lead us to Pendell Manor?

NEEDHAM (*aside*).
                              Not if I
Can help it. (*Aloud*) No, sir.

HOPKINS.
                              Know you an old hag,
One Alison Devise?

NEEDHAM.
                    The honest soul
Dwells yonder.   (*Pointing.*)

HOPKINS (*grinning*).
Honest, eh, Paul?

Follower (*gruffly*).
                                        Humph !

Needham (*aside*).
                                        I'll lead
These gentlemen a dance.   Well, sirs, for love
Of such society, I'll be your guide
To hut and manor both.   Come, master Gabb,
Go with us.

Gabb (*aside to him*).
            Hang me if I do.   Just leave
Your friend in some convenient ditch, and earn
The county's thanks.
            (*Exeunt* Needham, Hopkins, *and followers.*)
Now, Anthony Gabb, sit down,   (*Sits.*)
And listen.   Sir, should fortune, yet untired
Of lavishing fair opportunities
On such a recreant knave—bring that sweet soul
Across your vision—try, sir, to reflect
That legs were given for nobler ends than that
Of simply taking flight ; that tongues should speak,
And lips— Confound this fellow !   (*Re-enter* Martyn.)

Martyn.
                                        Still alone ?
Why, where's the nymph ?

Gabb (*sulkily*).
                                        Not come.

Martyn.
                                        How's that? I saw her
Approaching, through the trees.

Gabb (*starts up*).
                                        The deuce you did !
Good night.   It's getting late.

MARTYN.
What, don't you want
To meet her?

GABB.
Ye-e-s—I *did*—but now,—

MARTYN (*laughing*).
She's here!
Stand, or she'll think you're drunk.

GABB.
I wish I were.
No man's afraid in his cups.

MARTYN.
Then counterfeit—
You'll do it to the life.

GABB.
Good thought! I will—
But stand beside me.
(*They retire.   Enter* CECIL, *leading* ALISON
DEVISE.)

ALISON.
Fie on this drear place!
And on those aches that force me drag my weight
Of years, so tardily.   Now must thou return
With those poor feet threading the long, dank grass,
That teems with agues.   Well, wit comes with age,
And soon you'll hate me.   They'll compel you.   I'm
An old witch, am I?

CECIL.
Come, be calm, dear Alise.
If I believed them, I must pity.   Now
You've love and pity both. What creature's this?
Ah! 'tis my mute adorer—but bewitched,
And *talking!*

(Re-enter GABB, *stumbling as if drunk.   He reels
against a tree.)*

GABB.
Sir, I really beg your pardon.
'Twas awkward.   I ne'er saw you, till my nose
Struck yours.   Why, what a labyrinth is here !
Nettles and briers !   Where's my brother-owl ?
Oh, here you come, you mouser !   *(Re-enter* MARTYN.)

MARTYN.
Whither now ?
Madam, excuse him,—a poor, harmless soul,
When he's not drunk.   Come on, sir.

GABB.
Drunk, sir ! drunk ?
Have you the—ears—to say so ?   This fair dame—
This grandame of the wood-nymphs—shall be judge.
Fair Dryad, am I drunk ?
(Falls on his knees before ALISON.)

ALISON.
He ! he !—He seems
A merry gentleman !   Stand up.   Poor thing !
'Tis very much o'erta'en.

CECIL.
Away—nurse—come.

ALISON.
I am ready, darling.

GABB.
Darling !—A sweet word. *(Sits down.)*
A frank avowal !   All my spirit owns
The sweet intoxication.   I—I choose
The sitting posture, having thus my legs
More, as it were, beneath us.   Now would men

Dwell in revolving tickets, *thus*, thatched roofs
Would soon be deemed luxurious.

MARTYN (aside to him).

       Courage. Speak
To your goddess, man, or leave her.

GABB (aside).

       'Faith, I dare not.
Look at that eye. By heaven, its glances seem
To thread one, and pass on.

MARTYN.

      Sharp vision, truly!
Madam, 'tis late, and these are no safe paths
For such fair pilgrims. Will you accept our escort?
We'll leave you at your pleasure.

CECIL.

      Go, then, *now*.
And for this gay, convivial gentleman,
Whose sin of drunkenness, I fain would hope,
Is no accustomed guise—so awkwardly
It sits upon him—take him with you. Look,
He's marvellously sobered!

GABB (aside).

      'Faith, she's right.

MARTYN.

We are both fools, and I the greater. Come,
There's comfort for thee. Heaven be with you, madam,
The field being lost, I yield it, and retire,
A wise commander, sending, as you see,
My heavier baggage forward. (*Exit, pushing off* GABB.)

CECIL.

      It has grown
So dark ! Lean harder, Alise,—I can bear
More than you think. How strange ! If I were one

T

To harbour gloomy prescience, I could deem
Some dark, unwonted, evil influence
Sat brooding o'er this wood.
> (*As they are going out, re-enter* HOPKINS *and
> followers, meeting them.*)

HOPKINS.
                    A pretty guide !
I never knew a fellow could discourse
In words of twenty syllables, like him,
Worth a cock's feather.

FOLLOWER.
        He deceived us.

HOPKINS.
                          Ha !
If I were sure of that—   Hallo ! here's game,—
Whirr ! *two* birds flushed together !

FOLLOWER.
                    Chick and hen.

HOPKINS (*catching* ALISON *as they try to pass*).
Stop, neighbour, not so fast.   A word with you.

CECIL (*agitated*).
What do you want?

HOPKINS.
        Why, firstly, child, to see
From what red, pretty rustic lip proceeds
So musical a query.

CECIL (*throws up her head with dignity.*)
        There, sir.   Back,
And leave me room to pass.

HOPKINS (*admiringly*).
        Eh !   By these hilts,

But you're a beauty !   No clown-architect
Built that brow's arch, I take it !   You may go,
Young lady,—I have no right to stay you ; but
This ancient fowl comes of another nest,
And I must hear her singing.

CECIL.
Sir—

HOPKINS (*laughing*).
Don't be
So haughty, little madam.   I am charged
To hunt up certain witches hereabout ;
Among them (where's the paper ?—here 'tis)—humph—
Among them (*reads*) one, " called Alison Devise,—
An ancient gentlewoman, rather lame,
Owning a slight obliquity of vision."
Hum !   " Causes of suspicion," hum ! ah ! " old,
Dwells in the forest, keeps a cat, hates beer,
Refused to kill a toad " (her imp, of course),
" Keeps a wax image" (vicious hag !), "prescribes
For cows in mortal sickness " (hum !), " which die."
Here's proof on proof.   Stand from before her, madam ;
Down hood, old girl,   If you're not *she*, I'll eat you,
Tough as you are, unsalted.   (*Tears off her hood.*)
Seize the witch !
I told you so.

CECIL.
Let her alone.   Stand back.
Sir, with your sex a woman's weakness is
Her best assurance.   *You*, it seems, would turn it
Against her as a weapon.   Where's your warrant
Thus to molest us,—none ?

HOPKINS.
That's soon repaired.
We will but ask this lady's company
To the next justice.

CECIL (*eagerly*).
                    That's Sir Gerald Mole,
My uncle, who, on full investigation
Of the rank follies that disgrace us here,
Has set her free already.

HOPKINS.
                    Humph !   Are you
Niece to that old curmudgeon—I—I mean
That learned and wealthy squire ?

CECIL.
                    What's that to the purpose ?
Yet, since you know me, sirs, in courtesy
Let us begone to-night, and take my pledge
That this poor soul be at the hall to-morrow,
There to abide your question.

HOPKINS.
                    No, fair lady;
You little know the malice of this kind.
We've stirred her venom now, and, ere the morn,
Backed by the devil, her lord, she'll scatter round
A tenfold mischief.   That is not my way
Of doing the work ; nor ever doth this hand
Loose its first gripe till the foul prey be brought
To that safe goal—the gallows !

CECIL.
                    She is innocent.
Heavens !   Can this be ?   It will not.   You relent—
You hesitate—

HOPKINS.
                    Not I.   Yet stay,—come nearer.
Don't be afraid.   Is—is your heart *much* set
On saving this old hag ?   Enough !—I'll do't
On one condition.

CECIL.
Well, sir, what ?

HOPKINS.

> A kiss.

CECIL.

Is the man drunk, or mad?

HOPKINS.

> Drunk, pretty one,

With love; and mad with fury if you baulk me.
You must be mine.   Tush!   I mean honestly.
We are alone, as 'twere, in the dark wood,
And you shall hear me what I list to speak,
And answer too.   I love you.

CECIL.

> *You!*

HOPKINS.

> Ev'n I.

No saucy glances,—no curled lips.   I warn you.
I am not that I seem.   I have a name
For courage, zeal, and sanctity.   I feel,
Within this rugged rind, a slumbering spell,
Awaiting but the charmer's voice to wake
Its fine and terrible action.   Girl, that voice,
That power, are *thine!*   I saw you, and my soul,
Never yet moved, shrank helpless.

CECIL (*faintly*).

> I—I pray you—

HOPKINS (*catching her*).

Stay—you must hear—must speak too,—for the game's
Begun, and must be played out *now*.   I love—
I love you, maiden!   I've no mincings, drawled
By feathered apes o' the world, but by this sword—
And that's a soldier's oath,—I'll woo you like
A soldier.

CECIL.

Will you?   Then begone, and know,

When you would practise on a woman's fears,
The true road to her heart—at least, to *mine*,—
Lies not through terror.

HOPKINS (*eagerly*).
The true road !

CECIL.
I'll not
Deceive you.   This is idleness.   To you,
And such as you, there's none.

HOPKINS (*furiously*).
Then (*checking himself*)
—stay,—so young,
And fair, and pitiless !   I was not always
The man you see me now.   My youth, stripped bare
Of all sweet subtleties that win mankind,
Was wasted in vain search for bliss.   At length,
I touch it, and 'tis ashes.

CECIL.
Am I free
To leave you now ?

HOPKINS.
You *are*, with this assurance,
That, as you scorn me, and reject my love,
So shall you find the hate you calmly dare,
As strong as love, but deadlier.   Our short strife,
Passed in the dull depths of the silent wood,
Revenge shall visit you within the gaze
Of gaping thousands, and before this sun—   (*Goes up.*)
Ho !   Michael,—Voules !
(*Followers advance with* ALISON.)

FOLLOWER.
Here, master.

HOPKINS.
Let her go.

FOLLOWER.

Eh?

HOPKINS.
Let her go, man.   Did your grandame never
Teach you 'twas wisdom to expend a sprat
To catch a grampus?   We have greater ends
To compass than are gathered in the grilling
This piece of parchment skin!

ALISON.
Heaven bless you, sir !
You're very kind.

HOPKINS.
Enough.   A witch's benisons
Are doubtful gifts.   (*Hesitatingly.*)   Madam, if I might
        touch
That hand,—mistake me not, the pact is made,—
Are we not foes ?

CECIL.
On that condition— (*Gives her hand.*)

HOPKINS.
Trust me,
I will fulfil it,—*to the death !*   Farewell.   (*Exeunt.*)

END OF ACT I.

ACT II.

SCENE I.—*Apartment in a Hunting Lodge, opening in the Forest.*

(*Enter* MARTYN *and* GABB.)

GABB.

I say again, I'm satisfied.   I say,
I've every reason to be no less pleased
Than flattered by such notice.   Why, you saw
Our meeting ?

MARTYN.
Plain enough.   If that meant *love*,
Heaven keep me from its tokens !

GABB.
I confess
My nymph is somewhat of the panther kind,
As stern as beautiful.

MARTYN.
A pleasant beast
For semblance—that accepts her love with growls
Below all vocal divings, and soft pats
Would smash a human occiput !   Come, come,
You're disappointed.   Own it.

GABB.
Not at all.
Last night I added to my calendar
A golden day.

MARTYN.
A what ?

GABB.
A golden day.
Those, sir, are golden days on which I hold
Converse with Mistress Cecil.

MARTYN.
So !   It seems
The ice is broken ?

GABB.
Not precisely.   She
Ne'er fails to greet me, but, to say truth, my tongue
Has, up to this time, steadfastly declined
Articulation.

MARTYN.
Then what passes ?

GABB.
This,—
" Ah, Master Gabb ! " or else, " Good morning, sir,"
Or, " Here's a fine day, Master Gabb ! "   For thus
(As though to keep me longer at her side)
She'll spin out commonplaces.   Sometimes 'tis
Most sweet, and graceful, and confiding, as,—
" Should you meet Goody Plumstick gathering wood,
Say that I have been at her cot, and left her what
Will cure her toothache."   These are golden days,
And so recorded.   Silver ones are those
On which we meet, but speak not ; and all else
Are of that blank complexion, that no base
Dishonoured metal's poor enough to note
Their sadness in.

MARTYN.
Why, then, in point of fact,
Your suit stands still ?

GABB.
Sir, on the contrary,
It flies—it rushes !   Hem !   (*Drops a paper.*)

MARTYN.
                    Holloa, there !   What !
                                        (*Snatches it up.*)
Another poem ?
                    GABB.
          Eh ?   Well, read.   I know
We are in honourable hands.

                    MARTYN (*reads*).
" He whose time-mellowed judgment, as is fit,
Holds passion reverence, and silence wit,—
He that hath love, hath courage, time, and power,
Should read the stars this night on Malkin Tower."
                                        And pray,
Where found you this mysterious bidding ?

                    GABB.
                                        Pinned,
Like a sweet postscript, to a loving scroll,
Whereon this teeming brain had lately spent
Some idleness in rhyme.

                    MARTYN.
          You'll go ?

          GABB (*gravely*).
                              I will.
Poor thing !   One can't do less, you know.

                    MARTYN.
                                        Perchance
Two can do more.   I'll go with you.

                    GABB.
                                        Why--eh !—
You see, she doesn't propose that—

                    MARTYN.
                                        As you will.
Only take care.

GABB.
Care !—eh ?

MARTYN.
                          You have no faith
In such things.   One in your lost state believes
In nothing but his mistress.

GABB.
                    Such things!   *What* things?

MARTYN.
Why, know you not that yonder Malkin Tower 's
A sort of witch-cathedral ?   All the hags
Of the district gather there to consecrate
Unholy sabbaths, raising, we may say,
In truth, the devil's own row,—since he himself
Presides there.   How's the moon ?   Why, as I live,
It is their very night—their storm—their revel—
Their St. Walpurga !

GABB.
                    Is it ?   Hang it now,
That's most unlucky !   Stay, I think I know
A counter-charm.   There's Matthew Hopkins !   I'll
To him at once, and bid him lay his nets
For a fine haul.

MARTYN.
                    A brilliant thought !   About it.
Why, there he passes.   After him at once !
The time draws on,—'tis noon already.

GABB.
                              No ! (*Exeunt.*)

SCENE II.—SIR GERALD'S *Study.*

(SIR GERALD *studying.*　CECIL.)

SIR GERALD.

Quod erat demonstrandum.　Wond'rous volume !
Thou philosophical magic !—mass of marvels !
How through thy clear, yet complex tracery
Of line and circle, mighty truths evolve,
And grow to life !　Why, pet !

CECIL (*starting, drops her book*).
Dear uncle !

SIR GERALD.
Come,

I've solved *my* problem, let's have yours.　It seems
The harder, love.　Why don't you talk ?

CECIL (*smiling*).
And spoil

Some great discovery ?

SIR GERALD (*gravely*).
You would not, Cecil.

Talk when you will, my child, I can resign
With ease the filmiest and most subtle thread
Of argument, and, when your voice has hushed
Its music, turn, old spider as I am,
To my unbroken meshes.　'Tis because
That happy spirit, like a hidden sun,
Is ever beaming on me.　So our blood
Runs its articulate course, dispensing life,
Vigour, and health through this wrought frame, the
　　while
The functions of the busy brain proceed,
And, feeling, heed it not.　Come, let me hear
Your voice.　Speak !　Ask !　Sometimes I cannot hold
Pace with your questions.

CECIL.
So I will.   Now listen.
Dear uncle, you are very learned?

SIR GERALD (*smiling*).
Indeed!
Who told you so?

CECIL.
But are you not?

SIR GERALD.
Well, well,—
A thing or so, perhaps.

CECIL.
Learned,—and kind,—
And just?

SIR GERALD.
I hope so, chick.

CECIL (*starts up and throws herself on his neck*).
You don't believe
Nurse Alison's a witch?   You don't believe
There's one in the wood,—in the county,—in the land?
In earth or heaven?   You, uncle, grave and wise,
Cannot yield up your great prerogative
Of reason, judgment, truth, to that wild dream,
Born of an idiot's fancy—nursed by knaves—
Insult to Nature, and to Nature's God,—
That hideous, writhing mockery of nothing,
That men call *witchcraft?*

SIR GERALD.
Soft—nay, soft, my child!
There, be composed ; I never saw you thus
Before.   These matters are too deep and strange
For your young judgment yet.   To Mistress Frill.
'Tis school-time, eh?

CECIL.
First, promise—

SIR GERALD.
What?

CECIL.
To give
No heed to any that shall seek to use
Your warrant, and the name of English law,
Against poor souls like Alison.

SIR GERALD.
Come, come,
What know you of these matters?

CECIL.
Till to-morrow—
That's but a day.

SIR GERALD.
I cannot promise, child.
I'm but a servant of the commonweal;
I trust to hear no more on't.

CECIL.
Wait, at least,
Till you've consulted Master Needham,

SIR GERALD.
I
Consult! Come, to your lessons! Stay, how dare you
Go without kissing me?

CECIL (*runs back and kisses him*).
There, there, remember! (*Exit.*)

SIR GERALD (*looking after*).
It's odd enough. I always thought, till now,
Dame Nature, through her fair gradations, glides

With step so slow and noiseless that no eye
Detects the stealthy movement.   Hitherto,
The babe we nurse on Monday is not much
Too big on Tuesday ; now, forsooth, it seems,
The world's received an impetus, a spur—
The toy we doat on goes to rest a child,
And rises *woman !*
                    (*Enter* HOPKINS *hastily;* STERN *follows.*)

HOPKINS.
            A fine dance, indeed !
High time I came among ye.   Here we've plumped
Into the heart of witchdom.   What d'ye say
To that, Sir Gerald ?

SIR GERALD (*abstracted*).
                    That, sir, if the bases
And altitudes of solid parallelograms
Be but reciprocally proportional,
The parallelopipeds are equal too.

HOPKINS.
'Tis most unanswerable. (*Aside*) The old fool !
As well accost a milestone.   Sir, I need
Your warrant to take certain rogues, suspect
Of devilish arts.   A warrant, and, perchance,
More power, to—

SIR GERALD.
Power, sir ?   Where's your lever ?

HOPKINS.
Lever ?

SIR GERALD.
Sir, the immortal genius, Archimedes,
Wrote ('tis in science' annals), " *Give*," wrote he,
" Give me a lever only big enough,
I'll move the world."   Great man !

HOPKINS.

                    A wizard, sir !
And that reminds me of the work in hand—
That warrant?

STERN.
        Haste.

SIR GERALD (*aside*).
                    Now, could I but divert
Their thoughts till Marchmont Needham comes !   Let's
        see—
Some lively problem.   Master Hopkins, one
Of your grave aspect cannot but have drunk
At geometric fountains—revelled in
The luxury of angles.

HOPKINS (*aside*).
                    Sir, I've given
My brightest years to mathematical lore,
And found all's nothing.   Algebra's a hoax ;
Euclid a humbug—a pedantic ass,—
I saw it—and exposed him.

SIR GERALD.
                    Did you so ?
Oblige me with a trifling illustration
Of his absurdities.   Just cause to meet
Two parallel lines.   Or will you square the circle ?

HOPKINS.

Square what ?

SIR GERALD.
The circle.

HOPKINS (*boldly*).
        Yes.

SIR GERALD.
                        The deuce you will!
Science has offered some ten thousand crowns
To him shall do it.

HOPKINS.
                She has ?   The liberal soul!
I'm half ashamed to take it.   Ne'ertheless,
Just to oblige.   Now, sir, attend to me—
              (*Takes the chalk and approaches board.*)
A is a country justice, kind, but weak.
B is a zealous witch-destroyer, thwarted
And crossed by A ; C is the public, looking
To both for comfort and protection.   Well?

SIR GERALD (*reluctantly*).
The point is clear—

HOPKINS.
            Most lucid.   Or, again,
Let A, B, C, be certain witches ; D,
The—hem—the devil—and E, a ducking-pond.
Now, then, 'tis plain that lines from A, B, C,
Produced to E, and there united, passing
Downward to D, get their desert.   And now, sir, we pro
      ceed
To business.   Sign.   (*Offers pen and paper.*)

SIR GERALD (*writes reluctantly*).
                  But you will need some aid
To back the warrant—eh ?   Let's see—let's see.
Old Simon Mopchase—bedrid, to be sure—
But then his name—as constable—

HOPKINS.
                No fear!
I've three stout villains—pious knaves enough—
Who put their trust in God, and carry cudgels ;
And Richard Stern, the eloquent.   Ere you sleep,
Look for some news, Sir Gerald.
                                  U

STERN.
>Plenty.
>(*Exeunt* HOPKINS *and* STERN.)

SIR GERALD (*alone*).
>There—

'Tis done—and now, as eager to reproach
My too precipitate yielding —here comes Needham!
>(*Enter* MARCH. NEEDHAM.)

Why, you seem breathless.   What's the matter, boy?

NEEDHAM.

Does yonder ruffian lie?

SIR GERALD.
>These walls contain

No ruffians, Master Needham.

NEEDHAM.
>True, Sir Gerald.

They have attained their object.   They have wrung
From your unthinking judgment what the law
Wisely withheld.   Ah! sir, this little pen
Has pricked a vein of innocent blood, will drain
The life from bosoms that ne'er beat with aught
But love to you—goodwill and charity
To all mankind.   Shame—shame, sir—

SIR GERALD.
>Master Needham,

I would forgive this speech—you 're hot and young ;
Age, sir, that dims our eyes, destroys, at least,
That fine, false medium which in early years
Clothes guilt in rosy attributes.   Enough—
Sit down, and I'll reward you with a problem
Unmatched in simple grandeur.   Let—

NEEDHAM.
>Excuse me—

This nonsense—

SIR GERALD (*starting up*).
    Nonsense! Look, sir—here's a problem
Asks no great wit to solve. See, from this point,
This centre, A (my manor-house), I draw
A circle, B, C, D, within the which
I do not ask your entrance.   (*Exit.*)

NEEDHAM.
        I was wrong
To cross his humour ; yet, so far, it spares
Expenditure of thanks and compliment,
For here's a more implacable summoner
Chiding me hence.   (*Takes out a letter.*)
     " What madness chains you, man ?
What spell beguiles you from the noble strife
Your soul was pledged to? Wherefore cast your staff
Aside, and like a tardy pilgrim sit
Dreaming beside the waters? Up! Awake !
Come to life's battle—and earn rest. The worn
And wayward sleep. Thou'rt neither."
        Good, blunt friend—
I love thee—have thy will. And yet, methinks
E'en thy stoic nature might discern
Discretion in my madness. Am I asked
What spell? Ah—*Cecil*—it replies !
    (*Enter* CECIL *and* MAGGIE.)

CECIL.
       Do that,
And then return ; I'll keep your skipping-rope—
'Twill bring you back the sooner. (*Exit* MAGGIE.)
      Master Needham !—
With that grave aspect ? What's the matter, sir ?

NEEDHAM.
I cannot laugh.

CECIL (*skipping*).
   Nor skip ? There—mind your eye,
I saw you wink. Keep off, then.
          U 2

Needham.

> Cecil—Cecil!—

Cecil.

Well—what's the matter?   O, I did not tell you
Our frolic for to-night.   'Tis all arranged—
Masks, dresses, broomsticks—

Needham (*amazed*).

> What do you mean?

Cecil.

> A feast

Of little witches, sir, is held to-night
In the dells of Pendell Forest.   There's a moon
Brightening expressly—dews will keep their distance—
And there's a band of merry forest-minstrels
(Led by one Signor Cicala), engaged
To dance to.   You'll be there?

Needham.

> Alas!   I must

To horse within this hour.

Cecil.

> To horse at once!

And make haste back, sir.

Needham.

> I shall be—

Cecil.

> Too happy,

Of course, you will.   Be back by half-past nine;
For at that wizard hour Sir Gerald Mole
Will be in the moon with Euclid—Mistress Frill,
In a laced night-cap, safe in bed—and I,
With twenty other madcap damsels, culled
Out of my village-pets o' the vicinage,

Holding a banquet in the Malkin Tower,
Shall craze the owls that mope there.

NEEDHAM.
                              Are you mad ?
Or jesting ?

CECIL.
          Neither, sir.   Ere now, you've told me
(More truly than politely) I was strange
In fancy, as in deed ; defying rule,
Marching to strange—not all unworthy—ends,
By quick cross-paths, while others will jog round,
Pay toll, and pass more safely.   And, in truth,
You're right enough, I fear ; for when at chess
I beat my uncle—with a quick thought, at once
Conceived and execute—he cries, " *Ah ! psha !
Absurd, unscientific*—"   So it was ;
But then it won the game !

NEEDHAM.
                              And may I know
The secret of your present plan ?

CECIL.
                              O, surely.
The plot, sir, has two branches.   Master Gabb
Loves me, and needs discouragement.   He, therefore,
Has been beguiled to meet—you'll not guess whom ;
And hear— I'll not say what.   A graver end
Is this—to prove to such as, on pretext
Of witchcraft, dog the steps and hunt the life
Of every lame and ancient gentlewoman,
That they are fools, and might as well harm *me*
For May-day masqueing and fantastic sports,
As those for sorcery.   Ridicule's the cure
For these witch-seekers.   Never trust my word,
If I don't make them dance to-night to a tune
Shall hiss them from the country !

NEEDHAM.
                              Would to Heaven
I might have stayed to-night, were 't but to mix
With this unmellowed plot a drop or two
Of plain discretion !   But I must begone—
Must bid *farewell !*   Sweet Cecil, will you hold
Your poor friend in remembrance ?   Will you, Cecil ?

CECIL (*faintly*).
You're saying this to vex me.
                    NEEDHAM.
                              'Tis too true—
I go to-night.

CECIL.
        Why, then, you're very cruel.
I thought you loved us all : that's why I've teased you.
You might have studied Euclid all day long,
In peace and comfort, else.   And now you leave
The hawk—the spaniels—Mistress Frill—and me ;
And more than these—than *all*—the kind old man
That loves and leans on you !

NEEDHAM.
                              But he himself
Desires it.   And, were that not so, a voice
As potent calls me.   Cecil—

CECIL (*passionately*).
                              Go, then—go !
Why do you wait ?—what care for here ?   O Heaven !
To dwell six happy months, accepting love,
Respect, and hospitality ; and when
You've stol'n our fancies, just turn on your heel—
And part !   'Tis cruel—cruel !   We're well rid
Of such a guest.   I'm very glad to lose you—
Only—it—breaks my heart !   (*Bursts into tears.*)

NEEDHAM.
                              What do I hear ?

Away, suspense !   (*Throws himself at her feet.*)
                    O, Cecil !   O, sweet bird !
Start not to hear this strange and sudden tongue—
I love you, Cecil !   Common love needs time
And grace to perfect it, but mine was born
Gigantic—sprang to manhood at a leap—
And stretches to you its true, honest arms,
Offering a refuge where *your* love shall, in
Its own good season, flourish too !   You blush—
You tremble !   Cecil, do you love me ?

CECIL.
                              I—
Perhaps—I—I'm not sure.   You needn't ask
Such downright questions.

NEEDHAM.
                    Cecil, I must take
My fortune with me.   Sweet one, can you guess
What love is ?   Cecil, darling Cecil, speak.
I love you—will you be my wife ?

CECIL.
                        You love ?
And you'll be gone to-night ?

NEEDHAM.
                        It is love's self
That spurs me.   Sweet, you shall know all—meanwhile
This scholar's gown grows threadbare.   I must woo
Dame Fortune for a fitter.

CECIL.
                    No—in *that*—
And *that* alone—approach me.   There's my hand.
Kiss gentlier.

NEEDHAM.
            Why, the eloquence that scorches
On the dumb lip can find no better vent

Than burning kisses.   O, be faithful to me—
Be kind—be loving.   But a few short weeks—
Then, re-united—passing hand in hand
Into that sunny vista, love's bright world—
We'll make its paths eternal.   Now, farewell—
Farewell!   One kiss, my Cecil.   O, the music
Of those sweet wedded words!   And you'll give up,
For my sake—will you not?—this wizard scheme
To-night?

CECIL (*smiling*).
        I've little heart for it now, believe me ;
But it's too late.

NEEDHAM.
        Indeed!   Well, dearest, may
The kind intent hallow the mystic means
You work with !   One word—and I go—Sweet Cecil !
There are some points in every life wherein
All wandering rays of happiness converge—
Ev'n in such haven, such sweet, sheltering bay,
We anchor now.   Then, loveliest, once more search
Thy heart.   If changed from its first prompting, here—
Here, in this quiet wilderness, my fate
Interpret to me.   So content I am
To know the world no nearer, here I'd pause—
Here, at thy feet, lie down—here rest—here die!

CECIL (*smiling*).
The search were fruitless, sir ; I never loved
Until you taught me.   Marchmont—oh, my Marchmont,
May Heav'n forgive you !

NEEDHAM.
        Sweet, for what ?

CECIL.
                You've spoiled
The calmest, sunniest, and most innocent dream !
I thought I was a child.   O love—love—love

If you enrich us, 'tis but a debt repaid.
I am a slave now—must be docile—grave—
Never climb trees again, nor care for skipping !
O, if you knew how I have nursed this dream—
This happy, careless, thoughtless, *tearless* dream—
You would have spared it for a while—not plucked
This young old age upon me !   Heav'n forgive you !
I won't—till you return.   (*Aside*) Who knows ?—perhaps
You'll come the sooner for it.

NEEDHAM (*eagerly*).
        Cecil !—

CECIL (*motions him away*).
            There !—
Leave me—don't speak !   Away, I say !
          (*Exit* NEEDHAM.)
          Gone—gone !
          (*Bursts into tears.*)

END OF ACT II.

ACT III.

SCENE I.—*In the Wood.   Near evening.*

(*Enter* GABB *and* HOPKINS.)

GABB.

In point of fact, then (do I take you right?
If not, correct me), witch or no witch, 'tis
My duty to mount guard on Malkin Tower,
And take what follows?

HOPKINS.
                    Every principle
Of love demands it, sir.   A man is bound,
Says Euclid, to keep love-tryst, though he stump
Bleeding and footless thither.

GABB.
                    Hang it, man!
Can't you use milder illustrations?   Well,
I must not quarrel with my monitor.
A confidant is, to a man in love,
Essential as a mistress.

HOPKINS (*aside*).
                    So 't would seem.
I'll wager, not a soul in twenty miles
But has been yours.

GABB.
                    'Tis almost time.   You'll walk
Some little distance, eh?

HOPKINS
I'll keep aloof.
My hounds are out.   If there's a witch i' the wood,
She'll grunt her vespers to the devil, her lord,
'Twixt four stone walls to-night.   Come, sir, away.

GABB.
I'm rather—nervous.

HOPKINS.
Have no fear.   You go
On a high mission, man.   The world's large heart
Expands with symp—

GABB.
The world's large countenance
Expands with *mirth*—when any great mishap
Befalls one.   So be near me, as you promised,
And if you hear me whistle,—so—

HOPKINS.
Or scream,
(That's better) we'll be with you.   All success.
How now?   Why, what's the matter?   Hold up, man!
Is it a witch?

GABB.
Yes,—or a woman,—now,
Should it be her—
        (*Enter* STERN *and two others, disguised as old
        women peasants.*)

HOPKINS.
Well done, my rustic beauties!
Here's masqueing, 'faith!   Pray know this gentleman:
Sir, Mistress Richard Stern,—Miss Sampson Voules,—
The lady Peter Bullman.   Covert, boys!
Stay, though,—I'll post you.   Master Gabb, you stare;
You'll see more wonders yet, sir.   Come along.
        (*Exeunt.*)

SCENE II.—*A glade in Pendell Forest. Exterior of the ruin called Malkin Tower. Moonlight. A village girl enters disguised as an old ugly woman with broom; her dress torn and disordered.*

GIRL (*crying*).
Fierce brute !   Yet he's a civil dog enough
By daylight.   (*Another enters suddenly.*)

SECOND GIRL.
        Judy !

FIRST GIRL (*starting*).
                Who—who's that ?   Dear—dear !
I thought it was a wolf.

SECOND GIRL.
                It's Katty Hewit.
How pale you look, child !   What's the matter ?

FIRST GIRL.
                                        Matter !
If you'd been half devoured by Burrough's mastiff
You might look pale.   Kate—I do think 'tis wrong,
A-flying, you may say, in the parson's face,
Pretending to be witches.

SECOND GIRL.
                Nothing's wrong,
Miss Cecil says.   I'd play the very—

FIRST GIRL (*stopping her mouth*).
                                Hush !
You wouldn't.   Here's some more.   Thank goodness !
        (*Enter* MAGGIE, *and several others, similarly
                disguised.*)

SECOND GIRL.
                Here's a repentant witch.   Let's send her home ,
Or she ll infect the party.

MAGGIE.
Little coward !
Don't mind. I'll give her heart. Take courage, Judy.
(*Aside*) You know the white-thorn on the Lowmoor, child?
Just think you're there, and young Will Peters—

FIRST GIRL.

Stuff !

He didn't.

MAGGIE.

What ?

FIRST GIRL.
Why, kiss me !

MAGGIE.

Well ? and pray—

Who said he had ?

FIRST GIRL.
You did, or,—eh,—perhaps
You might if I hadn't stopped you.
(*Enter* CECIL *disguised.*)

CECIL.

Scolding, children ?
Do you forget you're not mere flesh and blood,
But witches ? things that own no foe but truth,
Reason, and sense—ahem ! (*aside*) the last, I fear,
Is scarce upon *our* side. It's past the time ;
I stopped to listen to a nightingale :
He had a deal to say, and to my ear
Ne'er sang so sweetly. Well, he's flown. Let's see,—
Are we all here? What ! only ten in all ?
Where's my pet Rhoda ?

MAGGIE.

Frightened, and gone home.
And Polly Frere, in squeezing through the lattice,
Was caught by her mother, whipped, and put to bed.
Two witches less !

CECIL.
And Dorcas Eames ?

A LITTLE GIRL.
                                    She's got
The hooping-cough, my lady.

CECIL.
                        Little imp !
Give me a kiss.   Come, then, let's make the best
Of our scant fellowship.   Witches, I hope
You met some honest people by the way,
And let yourselves be seen ?   I've other ends
Than a mere moonlight skipping, clothed in rags,
I promise ye.   Have courage, and observe
All that I said this morn.   Maggie, the paper
I bade you hang on the oak,—did Master Gabb
Detect it ?

MAGGIE.
            Yes : I watched him from the tower :
He spelled it twice, then tossed his hat in the air,
So gaily that it caught upon the tree,
And he'd to climb—

CECIL *(hastily)*.
            Hush !   Skip !

*(They retire to the Tower and other spots, as
        GABB enters.)*

GABB.
                        The wood's asleep.
I wish I could say *snoring*.   Any sound,
How rude soe'er, were melody.   I'd sing,
But that the echoes in this cursed dell
Give one's own voice a witchy twang.   I'll try.
Halloo !

GIRLS *(within)*.
Halloo—o—o !

GABB (*starting*).
       I thought so. Hang it, now!
That echo's in the day-time a mere grunt,—
The north wind with a quinsy—a hoarse sob.
(*Calls*). *Don't—be—a—fool!*

GIRLS (*within from different parts*).
       Fool—fool—fool—fool!

MAGGIE (*from the Tower*).
       You fool!

GABB.
It is herself; she knows me! There's no echo,
Save in this bosom. Help me, Love! the path
Up to thy bower is dark, and (might I judge
By certain irritations), slightly fringed
With stinging-nettles. Hah!
       (*A bluish light seen within.*)
       Thanks, sweetest Hero!
Leander comes. My ancle! Ha!—a toad!
So, one more scramble, and all's safe. I'm—
    (*The interior of the Tower becomes suddenly
      illuminated; GABB starts and falls back to
      the ground.*)
       Help!

SONG (*within*).
Imp and witch, to the Malkin gate,
  In all strange shapes, assemble!
Gather, till with the fiendish weight
  The old walls shriek and tremble!
Snake from muddy pit, toad from tomb,
  Cat from the cottage ember;
Hurrah for the hell-broth, banquet, broom,
  Blue fog, and black November.

GABB.
Mercy! I'm in the witch-trap—caught—betrayed:
Poof! (*tries to whistle*) poof! My lips are parched; I'll
    creep away,
And give them notice.

Cecil (*within*).
Folly, in man's form,
Approaches! Rutterkin, out—out, good fiend,
And make it prisoner.
(*One of the girls, dressed as a huge rough dog,*
runs down and seizes Gabb. Cecil *and the*
rest following, enter on all sides.)
Gently, gently, fiend!
Seize, but don't mangle him at first. The wretch
Must have witch-baptism. See that's all prepared:
Then to your nightly pleasures. Tituba,
You're but a baby imp; stay with your mistress.
Cloyse, hunt the yellow raven. Hawthorn! Ball!
Burn Goody Joyce's haggard. Fancy! Fancy!
Bite the brown cow!

Gabb (*aside*).
Amiable pleasantries!
What mischief next, I wonder? They surround me.
Now for an incantation.

Cecil.
Join your hands.
(*In a low chanting voice.*)

All ye that have stol'n the miller's eels,
　Laudate Dominum de cæl's ;
All ye that have given consent thereto,
　Benedicamus Domino !

(*Aside*) Dear Marchmont!
Who taught me that rude rhyme? Now, Heav'n be
　praised ;
You cannot see this folly!

Gabb.
Worthy souls !—

Cecil.
He calls us worthy ! Tie a knot in his tongue
For lying !

GABB.
Mercy ! I retract.   Vile hags !

CECIL.
Vile !·

GABB.
I beg pardon ; mild, or mischievous,—
Lovely, or loathsome,—fœtid, or fragrant,—belles,
Or beldames : only let me 'scape you now,
And never shall this Christian hoof again
Impress your cursed precincts.

CECIL.
No, you've seen
Too much of our dark doings.   We must take
Judgment and memory from you.   Ho! there ! bring
The goblet filled with nightmare's blood and spiced
With acorns.   (*Cup brought*).   Drink, or die !

GABB (*aside*).
And die, you mean.
I am forbid fermented liquors ; pray,
Excuse me.   I've a bilious habit.

CECIL.
Come—
To supper, then.   We only staid for *you.*

GABB.
You're very kind.   (*Aside*) I wonder what foul dish
They browse on !

CECIL.
Wretch ! I read thy thought. To-night
We've got a sodden—*fool !*

GABB (*uneasily*).
A what ?

X

CECIL.

You'll know
In time, poor creature.   Does the cauldron boil?

MAGGIE.

Dread mistress, no.

CECIL.

Drop in the woolly knot
Pluck'd from a bat's left ear.   Now for a dance
To give us an appetite, and then—
     *A grotesque dance, during which several figures
     enter, and mingle with them.*)

CECIL (*pausing suddenly*).

Dark comers!
Whate'er you are, disclose yourselves!
     (HOPKINS *and the rest throw off their disguises;
     all fly, but* CECIL.)

HOPKINS.

That will we.

CECIL (*hurriedly*).
Stay, children, stay!   Flight ruins all.   Remain,
And you are safe.

HOPKINS (*aside to the rest*).
Disperse, don't *hold* them.   (*Aloud*) Fools!
You can't bestride the moon-beams.   Let them go;
We've got the queen-witch safe.

CECIL (*eagerly*).
Back, little fools!
Show what you are.

HOPKINS.
Why, so they do.   All vanish'd,—
Fiend, imp, and sucking-witch.   Ho! Master Gabb,
Stand up, man!

Gabb (*bewildered*).
Night-mare's blood!

Cecil.
                Good Master Gabb,
If I, and those poor frightened maids, have used
Some merry freedoms with you, pardon them,
And see us safely hence.

Gabb.
        I—I—eh!—I—

Hopkins.
Look how he shrinks and trembles!

Gabb.
             When she speaks,
Strange thrills come over me.

Hopkins.
            Yes, that's her spell!
Come, bring the witch along.

Cecil.
          The witch!   Keep off!
I know your ruffian leader.   But, for you,
Beware, sir, how you use me.   I am a lady,
Niece of Sir Gerald Mole.

Hopkins.
         Indeed!   Then—lady—
Niece of old Mole—but, ne'ertheless, a witch,
Will you be pleased to walk, or shall we make
A litter for your dainty ladyship,
To visit the town gaol?

Cecil.
        You dare not use
This vile indignity!   Nor, for the sport
We follow—

HOPKINS.

Pretty sport !　Who was't that bade
Fire Goody Joyce's haggard ?　See !

(A conflagration is seen rising.)

CECIL *(aghast)*.

Great Heaven
What have I done?

HOPKINS.

You hear?　She owns it.　Come—

CECIL *(faintly)*.

To the Manor.

HOPKINS.

What's the use?　Your worthy uncle's
In his first sleep ; but, if it's any comfort,
Here's his own warrant.　*(Aside)* Struggle as you will,
You're in the net.

CECIL *(aside)*.

O Marchmont ! had I ta'en
Thy counsel !

HOPKINS.

Come—*(aside to them)* Who fired the haggard ?

STERN.

I.

(Exeunt.)

END OF ACT III.

ACT IV.

SCENE I.—*Hall in the Manor.*

(SIR GERALD, *much altered, sits at the table, re-*
garding his books, etc., with a vacant and be-
wildered manner; GABB *and* MISTRESS FRILL
seated apart, watching him.)

MISTRESS FRILL (*sighing*).
I fear you're wrong.

GABB.
    Excuse me, I am clear
He did. He spoke distinctly,—" *Master Gabb,*
Sit down, sir; you're a fool."

MISTRESS FRILL (*eagerly*).
      Did he say that?
Gracious be thanked! I thought his wits were gone.

GABB.
At least, perhaps, they're wakening; and, of course,
At first see mistily. " Fool " is a word
That means so little! I knew a merry squire
Would pinch his wife by the ear, and called her "fool,"—
" His pretty, jealous fool." Well, I must take
My leave. I fear I tire you; but, in truth,
Since that accursed eve in the Malkin Tower,
I have no comfort, object, act, or thought,
Out of your presence! Dearest mistress Frill,
 love—

MISTRESS FRILL.
  Sir!

GABB.
Yes. Of course—to talk with you
Of mistress Cecil.   Idiot that I was,
Not to perceive 't was jesting!   *I* to bear
Witness against her!   May my tongue be seared first!
O, Cecil! Cecil!   Oh, my goodness!
(*Walks about much agitated.*)

SIR GERALD (*looking up*).
Cecil!
She's to be tried to-day.

MISTRESS FRILL (*aside*).
Who told him that?
Nonsense, my dear Sir Gerald!   Turn your thoughts
To rectinatural pipeds.

SIR GERALD (*sternly*).
Recti *what?*
You don't know what you talk of.   Never think
To play on me.   Alack, I know there's something
Gone from my brain!   I can't define a rhombus.
They'd whip a schoolboy for the faults I make
In multilateral polygons.   But one thought
Is nailed and rooted here.   I moan it o'er
Nightly before I sleep.   My darling's tried
To-day for witchcraft.

MISTRESS FRILL.
Heav'n protect its own!
We are powerless.

SIR GERALD.
Are we? Where's my mantle? Come,
Let's go.

MISTRESS FRILL.
But, dear sir, whither?

SIR GERALD.
        To the court.
I have a word to speak, if my heart hold.
But time grows brief. Good Master Gabb, you loved
My poor child, did you not? Be welcome, sir.
     (*Exit, leaning on* MISTRESS FRILL.)

GABB.
"*I loved his child,*" and "*welcome.*" Does that mean
Welcome to love her? Hem! I only wish
He'd found that out before. It's like a man
Bidding "Good morning" as one goes to bed,—
More courtesy than significance. Oh, brain,
For once be active for some good! Devise
Some means to save this angel. Would to Heav'n
Needham were still among us! To my mind
There is about him a plain, simple wisdom,
That, in his presence, really makes one feel
Almost an ass! If he should—
     (*Starts back from the window.*)
     Heav'n forefend
This should be witchcraft! Yes, one can't mistake
His eager step. 'Tis Needham, as I live!—
But spurred and cloaked.   (*Leans out at the window.*)
Hist! Hillo! Marchmont! Stop!
Don't you know Antony Gabb? I'm coming. Wait!
       (*Runs out.*)

———

SCENE II.—*In the Grounds.*

   (*Enter* MARCHMONT NEEDHAM.)

NEEDHAM.
When flight's impossible, 't is wise to show
A fair front to the enemy. Master Gabb! (*Enter* GABB.)
Welcome How thrives the Muse!

GABB.
								The Muse be hanged!

NEEDHAM.
So, so!	A lover's quarrel?

GABB.
								I shall change
Your tone, or I'm mistaken.

NEEDHAM.
							Pardon me.
I can be grave—and ought—for, to say truth,
Some strange misgiving has enticed me back
Long ere I purposed.	Prithee, what's the matter?
This Hopkins has not—

GABB (*eagerly*).
							Yes, he has.

NEEDHAM.
									Found out
Some grandame flirting with the devil, and clapped
His steeple hat upon them?

GABB.
						Worse.

NEEDHAM.
									Sir Gerald's—

GABB.
Mad—and no wonder.

NEEDHAM (*impatiently*).
						Out with your tale.	If 'tis
Of the wounding nature, use it like a sword,
Not like a gimblet.	Mistress—Cecil?	No,
They dare not do it!

GABB.
Mistress Cecil chose
To play the witch in the wood.   Upon the sport
Came Hopkins and his ruffians.   All were scared
And fled, save that sweet angel, whom they seized
And bore to prison.   And, with some few more,
By whose condemning they may colour hers,
She will be tried to-day—do you hear?—this day—
Monday—the last of beautiful May—henceforth
Accursed in Nature's calendar!

NEEDHAM.
                              To-day!—
To-day!   That's fatal.

GABB.
                              You will drive me mad!
Think of some remedy.   Let her die, *then* see
What all your learning's worth.   She wrote.   The clown
Showed me the letter.   I spelt it—" Marchmont Need-
     ham."

NEEDHAM (*starting*).
Now Heav'n forgive me! a more thoughtless fool
Never wore bells.   I but assumed that name
Worn by a scapegrace cousin.

GABB.
                              Then you're more
Villain than fool.   Do you indeed wear aught
So honest as a sword?

NEEDHAM.
You are mad!

GABB (*passionately*).
                              I am.
I love her, sir—whate'er you are—I care not
Who knows it now.   I'd give my life to save her,

And, with my last gasp, place her—in your arms,
For that's the home she looked for.

NEEDHAM (*pausing*).

You have learned
Love's lesson nobly.　　　(*Offers to take his hand.*)

GABB (*refusing*).

I believed you wise
And honourable ; now, sir, I would rather
Cross swords than hands with you.

NEEDHAM.

I offer you
A nobler contest—for a richer prize.
Advocate as I am, I cannot use
My calling now, nor with a bold truth scatter
This foul charge to the winds.　Yet there's one hope,
And time wanes fast indeed.　We will divide
The work between us.　Hie you to the Dolphin !
'Tis there the judges, Gayre and Howlett, lay
Last night.　Then summon patience and await
A mounted runner, bearing a sealed scroll,
Which, while in London, should have reached my hand,
But that my haste forbade.　Stay for no words ;
But force your way into the very court,
And place that scroll beside me.

GABB.

Is that all ?
Were but the rest as easy !

NEEDHAM.
We shall see.
I dare not promise.　At the worst, 'tis something
To *know* the worst.　Heav'n prosper all !　Away !

SCENE III.—*Room in a Prison.*

CECIL (*alone*).

Twelve days alone !   No knowledge of what's done,
Or what's to be.   No sign of sister-life
But the dumb wretch that doles me needful food,
And spreads the couch that brings not rest, but tears.
Where is my old kind uncle ?   Alice ! Maggie !
And—Marchmont—what of *thee ?*   Hast thou received
My earnest mission ?   Was the bearer true ?
Then why no answer ?   *Why ?*   So ever ends
My mournful questioning.   The twelfth eve, and lo,
There passes from the earth the golden smile
That kept my heart warm.   Linger in the skies !
There's a sad sweetness in the sun's farewell ;
'Tis a tried friend that leaves us, passing slow,
And often gazing backward.   So—he goes—
Slowly—how slowly !—scattering crimson light
On tree, and tower, then hill-top, and then cloud,
As one, in dying, turns on loftiest things
His latest aspirations.   Ah, farewell !

>   (*Enter* ALISON DEVISE ; CECIL *flies to embrace
>   her.*)

Ha ! a dear face !   Nurse—Alison !   Thank Heaven
That gives this comfort !

ALISON.
>   Comfort !—fool !

CECIL (*starting back*).
>   Why —nurse

ALISON.

Would I had nursed a snake, ere cherished thee
I'm an old branch, sapless, and winter-worn,
Fit for the burning ; but to slaughter *these*
Is more than murder.   Heaven assoil their souls,
The young unready things !

CECIL (*aghast*).
What mean you?

ALISON (*fiercely*).
Mean!
That you had better died in innocent sleep,
Than let your baby-fancies loose to ape
Witch-feasts in Malkin Tower?

CECIL.
Nurse! Alison,
Why don't they come to take me home?

ALISON.
They'll come
To —— psha! it chokes me. Why, poor, silly lamb,
You're penned for slaughter, or I'd thank you for
My death in other guise!

CECIL (*shrieking*).
Death! (*clasping her eyes.*)

ALISON.
'Twas fine sport
To fright yon silly gentleman; but stake
And chain are ugly toys.

CECIL (*still clasping her eyes*).
Death!
(*Several women and children brought in by
gaolers, prisoners.*)

GAOLER.
Come, no bawling!
Get to your cells; then bellow till the devil,
Your master, come to your succour. Hang ye all!

ALISON (*to* CECIL).
More of your victims, madam!

Cecil (*wildly*).
                              What are these?
What brings old age and childish innocence
To this dark house of grief?

Alison.
                Yourself.

Woman (*exultingly*).
                                  'Tis she!
Gossips, 'tis she!   Her frolics there i' the wood
Brought Hopkins' hell-hounds on us!   To her, all!
Give her a parting token.   (*They surround* Cecil.)

Gaoler (*driving them back*).
                Off, you hags!

Woman.
Well, we can curse at distance.   Pretty devil!
'Twill be like water on the flames, to know
Your delicate limbs must feel them!

Cecil.
                              Are ye mad?
My Lilian, little darling!   Sweet, come hither!

Gaoler.
Come, come,—in with ye!

Woman (*fiercely to* Cecil).
                Let my child alone!
Spit at her, Lilian!   She's a witch and murderess!
        (*The child repulses her.   Exeunt to inner cell.*)

Cecil.
Nurse, nurse! my heart is broken.
                (*Falls on the ground before* Alison.)

Alison.
                Psha!   Your tears

Won't melt stone walls.   There's your poor uncle, blind
With weeping for you : all his learning drowned
In helpless dotage.   Master Hopkins rules.
Fine sport, child, is't not ?

CECIL.

Torture me no more !
Oh, Alise ! Alise ! this from you !   Can fear
'Turn your old love to gall ; when *mine* defied
Malice and vile report, and left me your
Sole friend?

ALISON (*moved*).
Why, mistress Cecil—

CECIL.

Now, be mine.
This is the earliest home my memory claims.
'There, put my head upon your kind old breast,—
My night shuts early in.

ALISON (*passionately embracing her*).

Why, they shall rend me,
Fibre and vein !   This worn and worthless frame
Shall yield and crackle in the rustling flame,
Ere my vile, graceless tongue shall breathe again
One word of anger toward thee !   Oh, my child !
My darling !   Monsters !   Men of bloody minds !
If in the den of your steeled bosoms dwells
No touch of pity, then look up and *fear !*
You *dare* not cut this blossom from the earth,
Lest all else wither !

(HOPKINS *enters rudely ; Gaoler follows*.)

HOPKINS.
Turn the old witch in.
I'll have some chat with the other.

(*Exit Gaoler with* ALISON.)

Now then, girl !
Time's precious with us both.   No whimpering.   Come!
Is your mind changed towards me ?

CECIL.

Yes, from scorn
To loathing.   Why do you haunt me?

HOPKINS.

'Tis a folly;
Yet I would save you from a rougher grasp
Than that of Matthew Hopkins.   Can you,—come,
I'll not say *love*—but bear with me?   Who knows
What may ensue?   That's a fair offer.   Come!—
Age brooks no coynesses—those womanish toys,
The spurs to younger fancy.   Rude as I am,
I've some good points; and, at the worst, if Matthew
Be a grim bridegroom, Death's a grimmer.   Psha!
Marry me, and ha' done with 't.

CECIL.

I will first
Dig with these hands my grave.

HOPKINS.

Unhappy girl!
I am thy fate.   Trust not my pity.

CECIL.

Man,
I trust my innocence!

HOPKINS.
What's that?

CECIL.

A child
Of Heav'n—no kin to thee!

HOPKINS.

Poor witness!   Here,
You're innocent enough, child—if that's all!

CECIL.
And therefore you denounced me.   Well, you deemed

A name disgraced—fenced out, like some rude field
That no man owns—a haunt for thieves and beggars—
Was fittest for your wear.   Report bespeaks you,
Daring in purpose, resolute in deed ;
Yet, in the spirit of my soldier-sires,
I give you fair defiance.   What do you see
To gaze at thus?

HOPKINS.
   As fair a fleshly work
As ever Nature fashioned.   Silly one!
Had'st thou ambition mated with thy courage,
We two might rule the world!

CECIL.
      A child, bold man,
Reminds you that ambition, ill-directed,
First made, then peopled hell.

HOPKINS.
      Here's change, i' faith !
A week ago, you were a simple thing,
Trundling a hoop, or trembling at the frown
Of that sweet composite of starch and snow,
Your governess, Mother Frill.   Of late, I think,
You have found other teachers.

CECIL.
      Oh, I have,—
I have !

HOPKINS (*furiously*).
  I knew that scholar's frock concealed
Some crafty purpose.   Hang me, but I ever   '
Mistrust a man in petticoats !   You love
This Marchmont Needham?   No more trifling—come,
Confess it, or—   (*Grasps her arm.*)

CECIL.
How dare you touch me, fellow ?

Then, for reward of your vile insolence, know
I love, and am beloved.   Aye, more, I have sent
To warn him of his Cecil's danger here ;
And he will fly to rescue, or there's little
Of love or truth i' the world.

HOPKINS.
                              The devil you have !

Psha,—pedant coxcomb !

GAOLER (*entering*).
                          Here's a stuttering clown,
Charged with some message for the prisoner.
Should he have entrance, Master Hopkins ?

HOPKINS.
                                        Hem !

Is 't her familiar, think you ?   Hath his eye
An impish cast ?

GAOLER.
          It hath, sir, as it were
A smack of gooseberry—nothing more.

HOPKINS.
                      Admit him.
                      (*Exit Gaoler.*)

CECIL (*aside*).
And sunshine with him.   Marchmont !
              (*Re-enter Gaoler with Countryman.*)
                      Give 't me,—quick !

COUNTRYMAN.
There, take the 'chantment.   I'd 'a burned it, only
I veared 'twould do m' a mischief.   Sorrow on me,—
They tell me you're a witch !

CECIL.
                  If *you're a man,*
You served me, notwithstanding.

COUNTRYMAN.

                              Yees, I did.
They zent me to a place where Master Needham,
With other gallants, all in silk and lace,
Was playing bowls.   I poked the scroll in 's face.
He vrowned and laughed ; then tossed it to his vriends,
And bade me zay, for answer, he was then
Within five points of the game, and twenty crowns
Depending.   So I caught the letter up,
And left.   A witch, then, bee'st ?   (*Eyeing her curiously.*)

HOPKINS.

                              Ha, ha !   Discreet,
Courteous, and loving !   Well?

CECIL (*faintly*).
                              I am to be tried
To-day ?

HOPKINS (*aside*).
She's mine,—within this hour !

CECIL.

                              The haste
Is mercy.   Now you'll leave me.   Though six words
From yon poor clown have, in this heart of mine,
Stifled a lustrous world, there yet remain
Some earthly scintillations, which my soul
Needs *peace* to wrestle down.   Grant me so much,
And go.   I have chosen.

HOPKINS (*in a rage*).
                              Obstinate fool,—thou hast !
                              (*Rushes out.*)

END OF ACT IV.

ACT V.

SCENE I.—*The Justice-Room, representing the Trials of the supposed Witches.* A.D. 1634.

(*Before the Judges,* GAYRE *and* HOWLETT. HOPKINS, STERN, *Clerks, Officers, etc.* ALISON DEVISE *and others at the bar. The room lined with spectators of all ranks, among whom* NEEDHAM *is seated.*)

HOWLETT.

Set them all forward.   Alison Devise,
Rachel and Margaret Pinder, Lilian Grey,
Tried and convict of witchcraft—

ALISON.

Tried, my lord?

HOWLETT.

Most tenderly ; for 'tis a Christian land,
And you, inhuman, hellish, murderous—

GAYRE.

Sentence.

HOWLETT.

Nay, I must speak !   Oh, ye ungrateful crew !
Sit here ten hours !   Your fate, ten mortal hours,
Hang in the balance ; and, after that, not tried !
Not *tried !*

GAYRE.

Proceed to sentence.

HOWLETT.

So I will.
But such ingratitude! You, of all persons
Within this land, have the least cause to murmur,
Seeing what time and labour have been spent
In taking of your lives! Why, look around ye,
What persons, of your nature and condition,
Have with so gentle, soft solemnity,
Been graciously convicted? No, no, no,—
All your lives long, be—

GAYRE.
Hem!

HOWLETT (*quickly*).

Eh! That's to say,
Till you are hanged to-morrow; for the blood
Of many victims—

GAYRE.
Cows and horses—

HOWLETT.

And
Other his majesty's subjects, cries aloud.
Give Heav'n due thanks,—first, that your horrible sins
Have been so soon cut short. Then, that your end
Hath not been swift nor sudden, at a blow,—
But with the grave and gradual course of law.
And, lastly ('tis your sweetest consolation),
That the full record of your devilish deeds
Is left behind, as warning. You'll be hanged
To-morrow.

ALISON.

And 'tis time! Farewell, wise world,
Where every wrinkle on an old wife's face
Is brand of felony. Heav'n keep your souls
From taint of richer blood. My lords—

GAYRE.

Remove them.
(*Prisoners withdrawn.*)
Set Cecil Howard to the bar.

NEEDHAM (*aside*).
Hold—patience !
Death of my life !   'Tis she—   (*Starts up.*)
(CECIL *is brought in guarded, and placed before
the bar.*)

OFFICER (*to* NEEDHAM, *who presses forward*).
Stand further back.
Cork up your pity, friend, and hold your tongue,—
This trial's for life or death.

NEEDHAM.
Good fellow, are all
This crowd, or I, grown lunatic ?

OFFICER.   .
I thought
Your look was something wild.   Come, sit ye down,—
At least be mad like a gentleman.   Hush, hush !
Silence, behind there !   Ladies, I can't stop
Your prating but by cracking the man's head
That's nearest to you !

GAYRE.
Come,—proceed.

HOPKINS (*coming forward*).
My Lords—

GAYRE.
A moment, sir.   Why stands she thus alone ?
Have you no counsel, prisoner ?

CECIL.
Three, sir ; but

They're of strange speech, and in this court will scarcely
Stead me, I fear.

HOWLETT.
How do you call them ?

CECIL.

          Truth,
Reason, and Innocence.

GAYRE.
      Add another,—*Justice*,
For you shall have it to the full.

CECIL.
        It seems
You don't mean to keep faith, sir,—or what doth
This ruffian here ?   (*Turning on* HOPKINS.)

HOPKINS (*aside to her*).
    That shall you know anon.
Your wisdom, grave and learned Justices,
Lopping the infected branches, hath left bare
This trunk and root o' the mischief.   Ev'n to a source
So bright, we track the thick, envenomed flood
That taints our neighbouring world.   I see you gaze,
As doubting ev'n the devil's power to gain
Mastery of such fair province, whose good hap
Angels might sentinel.   But I, my lords,
Alas ! see deeper.   All the garden wearing
The stamp of Satan's hoof ; her spirit's soil,
Arid and curst ; her holy leaves stript off,—
All glory gone,—there stands before you, here,
A lightning-withered Eden.

CECIL.
      Turn this way.
Leave shuffling with your feet, and do your best
To fix that wandering, guilty gaze on her,
Of all this court, that knows you.   To revenge
A just repulse—

HOPKINS (*hurriedly*).
                My lords, she'd speak before
My charge be made.

CECIL.
                Lest that, the motive known,
No man accord an ear to 't.   In the dells
Of Pendell Forest—

HOPKINS.
                Listen,—only listen !
She'll have you think I hid myself in a wood
To court her,—whisper love !

CECIL (*quickly*).
                        No,—Heav'n forbid !
Love's empty *name* is yet too sacred for
Such foul association.   Look how close
Sin lies to the door !   I charged him not, yet something,
Beyond his nature's impulse or control,
From his own lips forestals me.   Yes, my lords,
In the twilight forest, this grave gentleman
Came on me unaware.   It seems my face
Had the mishap to please him,—for he paused,
And, as a schoolboy skips aside to pluck
Some red-lipped daisy, would have gathered *me*.
That honour I declined ; and therewithal
His lover's vows, to more congenial oaths
Of vengeance changed, find promised action *here*.
I pray your pardon ; I have done.   Henceforth,
Void on my name what poisoned drops they will,
I have deserved no worse report than one
Who, in the motley tumult of this world,
Is jostled by a knave.   (*Sits down.*)

HOPKINS.
                Poor soul !   Poor soul !
What virulence !   'Tis just their way.   Dick Stern,
How strongly she's possessed !

STERN.
Ah!

CECIL.
Gentlemen,
By what strange licence does this grey buffoon,
This solemn ape, chatter and grin unchecked,
Before our faces?   Fie!

HOPKINS (*furiously*).
A chit!   A child!
Not so young, neither, but she might have learned
The world's ways better.   That she eyes me thus
Askance, I can forgive.   No culprit thinks
The hangman an Apollo.   What's the matter?

OFFICER (*to* GAYRE).
Sir Gerald Mole, sir, claims admission.

CECIL (*starting up*).
Uncle!
Then all is well!

HOPKINS (*aside*).
The devil!   I thought I had
That old bird safe, at least.
(*Enter* SIR GERALD *supported by attendants.*)
No matter; all
The wit he owned lies dead in that dull eye.
He'll do our cause good.   Dear Sir Gerald—

SIR GERALD (*not heeding*).
Cecil!
Where are you, darling?   Why don't you come home?
You are the centre whence my circling life
Is drawn, and, lost, all's crooked.   There's no circle
Without a centre, love.

CECIL.
Oh! gracious Heaven!

SIR GERALD.

I'm very old—these three days—and I sit
Alone, with dry eyes, moping.   It is hard
That old age cannot weep, but must cage up
Its burning woes within the heart's dry veins,
Till time quench life and all!

HOWLETT.
Sir Gerald !

SIR GERALD.
All's
So dismal yonder !   Mistress Frill's heart-broken,
And wears her ruff awry.   What's this they tell me
Of people to be hanged ?

GAYRE.
Well, have you more
To say, Sir Gerald ?

SIR GERALD.
Oh! sir, *this*.   I've learned
Mankind as well as Euclid, and I know
The worst right-angle science ever drew,
Is made by the dangling criminal.

HOPKINS.
Poor soul !
He wanders.   If you listen, sirs, he'll prose
Till midnight thus.

SIR GERALD.
The fault is mine—'tis mine.
I cursed her.   When they said she was a witch,
And swore—I know not what—I—I—Alack !
Who deals in curses surely doth invade
The armoury of God.   I'll make it clear
With a short—I forget.   A sane man, sirs,
But with a wit grown wildered, and a heart
Too heavy for its fleshly home.   O, Cecil !

My child !—my flower !—fair, gentle, graceful, mild,
Full of sweet charities !   I should know, I think,
For she was seldom from me.   Mistress Frill !
Where's Mistress Frill ?   (*Turning, sees* HOPKINS.)
                    O treacherous, smiling villain !
Had you no means to work what you call justice,
But you must use the old man's trusting hand
To slay his darling ?

                    CECIL. (*eagerly*).
          Uncle !—dear, kind uncle !

                SIR GERALD (*struggling*).
Let me go to her !   Back, I say !   What, fellow ?
I'll brain you with my crutch !   I'll—Oh, I am weak—
I want you, Cecil.
                (*Falls back into the attendants' arms.*)

                HOPKINS (*eagerly*).
          Sirs ! my lords ! (*aside*) Pale fools,
They sit aghast.   In the king's name, my lords,—

                NEEDHAM.
The king's belied !

                GAYRE.
          What rascal's that ?   Look to 't.
Who spoke ?

                OFFICER.
          My lords, I did not notice.

                HOPKINS.
                              Sirs,
Let's come to business.   Yield not your grave ears
Captive to dotish wailings, nor regard
This fair illusion.   Crush the devil, ev'n in
His gorgeous palace.   Let the golden walls
Crumble in fires of earth, that the poor soul,
Once to a holier kingdom consecrate,

Be purified and saved.   Think where 'tis writ,
" *No witch shall live.*"

HOWLETT (*nervously*).
Yes, as you say, let's to 't.
There's no defence, I think.   So, Master Hopkins,
You must recount once more this dismal tale,
And 'twill suffice.

NEEDHAM.
I cannot hold.   (*Starts up.*)   My lords—

CECIL (*shrieking*).
Oh, Heaven !

HOPKINS (*angrily*).
What nonsense next ?   O, sir, tis *you* !
Here is a second gentleman to be soothed
Ere the king's work proceed.   (*Sits down sulkily.*)

GAYRE (*to* NEEDHAM).
Be silent !   Usher,
Look to that person.

NEEDHAM.
But the prisoner needs
Counsel, my lords.

GAYRE.
Have you a right to plead, sir ?

NEEDHAM.
I cannot claim it.   Still—

GAYRE (*loudly*).
Out of the court !
Begone, sir—
          (*Noise at the door.*   GABB *enters, forcing his way
          through all, and places a packet in* NEEDHAM'S
          hand.)

NEEDHAM (*aside to him*).
You have saved her.   At the least,
I pray your merciful and learned lordships
Read my petition.

GAYRE (*rejecting it*).
Fellow!

NEEDHAM.
Hangman !   Down.

GAYRE (*starts up in a fury*).
You insolent clown !   Here, marshal! beadles ! whip
This rascal forth !

NEEDHAM (*pushing them back*).
Not yet, sirs.   Stand aside.
I'll take that seat a moment.
    (*Walks up to the bench, and places himself in
    the centre.*)
It would seem
There's room for justice.   Sirs, I am Richard Bromley,
New Lord Chief Justice of the Common Pleas.
Here's the king's signet—here the warrant from
His gracious hand, that trembled as it wrote
With kingly passion, for his subjects slain
By blind and brutish ignorance, or, what's worse,
Witness suborned.   My lords, although my power
Extends not to unravel this foul web
Of sophistry and slander, miscalled trial,
I'll cut the sting out.   Bring all those condemned
Back to the court.
    (*Sits,* ALISON *and prisoners brought in.*)
Poor creatures, you are *free.*
Pity and gifts for all, and chiefly those
By your vile means convict.   (*To* HOPKINS.)

HOPKINS (*aside to* STERN).
A change of wind—
That always brings a gale.   Just wait the lull—
I've not done yet *with her.*

NEEDHAM.

      This court's dissolved,
Never again to test, on grounds so frail,
Issues of life and death. Mark, gentlemen,
Already in these fair and tranquil scenes,
Where, if at all, mercy and truth should reign,
There is a more enlightened spirit born—
Foster it, and farewell.
           *(All rise.   He descends.   Enter a Marshal
            hastily.   Alarm.)*

MARSHAL.

      May 't please your lordship
To pause some space, until your javelin guard
Have well dispersed a somewhat angry crowd,
Now thronging the court precincts.

NEEDHAM.

        What's their object?

MARSHAL.

Revenge, my lord, upon the witnesses.
They say the poor man's blood hath swelled the purse
Of Hopkins and his band ; that *these* are true,
And he's himself the wizard.

NEEDHAM.

        So doth crime
Fashion its proper scourge. (*To* HOPKINS) Get you within
Till night—then rid us of your presence.

HOPKINS.

           Psha !
Open the doors.   Come, Richard.

STERN (*drawing*).

           Ready !

CECIL (*eagerly*).

             Stay !

Stay, Master Hopkins.   Let your last act be
A gloss to its base precedent.   Some rude minds
May yet retain the poison your bold lie
And my own folly placed there.   Take away
This hideous stigma—and all wrong beside
I'll freely pardon you.

HOPKINS (*turns at the door*).
                    Good.   That's my duty.
                                        (*Advancing.*)
I'm glad you stopped me, madam.   I had gone else,
Leaving the fancies of yon fickle crowd
To goddess you.   If ever—as is writ
In terms that none dare question—our fall'n nature
Took service with the fiend—*behold*, for here
Stands one, who for three years hath practised charms,
Philtres, and all the deadly art of hell !
Yea—how much longer, she and the devil know best,
With whom she made her covenant.   Record
This in your souls—and wait Heaven's vengeance.   Stay!
Who's for a merry wager ?   Come, I'll bet
That, ere three months, Sir Richard Bromley, Lord
Chief Justice, weds a witch !   A legion imps
Dance at the nuptials—and the fiend himself
Be bridesman.   There's my blessing.
                        (*Striding towards the door.*)

NEEDHAM (*to Constables*).
                                    Go with him.
See him beyond their fury.   (*Alarm.*)

HOPKINS (*furiously*).
                    To the devil!
Show me the man dare lay his finger on me!
Come, Richard !   Back, thou *witch !*

              (*He rushes out,* STERN *following.   Loud alarm
                  as the doors open.*)

NEEDHAM.
Let him begone.
(*To the rest*)
Withdraw a little; but don't quit us.   Something
Whispers a sequel here.   Life of my heart!
But for that impulse unmistakable
Wherewith thy presence thrills me, this might pass—
The pageant of a dream.   Speak to me, Cecil.

CECIL.
You love me still ?

NEEDHAM.
From the heart's centre to
The utmost bourn of sense !

CECIL (*glancing at the spectators.*)
They look on me
With doubt; and yet you love ?

NEEDHAM.
What's that to me?
I'd clasp this lily hand, were 't stained with gore.
Slack not the grasp for any frowns of earth ;
And, if I have no power to clear thy name,
I'll even love thee more !

CECIL.
I thank you, Marchmont.
Now hear my answer.   For your sake, this hand
Shall wear its maiden honours to the grave,
Knowing no other lord.   But I'll not link
With thine, my soul—curse-laden.   Little know you
How deep and clinging are the stains imparted
Ev'n by a villain's hand.

NEEDHAM (*eagerly*).
You will not—

CECIL (*pointing to* SIR GERALD).
                                        Look
At that old man.   He loves me as his being—
Yet he's bewildered with an aching sense
Of wrong ; and, if there be a leaning, 'tis
To think me guilty.

                  NEEDHAM.
                  'Tis impossible.
Be that the test.

                     CECIL.
It shall.   (*They approach him.*)
                  Dear uncle, here's
An old friend come to greet us.

         SIR GERALD (*bewilderedly*).
                          She of Endor
Drew spirits earthward, and among them, *one*
More than she dreamed of.   Who shall trifle with
The powers of darkness ?   Let's to thought and prayer,
For Master Hopkins is a pious man,
And he has sworn to 't.

              CECIL (*calmly*).
                  Are you satisfied ?
Needham, forgive me, for the thing you loved
Is no more Cecil.   Since we parted, ages
Have swept above me with their wintry wings,
And blighted all my youth.   The dream has closed
As such dreams will—in darkness, and 'tis time
You left me.   Go.   There lies your world—and here
My sorrow's grave.   (*Turns away.   Alarm within.*)

              VOICE (*within*).
                  Open the doors !   Quick ! quick !

         (*The doors are thrown open, and* HOPKINS,
              *disordered and bloody, is borne in.   Many
         follow, kept back by guards.*)

NEEDHAM.

What wretched thing is that?

CECIL.

My witness !

HOPKINS (*hoarsely*).

Water !

OFFICER.

You've had enough, I think.   (*Gives water.*)
My lords—

HOPKINS.

Stand by,
Good fellow.   Let me tell it.   You shall sit
And drone and mope by many a Christmas fire,
When my pipe's stopped.
          (*Raising himself.*)   You told me true, Sir Richard
I found the county up—and bellowing
Death to the witch-informer.   What the deuce !
We could not fight the parish !   Awkward clowns—
They don't know how—to duck—a man—and yet
The pains—I took—to teach.   I think I broke
One fellow's head ?

OFFICER.
You did.

HOPKINS.

I'm sorry now.
But never mind him.   Now, what's more to the purpose—
Take all your eyes from me, and nail them *there*—
There, on that peerless piece of maidenhood.
Praise, pity, *love* her.   She's no more a witch
Than I'm an angel !   (*She falls in* NEEDHAM'S *arms.*)

SIR GERALD.
Erat demonstrandum --
In God's good time.   'Tis done.

z

HOPKINS (*lifting himself with difficulty*).
       Don't blind me. Ah!
'Tis the world that loses light. Help me—I reel—
And stagger through the gloom; but there's a speck
Cresting the darkening waves. Young, lovely one,
Give the old sinner pardon, and dismiss
His grey hairs peacefully.

CECIL (*eagerly*).
      Think not on me,
Nor man's forgiveness—but that's yours—
     (*To the attendants*) Good friends,
Look to his hurts, I pray you. The more guilt,
The longer respite's needed.

OFFICER.
      'Tis too late—
He's gone.

NEEDHAM.
    Remove the couch. One friend, sweet Cecil,
Awaits your kind remembrance ; and full well
Indeed he merits it.   (*Showing* GABB.)

CECIL (*giving her hand*).
     Dear Master Gabb,
Take all that's left me to bestow—warm thanks,
And earnest friendship.

GABB.
     Are you happy? Hush!
Don't speak. I am answered. All is well.

CECIL.
         It is.
And, thanks to Heaven, it shall be. For, as here
These curtains close upon each varied show
Of mimic mirth or anguish, even so
Hath growing Reason spread her vail between

Knowledge that *is*, and weakness that has been.
From heart to heart, on wings of mercy, flies
A free and brother spirit, and supplies
For sorcery, sense : malice, the will to please ;
For philtres, wit ; spells, smiles ; and witches,—*these !*

THE END.

PRINTED BY TAYLOR AND CO.,
LITTLE QUEEN STREET, LINCOLN'S INN FIELDS.